PROPER IMPOSTERS

PANHANDLER
BOOKS

UNIVERSITY OF WEST FLORIDA | PANHANDLERMAGAZINE.COM

Proper Imposters

FOUR NOVELLAS

Chaya Bhuvaneswar,
Mauricio Montiel Figueiras,
Jason Ockert,
and Jeff Parker

PANHANDLER BOOKS

Pensacola, Florida

Copyright 2025 by Chaya Bhuvaneswar, Mauricio Montiel Figueiras, Jason Ockert, and Jeff Parker
All rights reserved
Published in the United States of America

Front cover and interior novella covers by Rachel Howard.

30 29 28 27 26 25   6 5 4 3 2 1

The Library of Congress Control Number: 2024937436
ISBN 978-0-9916404-8-5

Panhandler Books
Department of English and World Languages
Building 50
University of West Florida
11000 University Parkway
Pensacola, FL 32514
http://www.panhandlermagazine.com

CONTENTS

Crowd 1
    Mauricio Montiel Figueiras
    Translated by Jen Hofer and Mauricio Montiel Figueiras

G v. P 51
    Jeff Parker

Lalita 93
    Chaya Bhuvaneswar

The Body Collector 153
    Jason Ockert

About the Authors 195

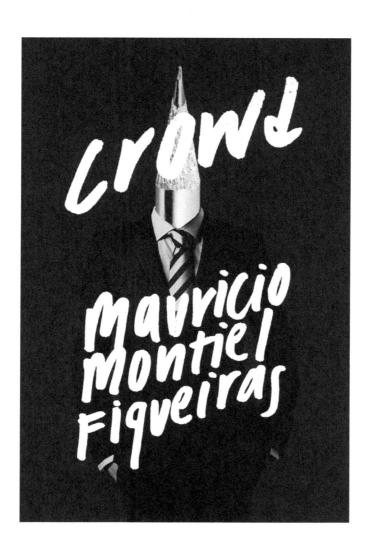

Crowd

MAURICIO MONTIEL FIGUEIRAS

Translated from the Spanish
by Jen Hofer and Mauricio Montiel Figueiras

The crowd is in all of us. . . . It is, like an appetite,
something in which dark satisfactions can be found.
Bill Buford

Like dandruff shaken from a thousand dark tresses, snow falls on the city: thick slow flakes, the ashes of a mute catastrophe freezing streets, doors, windows, awnings, cars and pedestrians into a postcard of nowhere. The night sky hides the source of this winter that doesn't seem to want to end, spreading its white empire into every corner of the country, only to be revealed by the first light of dawn. Day after day, the newspapers present the public with chilling, white images: sometimes one makes out a face buried inside the abyss of an overcoat or sometimes a tree crushed to the bone by the low temperatures; sometimes, only sometimes, the silhouette of a corpse against a mortared wall slips onto the back pages of a weekly, between endless advertisements for thermal clothing and heaters. Radio newscasts relentlessly transmit mortality statistics between bursts of static, peppered with musical notes from Kurt Weill; stations are rumored to have gone off the air forever, their antennas transformed by the ice into ominous sculptures, the voices of announcers mere vapors floating in front of the microphone. People talk of airlines going bankrupt from all the canceled flights, of an almost mythic North where hot water has been a fantasy for many years now, of a crisis provoked in some way by the pencil industry which the news media will not investigate but will reference obliquely, implying this crisis is to blame for the increase in riots and demonstrations of late.

In a taxi driven by an old man who talks through his scarf in a dialect full of textile fibers, Abel looks at his watch apprehensively, then slaps his knee. He'll get to work late. He knows perfectly, despairingly, what this means: Mr. Kane will deduct the day's pay and make him stay at the office three hours later than all the other employees; such are the unwritten rules of the pencil-manufacturing company where he has worked as an accountant for the past mechanical decade. If memory serves, only once before he himself had suffered this sanction designed, in Mr. Kane's own words, "for those goddam lazy-asses": one occasion when, just like today, his alarm clock had not burst his dreams of snow and dark tresses with the punctual force of a jackhammer. A knot of unease lodged in his throat, he awoke fifteen minutes later than he should have in the icy solitude of his apartment to face a morning which held in store for him a set of pipes that chattered like teeth, a cup of coffee reheated in the only clean pot in the kitchenette, a shirt from which a bit of cologne had not been able to eradicate the odor of armpit, a bowtie which he has kept wearing despite the fact that for some time now it had reminded him of a sad butterfly, a wallet with barely enough to pay for the taxi, which had now spent ten—no, eleven—minutes stuck in one of those epic traffic jams that the city, according to a celebrated cartoonist, has turned into an export product as important as the pencil.

Flicking an imaginary speck of dust off the cuff of his overcoat, Abel glances out the window. Snow piles up against the sidewalks where the crowd flows in a relentless stream of jackets and overcoats. The tips of shoes and the brims of hats, the car hoods that exhale clouds of steam in the shape of tremulous question marks—what are we doing here?, the hieroglyphs demand, what the hell are we doing here?—the heads and shoulders of mannequins carried by a group of workers in overalls who force their way through the morning bustle, the cheeks of a woman who stops for a moment in the middle of the street to consult a slip of paper and then gazes up at the misty heights of a brown building: nothing is exempt from the whiteness.

Abel sighs. He tries to concentrate on the crackling of the taxi's radio, behind which he can make out now a female voice intoning Kurt Weill's "Bilbao Song," now the freezing voice of an announcer reciting statistics, but after a short while he gives up. What he regrets most, he thinks, is not getting to punch in along with the rest of the employees who every day form an enormous line in front of the company's time clock. Few things move him as deeply as arriving early to work to line up in a hallway, to move slowly forward, to detect the last wisps of sleep that float off the bodies that crowd around him, to breathe in vapors of coffee and stale tobacco, to listen to murmurs that alternate between complaint and resignation; to feel, that is, part of a tumult of shabby coats which, time cards at the ready, pay homage to the imposing mechanical totem at the far end of the corridor, to be one more cog in the machinery that will be quickly distributed among the offices and cubicles immersed in an ashen light. For some time now—three, four years, a lustrum, two decades, his whole life? He really wouldn't know—he has felt a sort of terrifying security in a crowd. He has religiously followed the movement of many nomadic throngs through articles, photographs and special reports, and is now certain that only there, in the middle of a mob of people, wrapped in a chrysalis made up of homogenous threads which protects him and for which he must fight, is he safe from the world and its daily affronts, safe from the winter that has possessed the very soul of the city, safe from routine, safe from the small yet cyclic abuses that have found their most apt emblem in the erect figure of Mr. Kane, safe from an individuality which weighs upon him more and more each day as he sees it reflected in the mirror hanging above his bathroom sink like an impassive eye. Alone in the bitter dawn of his apartment, sitting in front of a bowl of oatmeal and a plate of ginger nut biscuits, sheathed in long cotton underwear which holds the secret of his nocturnal emissions, his feet bare and numb with cold, he is nobody, scarcely a first and last name on an ID forgotten in some drawer, a signature on a contract with its ink faded from the strenuous passage of months. Before the time clock, on the other hand, dressed in the tacit company uniform—overcoat, vest and suspenders, suit, preferably dark, glasses with round frames, felt hat—he is one of the cells that form a productive organism which functions according to its own codes throughout the workday. He is, simply, just another someone, something invulnerable: nothing can harm him without harming the whole to which he belongs. There are days when he wakes up with the comforting feeling that he was merely a statistic in another life—one of the fifty laborers gravely wounded when a section of the pyramid where they were working collapsed.

    A blow to one side of the cab brings him back to the pristine morning. Out of the corner of his eye he can just make out a burst of gray; a young man wearing a sweater and a wool beret tilted to the right stops for a moment to look at him, then proceeds with his mad race toward the front of the congestion. In no time another two, four, six, eight, ten, twenty, thirty, one hundred youths join this one: a gang of slightly tilted berets rushing headlong between cars and buses, conducting a concert of blows against hoods and windshields, reclaiming not just the spaces between vehicle and vehicle but the sidewalks as well, leaving behind a long trail of startled faces. Abel turns around in his seat, looks out the back window: like a textile swarm coming from adjoining streets and alleys, from doorways where the melted snow unveils a language of aqueous signs, the berets have usurped the avenue.

The radio crackles, erupts into a commercial for shoes at half price:

"Don't let winter get in through your feet."

"Janjthrj dejmojnstjajtion," the cab driver jabbers: another demonstration. "Gojdjaj lajyasjej," he adds: goddam lazy-asses.

Abel turns to look at him and for a second he thinks he recognizes, in the depths of the pupils which scrutinize him from the rearview mirror, awaiting his response, the signature glacial brilliance of Mr. Kane. A familiar image flashes across his mind: a just-sharpened pencil, similar to the one he always carries in the inside pocket of his suit jacket, plunging into the ocular jelly.

"Yes," he murmurs, "goddam lazy-asses, it's not our fault," and then he focuses his attention once again on the street.

The berets are now an army trotting in tightly packed lines through the whiteness. The hint of a tremor caused by the mad dash of a few boys is now something unmistakable: the presence of the crowd, the chronometric rhythm of the crowd. Pedestrians, drivers and passengers have all been bewitched by the procession; from behind the fragile shelter of glasses and eyelashes, hundreds of eyes contemplate men of all ages who flow past, their gazes fixed on the horizon.

As if propelled by a sudden charge of electricity, Abel takes out his wallet, holds out his only three bills to the cabby and abandons the car. He isn't sure, as he starts to walk through the snow, if the shout which is quickly lost among his footsteps is inside his head, or if, on the contrary, it's the head of the old man that has leaned out the window for a moment: "Gojdjaj lajyasjej!"

By the time the last strands of the sentence dissipate into the air, Abel has dissolved into the march. He looks to the left and to the right, feeling, with a jolt of pleasure, the first impact of the tachycardia that usually assaults him in the large stores he likes to peruse on Sunday afternoons—the adrenaline of the crowd, the ritual drumming of the crowd—tilting his hat with an unconscious gesture as if to integrate it once and for all into the legion of berets in which he could already savor the sweet taste of anonymity. A few centimeters away from his right elbow a man moves forward with heaving breaths that belie his gradual ascent toward the heights of obesity, a man whose features, furrowed by veins of sweat, forms the same abyss which stares at Abel from many, many photos. It is a face whose distinctive features are reduced to the very absence of distinctive features, a face which registers a fascinating limpidity over which skim a myriad of faces, the numerous faces of the mob which since the dawn of history has packed coliseums, erected temples and aqueducts and pyramids and docks, unleashed wars, constructed and destroyed cities, spilled its singular blood, the same on sand and in mud, on steppes and on mountains, beneath bridges and beneath blinding white sails. Snow, Abel thinks, his eyes fixed on the man's eyes, which are fixed in turn on the horizon; the masses always run toward the origin of the snow.

The march turns left and begins to trickle through a narrow alley: shoulder to shoulder, beret after beret, their breath drawing ephemeral scribbles on the pages of the morning. A garbage can falls, two fall, eight fall; a youth falls in a pile of steaming viscera, an old man falls and feels the impact of a heel—of twenty, of a hundred—on his waist and on his neck, his buttocks, his legs. The march leaves the alleyway and its trot soon becomes a gallop, a swift yet ordered race toward another avenue where the traffic has also frozen. The symphony of horns accompanying this change of rhythm does not take long to succumb to a new concert of blows against car hoods and windows, joined by improvised notes: the whinny of a horse that collapses in a corner, spilling everything including the driver and his cart of tomatoes, the clatter of a shop window as it yields to the assault of a kid armed with an iron pipe.

Abel wipes the sweat from his brow and cannot repress a dark joy; there is something in these vegetables winding through the street like red blood cells, something in this storm of glass exploding on the sidewalk, that provokes in him an ominous sensation, the moment before a pencil plunges into the ocular jelly, the second just before someone pulls himself out of the crowd and, for a fleeting moment, remembers he is an individual—the prelude to mass violence. His joy, however, evaporates, leaving behind nothing more than a few stray flakes of anxiety; behind the march, somewhere on the horizon, a siren has exploded, signaling the nearness of a police threat. Abel turns to look back, to look up; he thinks he can make out, sliding across the front of a brick building, splashing the faces that hang like gargoyles from the windows, the first gush of blood spilled by an avalanche of squad cars. The berets tighten their steps and begin to snake nimbly between the cars, forming a serpent whose uniform skin only highlights Abel's hat.

And then, at the end of the avenue, the city opens its fist to offer one of its concrete oases: a plaza in all its white nudity. At one end, a platform has been improvised on which stands a podium that bears a curious symbol: a worker's face with his mouth distended in a scream, in front of which floats a pencil broken in half. Pennants with the same image hang from posts and lampposts, along with loudspeakers that look like sad hothouse plants. The berets silently invade the plaza and the serpent disintegrates into a thousand ants that slowly form lines in front of the platform. The foot of the podium is suddenly occupied by a bald man with a small, pointy beard, who wears a black frock coat and casts his gaze, kindled by the flames of leadership, in all directions.

The loudspeakers crackle; the snow and frost crackle under the pressure of a thousand rubber soles. The man on the podium clears his throat in front of the microphone, raises his right arm little by little, extends his index finger as if to proclaim the distance guilty. His voice, the croaking of a statue about to come to life, conquers the plaza, the streets, the entire city:

"Out there, in the woods, the enemy is still at work."

The sentence is a dike that collapses and gives way to a torrent of harangues and dissatisfactions, solidarity and reprimands, mingled with lyric bursts and prophetic notes, colliding with the fury of tree trunks ripped loose by a rising river. Opening a path through the crowd with his elbows and knees, Abel tries to get as close as he can to the front; he notices, sprouting out from among the berets like paper flowers, placards he's seen in the newspapers that bear the fruit of a phony inspiration: "Death to the pencil industry," "The trees belong in our fireplaces," "End the graphite oppression," "Writing in Winter is forbidden," "More heat, less writing." At regular intervals that seem perfectly measured, the man on the podium raises his right index finger to accuse the faraway snow which continues falling, undaunted, attenuating the applause which explodes from time to time against the crystal morning.

Abel is just a few meters from the platform when he discovers, to his left, a boy of no more than five, sitting on his father's shoulders; he, too, wears a beret and a sweater, dark pants, small rubber shoes, and from his vantage point he watches the man on the podium with the crowd's hollow eyes. At almost the same time, after a new round of applause and cold cheers, there is a stillness during which Abel senses, seconds before it materializes, the fatal presence of another mob. Suddenly, as the orator pauses, the sound of a police siren slips in. Suddenly, its ululating is doubled, quadrupled, reproduced in every corner of the plaza. Suddenly, the berets are bathed in intermittent blood. Suddenly, there is pandemonium, primitive pandemonium.

Protected by face masks and out-of-date shields, armed with clubs which they wield with obvious phallic intention, their hands sheathed in black leather gloves, the cops have established a ring of boots, eager to take action, around the entire plaza. Fleetingly, absurdly, in the blink of an eye, Abel's vision becomes that of a bird flying disoriented above the scene; from there, from those imaginary heights, the berets make up the pupil of an eye circled, suddenly, by an iris of authority. And then the iris charges toward the interior, invading the crystalline lens, and the pupil explodes into a jumbled mass of particles that flee in all directions, causing Abel to return to ground level and resume his fragmentary optics.

He sees, in this way, how the berets undertake a clumsy retreat, how the police raise their clubs in a sullen attempt to imitate the orator who someone—there are four overcoats flapping against the immobile air—has snatched from the podium. He sees, as the loudspeakers emit an out-of-tune Kurt Weill song, about thirty youths approaching the police fence with iron pipes; he sees the pipes crash against the shields like batons that cue the beginning of a violent symphony; he sees, or at least he thinks he sees, just when the first club makes contact with the first face, a huge snowflake landing on a nose which turns into a red fountain. He sees one beret, ten, fifty, fall just like spare change, to be trampled with the placards as the two crowds fuse; he sees one man, five, ten, stumble and become merely recipients of kicks and bludgeons; he sees an old man leaning against the platform trying to put his ear, which hangs from a crimson thread, back in its proper place; he sees various police masks succumbing to an onslaught of sprung switchblades; he sees two kids holding a third up by his armpits, his features an incomprehensible ink stain. He sees how the atmosphere is furrowed by fireballs that call to mind a rainstorm of dark stars, and through the curtain of smoke descending unexpectedly over the world, he sees: a line of demonstrators being handcuffed and guided to the north edge of the plaza; a dozen men, kneeling, wringing their berets and begging the shields standing before them for mercy; a club knocking the microphone from the podium; a young man with damp cheeks cradling an inert figure on the ground; a child's shoe—the boy sitting on his father's shoulders appears in the pupil of his memory—half-buried in the whiteness like a memorandum of lost innocence. He sees—after his wrinkled company uniform has, in the eyes of two cops, turned him into a journalist, and while he is leaving the steaming plaza where the sirens have defeated Weill—a body lying face down in the snow. From the pulp which now takes the place of the head sprouts a mane which extends across the ground; a strange, bloody flower peppered with snowflakes, floating up toward reality from the waters of a dream governed—as Abel well knows—by the queen of all tresses.

"Late again, eh? You know the punishment for goddam lazy-asses, eh? And yet, it doesn't matter to you. I don't understand you people, I truly don't understand you people at all. Get going, get going, we don't pay you to laze about, eh?"

Mr. Kane's voice rings out like a whiplash in the gloom of the corridor, which is interrupted at scrupulously measured intervals by insipid forty-watt bulbs.

Dusting the snow off his coat and hat, Abel begins to walk down the hall with a nervous step; he is afraid that someone will notice the bloodstain on the left leg of his pants that he discovered on his way to the office and has not been able to get out completely, even with the corner of a handkerchief moistened with saliva. Where oh where, he has asked himself over and over since he made the discovery, did the stain come from, this tiny corpus delicti? Could he have stepped on one of the many red blemishes that peppered the whiteness of the plaza; could some man whose face had become a damp scribble have leaned against him for a moment? Shouts and sirens, Kurt Weill chords, fragments of an impassioned discourse, the murky harmony of clubs biting into flesh, echo in his memory. Features deformed by anguish, berets and placards fallen like ancient and worthless coins and bills, a child's shoe, a scarlet mane remain etched behind his eyes. But no matter how hard he tries, he cannot divine the source of that small emblem of the crowd sticking to his clothes, to his spirit, as he advances toward the totem time clock and Mr. Kane extracts, from his vest pocket, a watch on a chain which glitters in the shadows like a flame shooting out from the blaze of his hair, barely placated by a layer of pomade. On mornings like this one, when winter is more than ever a state of mind, when his heart wakes up already turned into a wasteland where a grayish air blows, the two figures lurking at the end of the hallway might be interchangeable; no one can precisely determine where the time clock ends and Mr. Kane begins, to which of the two belongs the minute hand which abolishes external time and institutes the secret equilibrium of the company, whose is the gaze which sets the gears of routine in motion. At times like now, when the red-haired supervisor extracts his watch from his pocket, man and object fuse into a single monolith which opens its jaws to receive its daily dose of time cards.

"An hour and a half, eh? *An hour and a half late*. And you, so fresh-faced, eh, so calm. Hurry up, you're the last to arrive. Remember, eh, that the last ones to arrive will always be the first to be punished."

Abel nods, breathes deeply, quickens his step and dusts off his coat and hat once more, all in a single mechanical motion that under other circumstances would make him stumble. Nonetheless, propelled by the image of the plaza and the fatal tramplings in the snow—in his memory a child's shoe flashes like lightning, black against white—he manages to control his limbs and walk slowly toward the time clock; he extracts his card from the gigantic compartmentalized box hanging on the wall and inserts it into the totem's maw, which swallows and then expels it with a rapid crackling noise. As he returns the card to its corresponding slot, Abel is assaulted by a recurring idea: the company's employees are nothing more than scraps of cardboard which must, each morning, lined up against a wall somewhat reminiscent of the backdrop to a firing squad, be stamped in order to carry out a kind of atavistic sentence. How many times, standing in front of the only bathroom on the floor where he works, waiting his turn together with a dozen other near-bursting bladders, has he imagined that when he sees himself in the mirror above the sink, he will notice, slightly dim in the middle of his forehead, the impression of three dark digits? How many times has he lifted his gaze from the accounting book—which, at the end of the workday, must be locked away—and thought that he could distinguish, printed on his colleagues' brows, their various hours of arrival: 7:45, 7:48, 7:51, 7:54, 8:01, 8:07? How many times, mingled in his mind with his mother's flashing fingers as she sewed endlessly, has he not been surprised to recall that Catholic tradition of Ash Wednesday; how many times has he been certain that what is actually happening in his office is a mimicry of Lent, that his lunch—a cup of coffee, a sandwich—is another form of fasting dictated by an all-embracing entity? There is something of exile in the wilderness in the workday, he reflects, in the acceptance of an individuality reduced to a cardboard penitence. Where is the redeemer that in forty days' time will attend to the call of the crowd down there, out there, in the city of riches made of snow?

Mr. Kane clears his throat and plunges Abel once again into a world ruled by an implacable minute hand and, since just a short time ago, by a sense of guilt imprinted on the left leg of his pants. Abel mutters an excuse and slips into the hallway which, with its symmetrical arrangement of light and shadow, makes him think day after day of the first row of a chessboard on which an ever-unfinished game is being played. The elevator, as per usual, is out of service, which causes him a moment of unease; if someone asked him, he could not say when he used it last, or if, in fact, he had ever used it in his ten years with the company. Furthermore, he could not be sure that he knew of anyone who had ever gone up in it. He resumes his walk, however, and while his steps smack against the emptiness of the corridor and the lightbulbs stutter, his mind is flooded with the stooped figure of Mr. F., an authentic prototype of industriousness, who had passed away six months earlier.

Mr. F., known thus because even Mr. Kane did not know his real name, had won a certain fame for being the most veteran of all the accountants; he himself, Abel remembers, in the scant conversations he had had with the other employees, was unable to fix exactly the number of years he had served with the company—half a century? fifty-two years? fifty-six? His death was disturbing to everyone: a janitor found him one morning in the narrow cubicle crammed with papers which the management had granted him as a reward for his steadfast work—collapsed on his desk, his head submerged in an enormous accounting book, half his face stained with blue numbers, a bloody thread hanging from his nose. There was talk of a cerebral hemorrhage, of the sin of impunctuality he had committed the day before for the first time in half a century, fifty-two years, fifty-six?, of Mr. Kane's firmness the moment he input the punishment allotted to those goddam lazy-asses and of a quantity as anomalous as humiliation, which would never have had any place in a mind accustomed to exact figures. The company organized a memorial ceremony on the twelfth floor of the building, generally reserved for executive offices; through an elderly loudspeaker placed on a podium, the director—for many, nothing more than a pair of penetrating eyes in the depths of a portrait, copies of which were hung in strategic spots beside reproductions of office paintings by someone named Edward Hopper—gave a brief speech on loyalty, peppered with static and bursts of Kurt Weill. As a sign of grief—or of negligence, it was impossible to define it clearly—Mr. F.'s cubicle remained deserted for two months; those who peeked through the glass door discovered, with a start, the museum side of the company: Mr. F.'s suit jacket, his enormous accounting book, even his pen and inkpot, had not been moved from their places. In a sort of morbid tribute paid by the dust of every passing day, Mr. F.'s things remained untouched in the limbo to which the death of their owner had condemned them. Until suddenly, with no prior notice, another stooped figure brought the paralysis to an end: it was Mr. G., who, upon earning the title of most veteran accountant, watched over his exact figures like a raven.

Mr. F.'s voice, barely a tobacco scratch, reaches Abel at the foot of the staircase which spirals up toward the gloomy heights of the building.

"The elevator has always worked," the elderly man had said just days before his death, letting his words fall like stones into the well of silence which had suddenly opened amid a casual lunchtime conversation. "It has never been out of order. The thing is that it is reserved for the director. Only he can use it."

As he begins to climb, grasping the railing, Abel reconstructs that moment in the cafeteria: he sees, once again, half-eaten sandwiches seasoned by the radiant ash which constantly falls down from the large windows. He sees employees with their mouths gaping, their jaws stopped in the act of chewing, incredulous gazes concentrated on the figure—on the lips—of Mr. F. He sees himself, saying, "And what does that have to do with anything? We were talking about budgets," only later to catch wind of a story that starts with the elevator's grate opening unusually one afternoon on an indeterminate floor. He once again imagines the old man making sure there is no one in sight before entering the forbidden cubicle; he imagines him swallowing saliva, feeling the first palpitations of anxiety, closing the grate with a metallic clang which alters the very innards of the building, pressing a button, sighing. He begins to see entire floors abandoned to their fate of dust, damp, and silken spiderwebs; he sees a chair and a table given over to the solitude of objects that await the return of their dead proprietors; he sees a chalkboard where the chalk of the years has drawn a work schedule stopped short by some uncertain war; he sees a pile of clothes—shoes, skirts, jackets, pants, ties—which has attempted to nourish an entire generation of rodents. He sees the offices of a company on the brink of bankruptcy whose name is just a smudge on the bronze directory that hangs in the front vestibule of the building; he sees a secretary who seems to melt into the decrepitude of her surroundings, a man in a dark suit overcome by the weight of waiting that bows, also, the sofa where he sits; he hears a telephone which rings ceaselessly in the distance. What he does not see, oddly, are the offices of the company where he works: the elevator openings have been walled over on all of those floors. ("But how absurd," Abel remembers saying, "if the openings exist, if there is a sign saying 'Out of Service,' if I . . ." "They are false," replies Mr. F. in a low murmur. "The elevator has never arrived there, no one has ever seen it.") What he does see, at the end of his ascent, is a door slightly ajar boasting a plaque with the word "Director" in white letters. Through the crack, widened by a small current of air, he sees a vast expanse of crimson carpet, presided over by a desk which recalls a wooden islet; he hears, emanating from the man with his back to him who nearly overflows the armchair behind the desk, a series of furious growls directed at someone outside his field of vision; he catches, while the armchair turns as if by its own will, some isolated terms: "strike," "red numbers," "physical sanction," "crowd." When the chair ceases to turn, he sees the director for the first and only time: a baldness that radiates with the hard brightness of a fist, a face across which a thin scar slithers from side to side, some fingers manipulating a case from which they extract a crystal sphere which flashes beneath the lamp on the desk before being slotted into the empty space of his left eye. Just then, the director also sees, and fires off an order that sounds more like a bark; just then, Mr. Kane bursts into his field of vision with his eyes popping out of his head, his hands extended, his hair a raging wildfire.

Just then, memory closes its grates. Abel is left on a staircase landing from which he perceives a faraway buzz that from time to time, throughout the day, reaches the accountants drifting in their numerical surf. Some, the few who surrounded Mr. F. that day in the cafeteria, attribute the noise to the elevator, which Abel has come to imagine as a bolus eternally circling a dark esophagus. Others, greater in number, speak of dilapidated pipes, of an ancient lift system that raises and lowers pencils to different floors, sharpening the smell that daily invades their olfactory passages like an infection.

Indeed: although the company's manufacturing plant is on the outskirts of the city, the smell of graphite has taken root in the administrative offices. More than once, Abel has thought that the atmosphere where he works is nothing more than a drawing done with a poorly sharpened pencil, a sketch whose background is the gloom which in every corner, every passageway, seems like an omnipresent reticle. In that drawing, employees move about with the slowness of tiny charcoal figures; his hand, for example, now that he stands immobile halfway up the staircase, is an indecisive line which grazes the handle of a faintly rendered door. What, he wonders, is on the other side of those sealed sketches on almost every floor? If Mr. F.'s account is to be blindly believed, must he assume he will find etchings of ghostly furniture, a draft of a woman and a man bent under the weight of waiting? Must he think of the director as the Supreme Draftsman, each morning drawn in turn by a Greater Pencil, fixing his glass eye in place so he can trace his employees' destiny with his own lead? Must he see Mr. Kane as a ubiquitous silhouette marauding on the periphery of the Great Plan of the Day? What might there be on the other side of those sketched doors which do not yield to the pressure of a hand drawn with a trembling pulse?

Abel leans against the door, feeling beneath his ear the swarming patterns of wood eaten away by time. The silence's response, punctuated with a quick series of scratches, is eloquent. Nothing, says the silence, there is nothing here, don't search any further. Here there is no solution to the mystery of the crowd; here you will not find that charm. Here you will only find what was left behind by the masses, now a tribute to prowling vermin. Go away, get the hell out of here, go out into the street.

A child's shoe atop a pile of old clothing and a scarlet mane combed through by insects accompany Abel as he continues to climb, floor after floor, door after door, a shadow melting into an architectural drawing. His steps echo the gloom itself: dulled, muddled, more confused with every stair.

The morning has been buried by a snowstorm of numbers, perhaps the worst in recent memory. Every time the accountants lift their gaze from their notebooks, which have become a mathematical wasteland, seeking a moment of rest through the bay windows that dominate the enormous office, they invariably encounter the same view: transformed into numerals, snowflakes cover the city with a blanket of unsolvable equations. After blinking, after rubbing their eyes hard enough to wring tears from them, the accountants resume their tasks with the certainty that down there, out there, are pedestrians who stop in the midst of the crowd to shake digits off their overcoats and hats.

The storm, however, does not prevent Abel from following the news, broadcast over a radio off in some uncertain corner of the office. With Kurt Weill in the background—now "Alabama Song," now "Nannas Lied"—and with growing astonishment, he listens to the official reports of the demonstration in the plaza: thirty policemen seriously wounded, another group with contusions and even knife wounds, minor property damage, forty-three demonstrators arrested, and luckily—the announcer's voice trembles—no civilian casualties, just another rally in our very own rally capital. Pencil industry spokesmen comment that their companies, far from being affected by the uprising, continue to push on full steam ahead. "Despite illiteracy's efforts to eradicate it," said one impresario who refused to give his name, "writing will exist for some time to come." A parade of black and white images slide across Abel's mind: a child's shoe and a mane of dark hair, yes, but also a forest of clubs, a field of berets, an ear hanging from a thread, noses reduced to thick streams, figures cradling inert bodies. Taking advantage of Mr. Kane's absence, he gets up stealthily to go to the bathroom—each employee is entitled five such trips a day—to take care of the bloodstain on his pants, which finally vanishes after a frenzy of soaping. As he returns to his desk, with a damp oval on the hem of his left leg, he wonders if a little detergent might be enough to erase the crowd's imprint on history.

As always, the lunch hour is preceded by an ashy paralysis, a stupor that turns the accountants to statues for a few moments: pencil or pen raised, they await the liberation signaled by a bell reminiscent of a raven's caw. And then they scatter, a symphony of chairs pushed back and notebooks being closed, a rapid yet ordered stampede of wire-rimmed glasses walking downstairs, glinting as they melt into the wide shadows of the cafeteria.

Abel knows that "lunch hour" actually consists of barely thirty minutes to choke down a sandwich and a cup of coffee—one might say that time is another of the materials the company is able to mold to its whims—yet he remains glued to his seat and pretends to be buried in his numbers until the office empties. Then, warily, leaving his pencil in his notebook as a kind of bookmark, he stands up, trying not to make too much noise with his chair, and turns toward the half-open door to reassure himself that only the half-light is wandering through the hallway. He walks out of the office and begins to tiptoe toward the elevator's metallic door; every five or six steps he stops and listens closely, aware of the reprimands he will have to endure if any of his superiors discover him roaming the corridor during lunch.

Though for some reason he had imagined it would be different—perhaps slightly warm, like an organism about to breathe—the elevator door greets him the same as ever, obstinately closed like a long-shut eyelid. Abel looks right and left before reaching out a hand to stroke the metal, which is as frigid as only a dead thing can be. As he takes his hand away, two images flash clearly in front of him: one, of his own fingers darkened by a mix of hair and blood, forces him to check his pants until he is absolutely sure that the damp oval has disappeared; the other—lips unfolding like gray petals—makes him remember that Mr. F.'s anecdote involved an elevator with a grate, not a door, an antique grate through which one could glimpse the twinkle of a glass eye. Where, Abel wonders, might that grate be? In what section of which floor was Mr. F. when he crossed the forbidden threshold? Why had he not realized until now that the "Out of Service" sign hung on doors and not on the grate of a bygone elevator, betraying the late accountant's tale? And why had he not concerned himself until now with these trifling details—grate, door—that were making him think of an elevator to the gallows, of a shapeless mass stirring in the depths of the building? The crowd, I've been bewitched by the crowd, Abel tells himself as he begins to push against the metallic door—but not the grate—with both hands, trying at all costs to open it, to wrench it from the wall, to rip the secrets from it one by one as if behind it throbbed Mr. F.'s voice, Mr. F.'s face half-stained with blue numbers, and not that clamor that begins to rise from somewhere within the building, the boiling din that reduces, little by little, until it becomes a pair of syllables—A-bel, A-bel, A-bel—carrying with it images of chaos: workers in a snowstorm with their mouths open in a shout, women lined up on sidewalks with their hair dyed with blood, white plazas strewn black with children's shoes—

A-bel, A-bel—avenues carpeted with berets and clubs, cities populated with bodies that have frozen in the form of question marks, fields where instead of bushes grow mounds of clothes—A-bel—maps of pain and anguish that diffuse when the elevator door yields with a deafening noise that reverberates down the entire length of the hallway, emitting a cloud of dust behind which Abel manages to make out not the empty space he had expected but rather a brick wall to which he stretches out his hand in order to feel the vibration of the cubicle which has begun, out there in the building's esophagus, to move with an ancestral weight.

"What's all this racket?"

The voice, ringing out like a whiplash from one end of the corridor, belongs to an executive who, silhouetted against the light of an office, his arms akimbo, a half-smoked cigar stuck between his lips, shoots a furious look that sets the shadows around his face ablaze. By some sudden survival instinct, Abel moves out from under the beam of light falling from the bulb that swings slowly, strangely, above his head; he turns his back on the figure with the cigar and, whistling a few notes of Kurt Weill, he pushes hard against the elevator door, closing it with a new deafening noise. Then, still whistling, he starts to walk toward the stairs with an indifferent step.

"Hey!" the executive shouts. "I'm talking to you! What's with all this commotion?"

"Inspection," Abel answers, without turning around and without slowing his pace, "it's the monthly inspection."

"Inspection? Inspection of what?"

"Of the elevator, what else?" Abel reaches the stairs. "It needs regular maintenance to avoid accidents. You know, orders from the top so we don't sink down to the bottom."

"But if the elevator doesn't . . . Hey! . . . What's your name? . . . I haven't seen you around here before . . . I have to report you . . . Hey you! . . . I'm talking to you! . . . Who . . . ? You aren't a technician! . . . Hey you! . . . Why all the racket? Hey! . . ."

The hubbub of the cafeteria envelops Abel in a chrysalis within which he feels safe enough to take off his sweat-fogged glasses and clean them with his handkerchief. Two of his officemates lift their eyes from their disposable cups to look at him curiously. Abel moves toward them noticing that other, equally curious gazes are glued to the back of his neck, his shoulder blades, his waist. When he gets to the high table—the stools have been taken away in order to guarantee that the lunch hour will pass rapidly—he claps his youngest colleague on the shoulder and, feigning a nonchalant air, asks no one in particular:

"Any news?"

"Any news?" repeats his eldest colleague, without hiding his surprise. "What's the news with you? Are you fasting? There are only nine . . . no, eight minutes left until lunch hour ends, and . . ."

"My stomach," Abel interrupts him, pointing to his belly. "Something didn't sit well with me last night, I had to go to the bathroom. Just diarrhea, nothing serious."

"So now you've only got three trips to the bathroom left, right?" says the young colleague, shaking off the shoulder that Abel had slapped as if it were covered in dust. "And don't forget that you're being sanctioned. You were late to work today, right?"

"What's all this?" Abel pulls back, looking at him with disgust. "Are you in charge of accounting for all our sphincters?"

"No, nothing like that, right, I just wanted . . ."

"Mr. Kane was asking about you," the elder colleague intervenes. "He thought that you might have left the office without permission. You know, because of the sanction. And also . . ."

"Also what?" The sentence left hanging in the air like a wisp of smoke makes Abel anxious.

"Also," the young colleague interrupts, lowering his voice to a conspiratorial tone, "there's a rumor that you took part in this morning's demonstration. In the plaza, right, and that that's why you got to work late. How ridiculous, who could be interested in demonstrations, especially as an accountant. The thing is, right, that a little while ago they announced that one of the policemen wounded in the demonstration died. On the news, right, we all heard it. The mayor expressed his condolences to the family and proposed a citywide day of mourning for him tomorrow. How ghastly, about the vandals, right, no one's safe. Violence, right, violence . . . The thing is that the company doesn't want any of its employees to be involved. In the death of the policeman, right, we all heard it. On the news, right?"

While his young colleague continues to spin out his tiresome telegraphic spiel about vandalism and the disadvantages of living in a big city, Abel casts his gaze around the cafeteria, gathering new looks of curiosity that slide up and down his body; he finally rests his eye on the niche in the corner from which a radio unfurls, between bursts of static, a version of Kurt Weill's "Surabaya-Johnny." For an instant, behind the worn cloth that covers the speaker, he thinks he glimpses a glassy shine, the glint of an artificial eye. The vision shatters when the same bell that proclaims the beginning of lunch hour sounds once again.

    Joining the orderly stampede of eyeglasses abandoning the space, with its fragrance of fried ham and tepid clothing, Abel thinks of ravens flying over a snowy plaza covered in footprints which become figures in an accounting notebook. He thinks, as he once again climbs the same stairs as always behind the backs of the same necks as always, of a face stained with blue numbers blinking in the depths of an elevator, calling him, invoking his name, urging him to act: A-bel, A-bel, A-bel. He thinks, as he once again melts into the twilight that reigns over the office, of the winter queen whose bewitching tresses coax him, like an explorer with no lamp to light his way, into a dizzying abyss of dreams.

The sensation is extremely familiar: a sort of gradual coming loose, a disjointed forward movement as you slip through the narrow space of the abyss attached to a rope that your unconscious has turned into an umbilical cord. Moisture runs down the walls of the pit, similar to that which soaks the cord; despite the way it drips into the depths, with the cadence of an underground leak, it has only one single explanation: snow, melting snow, snow from the ever more distant surface. To descend into that dripping and precise, almost spherical darkness, is the same as slipping backward down a path on a snowy peak during the night thaws: the moon has disappeared, and there, down below in the valley, the encampment lies in wait, roiling pots and elixirs lie in wait, the bonfire surrounded by shadows lies in wait, as it does on Walpurgis Night, celebrated—a voice inside your head notes—on May Day, the very same day as International Workers Day, when no one labors save the witches and their accountants. Here, however, there are no witches and there is no bonfire: only shadows upon shadows, layers on layers of blackness, and that liquid rumor that suggests a nostalgia for the light more than for the snow. Looking closely, though—it is possible now to make out the curve of the walls, a viscous vibration of vermin—there is actually a glimmer at the bottom of the abyss, an exact circle of whiteness that grows while the umbilical twine slides through your fingers, cold and nauseating, a circle that becomes your last hope for salvation when you abruptly reach the end of the rope and begin to fall freely, tumbling down a shadowy throat, uselessly flailing your arms and legs in search of some hold, a circle that suddenly explodes before your eyes, dissolving into a white avenue along which—in the most rigorous slow motion—men and women move, escapees from a silent film. These are the historical masses, those of yesterday and of today, of magazines and newspapers, of books and documentaries, those that march, impassive, toward the origin of the snow: figures whose features and clothes belie their legacy of anonymity. To walk among them, to become confused with them, produces a joy that quickly ceases to be merely an abdominal spasm and begins to flood one's entire body, the entire panorama, becoming absolute communion. It doesn't matter, as they file past the windows of shops that have been closed for centuries, that their reflection shows nothing more than a deserted street populated only by aimless white ashes: who could possibly care about reflections, especially as part of the mob. Especially if in the middle of the sidewalk, among overcoats and hats, it is possible to glimpse a mane stretching out like a dark jellyfish going gray with the snowflakes that begin to fall more insistently. In fact you have to blink energetically, or, better, close your eyes for an instant so no particles blow against your irises; and when you open them it doesn't matter that the crowd has become paralyzed and you are the only person still moving in an opaque sea of statues, a frigid and patient sea under the drizzle of shavings that calls to mind a band of angels sharpening immaculate pencils among the clouds, forcing you to lift your gaze—using one hand as a kind of visor—to observe that the sun, the mere intuition of a sun, has been replaced by a black hole in the middle of the sky, undoubtedly the mouth of the pit from which you've only just emerged. Blinking your eyes you can just make out, way up there, at the other end of the opening, an office with various rows of desks, empty except for one on which a man sleeps with his head down on his arm. The sensation transmitted by that opaque medallion hanging from the heavens is extremely familiar: a kind of abrupt numbness, a disjointed forward movement toward sleepless vigil as your muscles and tendons give way under their cranial load. But now you must bring your gaze back to earth to discover with a sting of terror, while the scene in front of you begins to dissolve at the edges, that the snow is stained red: large clots of blood pepper the avenue, the sidewalks, the clothes of the petrified crowd, your own pants, part of your vest, the tips of your shoes, the palm of your right hand. You must rush now, you must ignore the blots of scarlet and the metallic stench that takes possession of the street, you must hurry your step because over there is the queen of all tresses and the scene is dissolving, the scene is vanishing as if an enormous eraser were being rubbed over it so you can just glimpse the edge of a desk, the sleeve of a suit jacket stained by an ellipse of saliva but there is the mane, there is the jellyfish unfurling her tentacles colored white and crimson, there are the first pains shooting through your numb arm although not preventing your hand from reaching out to lift with one motion the woman's head from where it was lying on the snow, there is the desk more and more clear, superimposed over the scene which dissolves into tattered fragments among which the woman's face flashes, her features almost supernaturally vivid while beneath them a mob of indistinct faces seems to stir, her blue eyes like unfathomable depths out of which any glimmer of humanity has fled, her mouth that opens like a third hollow in the middle of that convulsed mask to let out a whisper that brings together a legion of voices:

"Abel."

Then a pause and again the whisper, the multiple whisper:

"What are you doing here, Abel? This is a dream. There's no use for you here. Go away. Wake the hell up."

His abrupt awakening has failed to suppress the impression of his dream. Although he's stood up from his seat to rub his sleeping arm and start his blood circulating again, although he's gone to the bathroom to wash his face—after all, there's no one to count that as one of his allotted trips: the office is empty, and all that's left of Mr. Kane's presence is the odor of old clothes in the air—although he's returned to his desk with the cold studding his face and charging him with a blurry wakefulness, when Abel turns his gaze to the large windows, he encounters an image from his dream: a face hanging in the glass, pale like a paper lantern, a mane of hair woven with streaks of snow and twilight, a pair of eyes that scrutinize him like twin hollows in the gloom. Nothing, not even the lights which someone has turned on and which remind him of a dissection room—the desks are slabs waiting for dead bodies after a demonstration—can reach the depths of those eyes that float in the emptiness outside. Those are Mary's eyes, her mane, her invented face.

"Mary," Abel murmurs, and the name reverberates in the glacial office before merging with the snowflakes falling outside the windows, on the other side of the world, far away from reality. Mary, queen of tresses, mistress and lady of his deepest nightmares.

"Mary," Abel mutters again, walking now to the window, and this time the name collides with the snowy face, which quickly disappears as his hand strokes the glass where the shadow of a pair of implacable eyes remains, and from somewhere in the building the rumor of the elevator, going up or down with its ghostly cargo, reaches his ears.

Who, Abel thinks suddenly, deals with the objects that the dead leave behind? Where do they end up after the grieving, after the formalities that lead slowly, inexorably to that dead end that is any testament? Is there some limbo in which dead people's things lament their orphanhood while they await the sentence that will determine their next destination: a niece's living room table, the closet of the relative who wept through the burial, the dark attic of abandonment where the spiders have the last word? Abel watches the city shrouded in snow, the evening crowds swept along in a stream of scarves and overcoats that look like sorrowful birds. His memory is an eye that can now see only Mary, Mary's body like a broken scrawl under a newspaper headline: "Another Demonstration: 22 Dead." Abel has kept a clipping of the image for seven years; time has made its mark on it in the form of a yellowish gloom staining the corpse of the anonymous woman he decided to call Mary because of some fixation—perhaps more Oedipal than biblical—whose blood sketches a second mane, now sepia, next to her hair on the snow-covered avenue to which an equally anonymous photographer condemned her forever. Who, Abel has wondered on many afternoons just like this one, might have taken over Mary's belongings? After she was yanked into statistical anonymity, after she was dissected in the miniature morgue of that photograph, what might have become of her skirts, her favorite pillow, her family photo album? Did she wear rings, mascara, high heels? Did she wear lingerie? What might have happened to, say, her perfume, perhaps a long-ago Christmas gift? Might it have remained on the corner of her dressing table, an ancient bulb that struggles to emit brownish globules of light? Who will the portraits watch—her recently married parents, her aunt in a party dress—now that their only interest is the slow fall of night on a damp, humid wall? Might there be other eyes that peer into her closet mirror, might there be other hands that caress the arm of an easy chair, the edges of a rug? Might there be someone who nears Mary's house at dusk and thinks they can distinguish, behind the naked branches of a tree, the glint of a face in the bedroom window, a face similar to the one that appears from time to time in dreams, a jigsaw puzzle of feminine features glimpsed on the street and in the papers, Mary's fictitious face, since her real one was crushed by a club—it's possible, at times, to hear the cracking of cartilage, the fracturing of bone—and left hidden to everyone other than the snow and some forensic doctor who by now has perhaps passed away as well?

Tomorrow, Abel says to himself, tomorrow is the seventh anniversary. Year after year, ever since he came across the photograph of the face-down body, he commemorates Mary's death; though written in slightly faded blue ink, the date is still discernible on the lower left-hand corner of the clipping. As he settles himself in front of the accounting book, Abel recalls his first fruitless visits to the city's cemeteries; his examination, facilitated by a small tip to the guard, of endless registries where the dead were reduced to a collection of illegible scribbles; his walks along tree-lined paths—it was a figure of speech: the weather had done away with the foliage some time before—searching for any Mary whose death might coincide with the date on the clipping; his frustration at seeing graves where stagnant water filled flowerpots and vases, an eloquent kind of desertion; his nostalgia beside mausoleums frequented only by birds who left their excrement as an offering to the indifference of angels and virgins. And then, with no warning whatsoever, without even the slightest premonition—perhaps only, if he thought very hard, something from the depths of a dream, a stony glimmer in the multitude—a discovery under the obstinate snow: a gravestone half-overtaken by the brush, an epitaph whose lines suggested not the slow decanting of pain but the urgency of oblivion: "Mary, faithful wife of Saul, lovng mother of Paul." Underneath, in small lettering, the exact date of her death: Mary, dead at thirty-three.

For some reason he can't quite recall, Abel interpreted the orthographic error, that missing "i" in the word "loving," as a good omen, a sign from the anonymous woman. He imagined Saul, more stunned than in pain, writing out the epitaph as fast as he could on a sheet of paper torn off a pad while Paul—he imagines him now in a sweater and a beret, dark pants and rubber-soled shoes—watched him, hidden behind some indefinable toy. He imagined Saul's dry gaze during the funeral, Paul's eyes slightly damp every time someone came up to give him a hug and whisper in his ear that his mother had been a very brave woman, an exemplary person, a wonderful human being. He imagined Saul at home, distractedly caressing a skirt and remembering the slide of hips against the fabric while wondering what the hell his faithful wife had been doing at a demonstration that had left twenty-two dead. Finally, he imagined Mary—her face like a dress made of patches—at the moment she received the first blow and decided, standing in front of the gravestone with its orthographic error, that it would be this woman whose death he would commemorate year after year, that it wouldn't matter if she wasn't the same woman who had perished on that snowy avenue. This would be the tomb he must visit punctually each year, the tomb that from now on would act as a common grave for the crowds of history. It wouldn't matter to him, just as it didn't matter when it actually happened, when he was surprised at the deceased's grave by her relatives: a man in a wheelchair, for example, a man with a scant mustache—he could easily be Mr. F.—accompanied by a young man who on the fourth anniversary approached Abel wanting to know if he had been acquainted with his aunt, if he had known her for a long time before the accident. It wouldn't matter to him to then take a moment of silence, leave his white flowers on the white grave, and turn toward the cemetery exit, ignoring the kid's uncomprehending voice and Mr. F.'s sobs, which little by little would become the very thinnest wisps of the afternoon turned shroud.

Abel wakes up, abruptly and definitively, with the certainty that someone has been spying on him while he dozed on his desk.
On the other side of the windows the twilight has dissolved into the beginnings of night: specks of shadow alternate with the ceaseless snow, making the city into a bad copy of an old movie. The atmosphere in the deserted office, which also makes one think of a strip of celluloid, has become charged: the vibration of a nearby presence raises the hair on the back of Abel's neck, and he looks around the room. Mr. Kane's odor of old clothes—or was that only a dreamt odor?—has been substituted by another smell, analogous but more penetrating, a stench reminiscent of a body confined to a narrow cubicle. A body with a bloody thread hanging from its nose.
As if electrified, Abel stands up and turns, knocking over his chair. The door to the office sways imperceptibly. At the threshold there has been a moment's activity; a slow concentration of particles swirl in the vacuum of where someone has just been. With his nerves on edge—he can feel the tickle of almost every single nerve ending—Abel waits. He thinks he hears the friction of the snow, the touch of the night against the windows. He thinks he can sense at exactly what moment the swing of the door stops.

He thinks he can perceive something like a dark wing beat in the doorway; for a second he sees the building full of birds, taken over by feathers and beaks that pierce the air like sharp pencils. He thinks he hears a voice calling him from the corridor, barely a tobacco scratch—"A-bel." But no, now it's not his imagination, there's the scratch again—A-bel—two syllables flung into the gloom that yawns behind the half-open door.

With a shrunken heart, Abel separates himself from his desk, takes one step and then another that echo in the stillness. He stops. When he hears his name a third time, he goes to the door and yanks it open. The lights in the hallway quiver before reassuming their useless task of relieving the blackness that spills from the ceiling and walls like a thick broth. In this broth, floating aimlessly, a thread of light emanates from an office at the other end of the corridor, a filament that grows as the door of the office opens and hits the wall. In the doorway, a man's lean silhouette turns toward Abel and waves a hand—the sketch of a hand—by way of an invitation: come here, come here. Then both hand and man vanish, leaving the trembling of nicotine-stained fingers, the radiance of features tinged with blue numbers, to linger in the air.

Abel walks out into the hallway, his stomach weak, and heads for the light. At the entrance to the office he hesitates, and an image flashes in his mind, the figure of an executive with his arms akimbo and a half-smoked cigar clamped between his lips: "What's all this racket?" The room is submerged in an opacity cut by a single library lamp, an eye covered by a green eyelid that emits its warmth from the only desk, outlining shapes of leather and dark wood. The aroma of tobacco dominates the room: something almost solid that underlines the lack of living elements, something almost like a finger that hangs in the air, pointing toward the elevator grate just a few meters from the desk, closed like a set of dentures. Of the lean man there is nothing left but a hint of a smile: the sparkling of mahogany among the shadows.

Despite his stupor, Abel closes the door. He imagines the punishment he'd receive if anyone—the cigar-smoking executive, for example—came back to the office for some papers and ran into an intruder marauding in the dark. The tobacco scratch returns, but this time the words are unconnected, ricocheting against the walls of his mind: "strike," "red numbers," "physical sanction," "crowd." The silence becomes an oppression in the center of Abel's chest. Asthma, he thinks, so Mr. F. was asthmatic. With cautious steps he approaches the grate—not the door—of the elevator and grazes it with his fingers as if to prove its existence; then he pushes the first button on the panel. With the hum that has forever punctuated the company routine, the elevator comes out of its lethargy and begins to climb the building's esophagus; it appears, the age-old source of rumors, with a whisper of rusted gears and a metallic sheen. Abel opens the grate and walks in slowly, as if he were entering someone else's dream: the transgression is finally fulfilled, he has tread on ghost territory. Before he can close the grate he glimpses, once again, in the gloom of the office, the triumphant glimmer of a smile.

    Then the elevator begins to vibrate, to move, and Abel becomes a component of the legendary hum, Abel is now part of a gleaming breath rising up through a black trachea. Whole floors abandoned to dust and spiderwebs begin to reveal themselves to him and so he detects a chair and a table given over to the rites of solitude, a desk missing a leg whose lameness seems to account for the destiny of its proprietor, a chalkboard where the years have inscribed a work schedule stopped short by a war remembered only in newsprint. He detects a mound of clothing, a sofa bowed by the weight of magazines leafing toward decrepitude, the reception area of a bankrupt company whose name has been chiseled off the bronze directory hanging in the building's entryway. He hears a series of scratches inside the elevator and turns, expecting to be confronted with a numerical mask which ends up being just a cockroach struggling to climb up the wall. He sees, or thinks he sees, the insect's feet moving agitatedly and suddenly feels invaded by nausea, a mixture of sadness and repulsion for this other organic intruder, a universal disgust that crashes like a wave in his mouth and forces him to stop the elevator and lurch out to vomit into the shadows, a flow of discharge that might sum up his pity for the agitated crowds struggling to climb the walls of history.

    His retching ends in a shudder, and he remains crouched for a moment, looking down at the floor where—he hadn't realized it until now—there is a creeping glow that doesn't come from the elevator. As his eyes adjust to the darkness, he discovers that he has arrived at an enormous, unused office, empty except for a few lame desks and an imposing metal file cabinet indifferent to the light offered by a small shadeless lamp flickering timidly in the middle of a table, turning on and off as if struggling to bear the onslaught of blackness. Next to the table, dwarfed by the filing cabinet, is a filthy chair that barely supports the weight of the figure sitting in it: a man, with his back to Abel, hands tied and head bent in a reverential attitude, a faithful acolyte addressing his prayers to a metal monolith.

Abel approaches the chair. He thinks he can hear the cockroach's ever more useless scratches in the elevator. He sees, or thinks he sees, large notebooks on the desks where grime and oblivion keep their own accounts. He sees the man's hands, two globs of bloodless flesh tied at the wrists with a piece of telephone cord. He sees hunched shoulders, a shirt unbuttoned and bloody, suspenders that hang like flaccid appendages. He sees, in the fragile light of the lamp—off, on, off—a face become an inventory of tattered vermilion, a mouth open in a cloth-filled scream. He recognizes, among those swollen features, the eyes of his eldest colleague— "Any news? What's the news with you?"—and the cloudy, semiconscious gaze that remains fixed on the gloomy reflection of the lamp on the surface of the filing cabinet that turns on and off, on and off, on and off. He hears, with a fresh surge of horror, the hum of the elevator set into motion by an impatient finger on some other floor; he turns around just as the brightness of the cubicle disappears, leaving him alone with this red mask that seems to be asking for mercy from the totem—a bureaucratic god, he suddenly thinks—illuminated by the lamp. He tries to remember his colleague's name and when he fails—his memory is a vertigo of snow and blood, a labyrinth of words with no thread to connect them—he starts to shake him gently by the shoulders and tell him, in jagged breaths, to move, to wake the hell up, to do something and quickly because the elevator has stopped on the floor above them—the top floor of the building, patrolled by the glint of an artificial eye—to get going once and for all if he doesn't want them both to pay the consequences. The only response he gets is a trickle that emerges from between the lips and hangs there for a few seconds before melting into the puddle at the man's feet and there's the hum of the elevator again, there's the cubicle on its way back, and in one bound he leaps away from his colleague and looks around for a place to hide, a door, an access to some possible staircase that won't yield to the pounding of his hands bathed in light that flickers on and off, on and off, on and off announcing the arrival of the elevator, the imminent appearance of the owner of those shiny shoes that Abel can already picture, the suffocating presence of the monolith behind which he must slip, merging with a dusty darkness that smells of dead insects.

From his makeshift shelter, Abel detects a mixture of sounds: the thud of the elevator as it stops, footsteps that echo in the empty room, sobs enveloped in cloth, the chattering of teeth—his own—which he silences by clenching his jaws. As the footsteps draw near, he shimmies to one side of the filing cabinet until he can slip one ear out, then the edge of his glasses, so that he becomes a furtive eye studying the scene. He sees the upright figure of a man moving forward like a cutout against the light of the elevator; he sees a long object that deforms the man's right hand; he sees his colleague's face a few meters away, contracted in a convulsion accentuated by the blinking lamp. He sees the man from the elevator reach his colleague and lean down as if to whisper something to him and the figure turns into Mr. Kane: his shirtsleeves rolled up and flecked with crimson, his hair a chaos of flames, his sweaty features swirling with boldness and hesitation, mercy and rage. With a shock he hears the voice of this new Mr. Kane, a murmur which gradually becomes a series of demands, a terrifying familiarity: Tell me who is planning the strike, tell me who took part in today's uprising, tell me who deserves the beating I'm giving you. Tell me why you won't answer even though I rip the cloth from your mouth, why you instead spit blood and even a couple of teeth on my shoes, what language do you moan and jabber in because I can't understand you. Tell me why someone might be interested in these demonstrations especially if he's an accountant, why instead of replying you sob and beg for help with the thread of a voice that no one hears and you squirm around in your chair as if you didn't know that I've already broken one of your collarbones and both your knees and even if you did untie yourself you'd be quite the sight, just a scribble trying to slither toward salvation when here there's nothing more than gloom lit by a lamp that turns on and off, that will turn on and off century after century until you stop coughing and puke out more names and fewer blood clots. Tell me why you force me yet again to raise this club that makes my hand look deformed, where you get the strength to resist these blows to your face and your shoulders and your chest and your thighs, why you don't get sick of hearing the damp crack of flesh and bone, when you'll answer me instead of putting your head down and fainting and leaving me to talk to the shadows alone. Tell me what entitles you to share the weariness I suffer, which makes me lean on the table to mop my sweat and breathe shakily while the club escapes from between my fingers and hits the floor with a noise that makes me tremble and whine as if I were the victim and not the spontaneous executioner. Tell me why I haven't noticed until now a pair of glasses flashing from behind the filing cabinet, tell me whose figure suddenly emerges from the darkness and rushes toward me and knocks me down, overthrowing me and the table and the lamp, and clubs me on the back of my neck and I sink into a dazzling shaft of pain out of which I climb little by little to glimpse a man going into the elevator, a man whose features seem familiar but who I can't place because my memory is a whirlwind of luminous points, a man who closes the grate and vanishes stealing the light from me, a man who undoubtedly will return to some office to collect his overcoat and hat and turn out the lights and erase all trace of his presence. Tell me, please tell me who that man is, who will fearfully go down the stairs and leave the building without anyone noticing him, who with ghostly steps will become lost among the thick snowflakes in the night.

Hours later, in the midst of his insomnia, Abel turns on the bedside lamp and sits up with the covers pulled around him.

    He thinks he has detected the sound of blows coming from the next apartment, a sound that makes him think of a club sinking deep into someone's flesh. He pricks up his ears: as a matter of fact there it is again, that pounding, one two, one two, a syncopated anguish that speeds up the rhythm of his heart. After emptying in a single gulp the glass of water he always keeps on the night table, he starts to perform rapid mental operations—additions, subtractions, square roots—until his breathing normalizes. He recalls his neighbor then, an elderly man he runs into every day in the lobby when he comes home from work. He recalls his neighbor complaining about the dampness that infests his apartment, cursing the plague of cockroaches that he has not been able to eradicate, not even with insecticides, and which—I swear, Mr. Abel, I swear it—seems to be the legacy his wife left him when she died seven years ago. Abel imagines him in the long night of old age, his slipper raised high, hunting down the bugs that slip between the furniture and the curtains and hide in the dresser that holds a few of his dead wife's belongings. He imagines him sitting in an armchair as dawn breaks, crying as he caresses a dusty dress and searches out the vermin.

    Abel pushes the covers aside and gets out of bed. In the kitchenette, as the glass fills under the tap, he watches his breath rise in vaporous clouds that hang in the atmosphere before dissolving; he discovers he's shivering, that the cold enveloping him is, more than anything, internal, an iciness that cinches his heart with the ferocity of a fist. He goes back to the bedroom, pulls a blanket over his shoulders, and turns to the wobbly chest of drawers that sits across from the bed like a rickety idol. He opens a drawer and extracts one of his many albums of newspaper clippings, a secret that he hides with a zeal more befitting a voyeur than a collector. Still shivering, he sits at the foot of his bed and begins to turn the pages of the album. He vaguely notices that the pounding in the neighboring apartment has finally stopped.

 As always, the spell of the crowd is instantaneous: a dizziness that blurs his surroundings, a smell of ink that hurls him toward a new sepia-bordered reality. Some nights he recognizes himself in one of the hundreds of tiny faces that populate streets, bridges, plazas, stadiums. Some nights he sees himself shouting at a rally, raising a banner over a sea of heads, protesting before a row of impassive shields, receiving the impact of a club. He thinks he sees the silhouette of his own arms reaching out a window in support of a protest in Iran, the flash of his glasses among the commotion caused by a tsunami in Japan, the rush of his legs during a stampede of American racists, the restlessness of his gaze at a line of striking workers in front of a turn-of-the century factory, his coattails in the photograph of the unknown man who, each year—as punctual as a raven—leaves three roses and a bottle of cognac on a famous writer's grave. He thinks he hears, as he does now, a clamor that begins to rise up from the depths of the clippings, a roar that slowly reduces itself to a pair of implacable syllables: A-bel, A-bel, A-bel. It is this clangor that has him dazed by the time he reaches the page devoted to the portrait of Mary, to Mary's corpse in eternal repose on the yellowish snow of oblivion, to Mary's blood which seeps from her head in languid tresses. It is this mixture of voices that accompanies him as he descends laboriously into a dream in which he is Mr. Kane, an executioner using a pencil to flagellate a shadow which is first Mary and then Mr. F. and then Abel himself and then nothing, the empty space occupied only by the unmistakable breath of the crowd.

The next day, faking a stuffed nose, Abel calls in sick from the phone booth on the corner. The company secretary who takes the call listens to his explanation through a silence peppered with crackling noises and voices that break into the line and then disappear; in the background, far in the background, a Kurt Weill piece can be heard. When Abel's excuses come to an end, the secretary reminds him in a mechanical tone that the day will be discounted from his salary and that he should speak with Mr. Kane—who has not arrived yet, something truly unheard of—sometime during the morning. Before he hangs up, compelled by the memory of a face ripped to shreds, Abel asks after his eldest colleague. The answer, equally mechanical, takes a moment to cross the abyss filled with static and short bursts of music: no one knows anything about him, he has not reported for work, his time card is intact in its slot, perhaps he, too, caught one of those flus so common among lazy employees. Abel thanks her and hangs up with a sneeze; his robe, pajamas and cotton underclothes are no match for the phone booth, which has become a geometric igloo. For several minutes he observes the street: there is something strange in the crowd, something ominous in addition to the mourning imposed by the mayor in honor of the policeman who died in the demonstration at the plaza. There is something demanding in the gazes that seem to be directed at him—only at him—something beginning to spread like a stain against a backdrop of newspapers and snow, the obstinate snow that keeps trying to cover the city.

The rest of the morning is concentrated on Abel's hands, which do not stop shivering as he dials through stations on his radio huddled in a corner of the living room that gives off the sheen of an ancient skull. He searches for a voice that might explain the oppression that has settled over everything, including his apartment, hoping for a sign that steadies the tremor that three cups of tea and two blankets haven't been able to control; his fingers move the dial as if it were the knob on a door into the unknown, the entrance into the secret world of the crowd. All the news reports, enveloped in fragments of songs that make him think of a beggar's rags, deny any civilian deaths from the demonstration at the plaza, applaud the heroism of the agents involved, wonder as to the identity and whereabouts of the leader of that "ridiculous illiterate riot"—a small, pointy beard flashes in his memory, an index finger extended as if to declare the distance guilty—and underline that the tranquility in the streets today is possible thanks not only to the official day of mourning decreed by the authorities but also, and very especially, to the deployment of police units that have left the warmth of their offices and precincts behind in order to make sure that the law is obeyed even beneath the snow that will not leave us alone.

Around noon, however, Abel stumbles across a station that erupts from a far corner of the dial. The announcer's voice, sputtering with gusts of static, transmits both extreme agitation and extreme weariness: the agitation of someone who knows he is condemned for what he must say before he even begins, the weariness of an insomniac who has made one final, desperate decision in the depths of the night. The unofficial statistics, the announcer says—whispers—are revealing: thirty-three protesters dead in the plaza, including a number of women and even a five-year-old child, and sixty-six arrests, I repeat, sixty-six arrests and not forty-three as the news reports announced yesterday. Thirty-three bodies which, according to the rumors, have been taken to a mass grave on the outskirts of the city; twenty-three protesters who have disappeared from the official records and have surely been doled out to various interrogation rooms. Family members of some of the victims have called this station seeking information about the bodies, asking the listeners to do something that Abel doesn't quite catch because the sentence is left unfinished, a tattered thread that dangles in the radiophonic chasm while the announcer coughs and seems to be about to suffocate and noises of a struggle can be heard—perhaps a chair falling over, a club imprinting itself on a jawbone and then knocking down the microphone—and the station goes off the air, substituted by a torrent of static, a gap which will be filled by sad piano chords, the droplets of a Kurt Weill piece flowing into the waters of the silence out of which the jingle of a brand of ginger nut biscuits will surface.

Afternoon comes with a shiver of clouds that smear across the highest windows of the city like furtive oil paints. After appeasing his hunger with a bowl of soup and attempting uselessly to reach Mr. Kane—the emergency meeting he was called to attend, reports the secretary, has lasted longer than planned—Abel gets in the shower. Amid the steam that dissolves the contours of his bathroom, amid the clacking castanets of the hot water pipes, he sees himself once again in the phone booth on the corner, dialing the number of his company inside that igloo, isolated from the mournful traffic of the crowd, awaiting Mr. Kane's voice not so much to explain himself as to murmur I know who you are now, I know what you do in your free time, I know it's very easy to be the occasional executioner, just give me a club long enough and a face in which to smash it and I shall move the world. He sees himself once again biting his lips when he hears the secretary's mechanical words, making an effort to control his fury—the fury of God knows how many years in front of an accounting book—so that it won't explode into a steaming frenzy against the glass of the booth, and then a rough towel rubs against his skin until it's red. As he shaves in front of the mirror, taking care to steady his traitorous wrist, Abel concludes with a shiver that his face no longer belongs to him: the exhausted eyes, the wide forehead, the twisted nose, even the blonde hairs the razor erases, are substantially part of the crowd. They are, in and of themselves, the crowd: a conclave of undifferentiated features, the refuge of anonymous entities.

This sensation follows him as he dresses in the tacit company uniform and sharpens the pencil he'll put inside his jacket pocket and takes a sip of water—the last sip I'll drink out of this glass, he thinks nostalgically—and leaves his apartment without looking back, imagining the atoms repositioning themselves within objects that will take a while to adjust to his absence. From the taxi he hails, he observes the late-afternoon mob and glimpses his face in storefronts and bus windows. What would the crowd think, he says to himself, to see itself assembled as one, riding in a single taxi? The car picks up speed and the city becomes a pale tapestry, laced with dark threads.

At the entrance to the cemetery, as a prologue to the ceremony he's been celebrating for the past seven years, Abel buys a bouquet of flowers—the whitest you have, he insists—from the old woman who always looks at him with a mixture of tenderness and compassion. Her eyes are the last stronghold of youth: a restlessness shining in her pupils, a lightning flash chasing the shadows from her lashes, reveal the young woman who long ago became lost in a labyrinth of wrinkles and varicose veins. Obeying an odd impulse, Abel reaches out and caresses the old woman's cheek. The flower-seller's reaction takes him by surprise: the youthful bolt of lightning vanishes and gathering stormclouds quickly obscure her features as she rises from her bench and begins to jabber in some toothless tongue. Abel retreats, backing away from the verbal barrage which increases in volume until it becomes a string of insults that escorts him as he crosses into the cemetery and disappears down a lane where the old woman's voice mingles with the rustling of air in the naked trees, with the caw of some invisible bird.

Beneath the snow, the angels watching over crypts and mausoleums seem gloomier, their edges more defined, as if they were about to lift into flight in order to guard some purgatory. The few people meandering through the whiteness—a couple of women, some solitary men, a boy dressed all in black, holding his father's hand—seem oblivious to the imminent wing-flapping, absorbed in their own plots of sadness where there is no room for the snowflakes that feather from the sky, gentle as pencil shavings. Abel looks up and sees a vibration at the top of a eucalyptus like an enormous beating of wings; he imagines the face of a seraph, a marble mask with the flower seller's bright blue eyes, before a pair of ravens abandon their hideout. He thinks of the unknown man who, like himself, fulfills a funerary protocol every year, involving three roses and a bottle of cognac; he thinks of the accountants at his company, leaning down over their desks like fatigued, myopic birds; he thinks of Mr. F., of Mr. F.'s beak buried in his notebook as if it were a large dish of mathematical birdseed. Then he jams his hat on his head, clutches the bouquet of flowers and begins his own personal ritual: to wander unhurriedly down ever more desolate paths and get lost in the cadence of his stroll; to pause in front of gravestones that attract his gaze and searching for memorable inscriptions; to study the features of the mourners sitting next to graves which welcome them in hope of tears, of that wet glimmer that oils the turning cogs of memory; to trap a snowflake on his tongue and savor the taste of the cold; to interrupt his trek from time to time to enjoy the silence and become just one more thread in a shroud of stillness.

"Mary, faithful wife of Saul, lovng mother of Paul." Abel doesn't know why he feels offended by the error in Mary's epitaph. Unlike the first time he came, when it seemed like a good omen, the missing "i" in the word "loving" now seems unforgivable to him, an obscene oversight that no one has deigned to correct in over seven years. What could the man who chiseled those lines—just three lines—have been thinking when he came upon the "ing" ending? Wouldn't he have consulted the paper with Saul's faltering handwriting—would that scrap of paper have even existed? What could Saul have thought when he discovered the error; would he even have seen it? And Paul? How old would Paul be? Would he wear patent leather shoes, a bow tie, or just a school uniform? How often would he visit his mother, buried beneath an egregious misspelling? As he pulls thistles away from the grave in search of a space to deposit his floral offering, Abel recalls the fourth anniversary of Mary's death, the man in the wheelchair who might have been Saul—or Mr. F.—pushed along by a nephew. He recalls the paralytic's sparse mustache, the sobs that at first refused to surface as if the stone's absent "i" were obstructing his larynx.

He recalls the nephew's questions—what accident?—his own refusal to respond and subsequent escape, just as a gust of icy wind seizes his hat and forces him to his feet.

The hat rolls away and stops at the edge of an open grave. Abel picks it up, but before he walks away, something—a tremor of roots—makes his gaze drop into the depths of the chasm, into the gloom, where he catches the glint of a formless mass. A mass that slowly acquires contours, dimensions, until it becomes a pile of bones, a bony pyramid crowned by a few skulls in whose sockets shadows seethe, an impatient larvae of darkness. Mass grave, Abel thinks, not even realizing the phrase has left his lips, and he remembers the hiss of a station as it goes off the air. And at that moment a voice explodes behind him.

"Abel? What are you doing here?"

First comes the chill: an icy current that envelops his chest like the promise of a heart attack, only to fill his body with a persistent drip. Then comes the tingling sensation at the back of his neck, the slightly comical feeling that his spine has become a hat rack for stalactites. First is the certainty of total petrification, the image of a man who will merge with his fellow statues and who the gravediggers will learn to protect from dust and bird droppings. Then comes the muscle spasm that makes his body turn, the blinking that focuses his eyes on Mary's grave. Next to the gravestone—only now is it possible to make it out—there is a vase with a few stems sticking out of it. Next to the vase, the recently deposited bouquet sparkles like a handful of knives. Next to it, standing on the grave, there is a silhouette, clearly a feminine silhouette, sheathed in clothes that seem to be made of newspaper. A woman who couldn't be more than thirty-two, thirty-three years old. A woman with long hair, whose face recalls a dress made of changing remnants of fabric. Remnants of magazines. Remnants of features lost in the labyrinth of the city. Remnants of imagination.

"What are you doing here?" the voice demands again. "Go away. There's no use for you here."

The woman's lips are sealed shut. Lips that seem made of earth, of aged parchment. Your lips, Mary. At long last your lips.

But soon those lips are nothing more than two leaves swept by a sudden breeze, and after a series of furious blinks, Abel must accept that the woman has disappeared.

The bouquet of white flowers and the vase with its stems remain on the white grave. And floating in the air like an absent "i," the thread of a voice: ". . . no use, there's no use for you here . . ."

There in the distance, among the naked trees, remains the impression of hair combed through with snow to which a second figure is added, a face covered in blue numbers. There remains the certainty that these figures will reproduce until they populate the cemetery with shadows made of newspaper. There remains the impulse to run, to escape the silence that precedes nightfall, to notice as he crosses through the heavy iron gate that the flower seller has closed her stand and put away her bench, her wrinkles, her varicose veins.

There, on the sidewalk, remains a rose which no one will claim and which will be the only light when darkness devours everything with unmuzzled jaws.

Perhaps Abel will never understand why he is not surprised by the spectacle which greets him when he opens the door of his apartment and turns on the light.

Perhaps, ever since he found himself next to Mary's grave, or even since he telephoned the company, a fraction of his unconscious awaited the chaos now illuminated by the indifferent light of his living room.

Perhaps he has already watched this grainy footage, projected on a dusty mental screen, of himself ambling through his vandalized house, picking up razor-slashed clothes, avoiding the pieces of glass and dishes that litter the floor and the shredded rugs, sighing as he faces his reflection smashed to bits in the bathroom mirror, picking up the leg of a table here, a bit of sofa stuffing there, stacking the clippings that survived the violation of his albums into a bundle that he'll set in a corner of the bedroom, sitting at the foot of his disemboweled bed, eyes scouting the room for any small movement—a chair that finishes collapsing, a piece of paper that falls from the top of the dresser.

Perhaps the vivid images that now bombard him have already flickered across the same mental screen: three men, their features hidden by their hat brims, who destroy everything they find in their path; three pairs of gloved hands that attempt to rip a confession from his things, any compromising tidbit, while Mr. Kane watches from the doorway, wiping the sweat from his brow with a handkerchief, lifting his hand to the back of his neck to pat a bandage stained with dried blood, combing his fingers through his hair without burning himself on the fire that crowns his skull.

Perhaps, as in the ledger of an evil Demiurge, Abel's next movements have already been accounted: rummaging around in the ruins of his drawers until he finds the money he keeps there in case of emergency; abandoning the apartment without forgetting to turn off the lights; double-bolting the door as he always does while ignoring his neighbor's complaints, the voice of the widower he'll never run into again as he's coming home from the office, demanding an explanation for the uproar caused by four men in suits, I swear to you, Mr. Abel; going down the stairs slowly and leaving the building without anyone noticing him, only to disappear with a ghostly step among the night's thick snowfall.

Perhaps, only perhaps, the hotel sign that interrupts his progress like a neon wound has already flashed in a dream where he was pushing the same revolving doors, signing the registry with the same name—A. Kane—going up in the same ironwork elevator, walking down the same hallway illuminated by wan bulbs and submerging himself in the abyssal gloom of the same room while having the same primal, exhausting certainty that waiting for him would be a mass of tresses combed through by the snow and the crowd.

The difference is that now, instead of surrendering to a sort of gradual coming loose, instead of making a disjointed forward movement as he begins to enter the pit of his unconscious, he opens his eyes to discover that he's inside a dream building that might house offices similar to the ones in his company's building, a concrete mass that he imagines is in the city center, standing erect with a severe, vertical silence. He's at a window, watching how the flakes flow into strands of white hair that cover the afternoon. In one hand he holds a pencil with its point bloodied and in the other a page—December 31st—apparently torn from one of the datebooks the company gives its workers every New Year's and which remain unused—other than the cursive reminders to run the monthly report—until the end of the following year. No matter how hard he thinks about it, he cannot explain the presence of those two objects; he looks at them, he feels them, he smells them, they seem magical to him, important in some way, and for that reason he doesn't let go of them: someone must have entrusted him with them. Someone—perhaps the woman whose voice trickles like an uncertain dream flow. Don't put them down, the voice murmurs, they're your strength: writing and time. Writing—true, unique writing—has been practiced with blood since its origins and it will continue being practiced that way century after century: the pencil is your jawbone. The time is here, the moment has arrived, your December 31st: blank slate, all accounts at zero. Get away from the window, the voice demands, slip down the corridor sunken in darkness. Knock on the doors and feel the canceled worlds that throb behind them. Listen to the elevator that hums in the esophagus of sleep, go down the stairs and out into the empty city, to the evening wasteland: the crowd has dispersed. May the cold air bite into your lungs, may loneliness envelop you with its mantle. May the ravens at their posts on wires and cornices remind you of the end of the world, of accountants with their beaks buried in the afternoon's figures; may the stone angels that adorn so many buildings watch over this cemetery of the masses. When you look up, may the sky not crush you with its gray weight: turn your head. Pages, it's snowing pages, sheets ripped from thousands of calendars, all dated December 31st; on each one a pencil has scrawled "Final Report." Look at your own page: the same two words written in blood. It's still snowing pages, bits of time; may they brush against you like feathers as they fall. Do you remember the ritual planned in secret a few years ago, the only outbreak of rebellion within the company? The last day of work, and the accountants heading neatly to the windows to tear out pages from their datebooks and scatter them over the city? The sanctions, the mutilated salaries? The street turned into a triumph of paper? Surrender to the spectacle of the afternoon sown with pages and understand once and for all that the diary of the crowd is written with blood, that all hair is braided through with the filigree of time. Search no longer for your lost jawbone because it's hanging from your hand right now; surrender yourself to its firmness.

 And now, the voice whispers, wake the hell up. There's no use for you here.

 Surrender, by God, your final report.

When he awakens, in the middle of the night, Abel reaches out his arm, groping for the glass of water on his bedside table. His fingers are an extension of the bewilderment that floods him as his hand grazes the edge of a notebook, the stump of a pencil, and a switch he flicks with his pulse racing.

 The flash of light brings him back to the narrow reality of a room with a single blinking lamp. Little by little that blinking becomes the fluttering of a moth trapped behind a fabric screen, a beating of wings that recalls angels and birds.

A seraph in a maze of jagged clouds.

A conspiracy of ravens in a tomblike space.

Perhaps a dream, a memory at the margins of his consciousness?

Perhaps.

Abel stands up, glancing at his watch—he's slept almost three hours—and goes into the bathroom, where he drinks until he is no longer thirsty. Then he splashes his face with water and urinates: an abundant flow, uncontainable, which cannot muffle the fluttering of the moth in the lamp, the collision of wings against cloth.

A captive bird in a numeric sepulcher.

A light that quivers in the shadows, bathing a tattered face in its glow.

The clash of wings.

The moth about to immolate itself in a forty-watt flame.

Abel doesn't notice the flare that gilds the curtains until he sits down at the foot of the bed, after fighting off the temptation to fill the bathtub and submerge himself in a liquid dream, clothing and all. As the beating of the moth's wings fades into the background, he thinks the light is from the hotel sign, its neon caressing the velvet of the night. Then he remembers that the sign was crimson, a hemorrhage from nowhere, and the curtains glow with a patina of tremulous gold.

He opens the window and sticks his head out. A glacial gust pricks his cheeks, reddening them. A crescent hangs over the roofs like an icy sickle reaping a harvest of clouds. It has stopped snowing, and in the calm the hotel sign seems like an alphabetic scar.

The buildings creak, and the windows of the closed shops, and the hoods of the parked cars.

The women's shoes creak—dozens, maybe hundreds of women—as they move down the street in a mute procession of candles and black clothes.

The banners bearing enlarged photographs creak: features ripped from cheap frames and family albums, eyes like graves that call out from the other side of death.

The entire city creaks, run through with a river of flames that helps the victims of the plaza pass into anonymity.

Hours later, as the first flakes of dawn burst against the windows and the heat of the body beside him dissolves into a sadness of dirty sheets, Abel will remember, as if it had been a dream, the impulse that drove him to leave the room. He will remember, through misty filaments of dust, having closed the door with no thought of the key, and having gone down in the elevator and crossed the lobby, deaf to the clerk's snores, and having left the hotel with his hands in the pockets of his overcoat. He will remember having walked along deserted streets accompanied by curlicues of breath and the sound of footsteps, prisoner to a restlessness that would dissipate the moment he encountered the procession of women.

He will remember having joined them in silence, without a single verbal transaction, a cell rejoining its governing body. He will once again see the women's faces, those pale, mournful ovals blazing like paper lanterns. He will see eyes that are pools where pupils swim like dark fish, fingers indifferent to dripping wax, candles that give ephemeral life to the mannequins and other inhabitants of shadow, banners that multiply the smile of a boy wearing a beret, and a child's shoe—black against white—will flash in his memory. He will once again understand that the procession could not lead anywhere but to the plaza, that the flames were destined to illuminate as on Walpurgis Night that clearing in the middle of a forest of concrete, and he will see himself recognizing or aching to recognize a mane of long hair amid a multitude of tresses, hurrying his ghostly step without anyone noticing him, extending a hand to grasp a shoulder and encountering a set of changeable features, a vertigo out of which emerge, pulling in and out of focus, Mary's nose, Mary's mouth and teeth, Mary's eyebrows and chin and cheekbones and ears which are transformed by a weak glow, the flickering of a candle in the depths of a gaze where tenderness has lodged like an insect in amber.

He will remember how his disappointment vanished at the sound of an unknown woman's voice, a whisper that shook him with its force—"What are you doing here?"—and he will once again see himself breaking into sobs, allowing the dam of numbers and shadows he'd constructed over so many years to crumble in a rush that could be contained only by Mary's fingers, by the comforting words spoken by Mary who wasn't Mary except in that beam of light shining from the depths of her eyes. He will see the woman tossing aside the banner on which a man slumped in a wheelbarrow seemed to challenge the night; he will see her open her arms to welcome him into her warm clothes that smell of musk and lye; he will hear the cooing sounds coming from her lips, sshh, sshh, everything's over now, everything'll be fine now; he will once again feel shocked at such an outbreak of intimacy between strangers, the woman's tears damp on his hair, her kiss on his forehead, and he will remember having thought that there in the middle of the avenue, far for an instant from the crowd that surrounded them, the two of them formed a strange pietà: she cradling him against her generous breasts, he fighting the confusion invading his throat. He will hear once again the woman's voice, her name—Eve—a tempting hiss, yet he will see himself locating the tiny yet luminous imprint of Mary that quivered in her gaze. He will remember having let his hand seek refuge in Eve's as they rejoined the crowd, a pair of mourners compelled by their private sorrows.

In his mind, he will walk the streets at Mary's side, glimpsing faces peering out from windows like drowsy gargoyles, noticing that the moon has embedded itself in an outcropping of clouds, sensing in the streetlights an imitation of the candles that violate the darkness. At his first glimpse of the plaza he will feel a chill that will make him let go of Eve's hand, and murmuring soothing words she will lead him forward into the clearing where all the flames converge. The platform and podium from the rally will have disappeared; the plaza will be an immaculate eye, whose pupil will shine thanks to the candles placed in a reverential circle that will seem like part of some secret rite. Standing at the edge of the circle, with Mary's fingers on his arm, he will let time pass until he can feel, even before it materializes, the fatal presence of another mob. Suddenly, as the wind flickering the flames pauses for a moment, a police siren will leak into the quiet. Suddenly the screeching will be reproduced at every corner of the plaza. Suddenly the women will be bathed in intermittent blood and pandemonium will break out, primitive pandemonium.

Wrapped in a sad tangle of dirty sheets, he will remember Eve pushing him toward a nearby alley and once again he will see himself running down icy sidewalks, beneath blind streetlights, beside shop windows that unfold the reflection of Mary's paper-pale face. He will see himself dodging trash cans and cardboard boxes, ducking down side streets beside Eve and running, running until they reach the doorway of a decrepit building into which Mary slips like a breath. He will see himself following Eve's shoes up a shadowy set of stairs, walking down a hallway similar to so many others, stopping in front of a door that Mary opens with a jingling of keys. He will see himself entering a living room lit by a shy lamp, catching his breath while Eve heads for the kitchenette, letting his gaze linger on the sofa with a plaid scarf hanging off it, on the umbrella forgotten in a corner like a plucked bird, on the rug that underlines the loneliness of a pair of slippers, on the framed photos on the wall where Mary stands beside a man and smiles against a rural backdrop, on a makeshift altar presided over by a portrait from which the same man—now slumped in a wheelbarrow—seems to challenge the night that has defeated him. He will see himself accept a glass of rum in silence and take a sip while Eve sits down on the sofa and empties her glass and caresses the scarf distractedly, allowing tears to moisten her cheeks. He will feel the impact of alcohol and he will see himself drain a second shot, a third and a fourth and a fifth—might there have been a sixth?—in the midst of a stillness cut through by Mary's weeping and the ringing of a telephone in the distance.

What he will never know is when exactly Eve's eyes set into his with a yearning where something was throbbing, something more than mere alcoholic warmth, something like an animal licking its pelt. He will never know what moved him to kneel down next to Mary and bury his head in her lap, that soft niche exuding lye and sweat. Nor will he know exactly when Eve's hands began to trace concentric circles on his back, why he found his tongue rubbing salt from cheekbone, what compelled Mary's hands to close like pincers around the erection that was swelling in his pants while their mouths fused in a tunnel of frenetic saliva. He will however remember, through misty filaments of dust, both their clothes falling to the floor, fluttering down and clouding the view of the man slumped in the wheelbarrow, their bodies struggling as they sought each other's deepest cavities, an armpit with a smattering of down that felt silken against his lips, the gloom of the bedroom set aflame by the friction of their skin and their panting, a pair of nipples flashing with a touch of rust, a vulva opening like a corolla of shadows before his eyes, two buttocks become a radiant marvel grazing his balls, a neck arched like a stalk about to break.

He will also remember the tresses and the tears, Mary's helplessness raining down onto his torso with the stealth of the snow that would be waiting for him on the other side of a dreamless sleep, in a dawn of clouded windows.

With the same stealth, Abel sits up between sheets which smell of grime and bodily fluids. He was awoken by the first symptoms of a hangover, a ring of thorns prickling at the base of his neck. Next to him the woman—Eve?—snores, and amid her booze-laden grumbles he detects the beginnings of emphysema, the tip of a pulmonary iceberg. Disoriented by his inability to locate his glass of water on the bedside table and because the age his memory ascribes to the woman—was her name really Eve?—doesn't match this death-rattle beside him, Abel rubs his temples and carefully pulls back the blanket that covers her sleeping body.

He discovers first a shoulder, the muscle scarred by a long-ago vaccine. Then an armpit out of which peeks a rough, woolly tuft; a back where time has left its creased imprint; hips which also do not match his memory of a pair of luminous buttocks; thighs which at some point were lost in a labyrinth of varicose veins. Abel feels the world blur and rests his head in his hands until the sensation passes and his cardiac rhythm is replaced by the patter of snowflakes against the only window. He covers the woman—what *was* her name?—and gets out of bed, walking into the living room where he gets dressed, without escaping the watchful eye of the old man slumped in a wheelbarrow who proffers a tender, commiserating smile.

Below the portrait, on the little makeshift altar, a candle sputters a weak flame.

Abel finishes tying his shoes and, failing to find his watch, goes to the altar and blows out the candle in a single breath while another candle lights up in his memory. He grabs one of the carnations, which leaks its contagious whiteness onto the empty bottle of rum next to the vase. He returns to the bedroom, walks over to the dresser, and just as he's exchanged the carnation for his watch he realizes that the woman is looking at him from the jumbled sheets. Her eyes, as required by déjà vu, are the last stronghold of youth—there's a glint in those pupils sinking like ancient coins in a frigid blue, a bolt of lightning that chases away the incipient shadow of old age. Her voice is a scratch against the air of the room:

"Still here?"

For an eternity during which the only sound is the brush of snow against glass, Abel imagines the girl hidden behind those vocal chords, inside that toothless mouth. Days in the country spent beneath a summer sun. The scent of hay and straw. Laughter like a warm stream that splashes the wagon pulled by a terra cotta horse. Her dress billowing in the wind. Her hair peppered with blades of grass.

"What are you doing here?" the voice demands again. "Go away. There's no use for you here."

Abel leans down over the woman, who has straightened up and covered herself with the sheet, and he kisses her forehead. Before he leaves the bedroom, from the doorway, he says:

"I know that, Mary. There's absolutely no use for me. Good-bye."

Then he walks across the living room, lifts her wrinkled dress from the floor, sets it on the sofa next to the scarf, and opens the door.

Two images will escort him down the stairs: the old man slumped in his wheelbarrow with a playful expression on his face and—he hadn't noticed it until now—one hand raised in a gesture of farewell and beyond him, in the background, the woman bringing the carnation to her sagging breasts which have been roughly exposed to the light of daybreak.

The city will greet him with an uneasiness that extends to encompass the day's first pedestrians, and even the heads of the mannequins watching him from a dusty shop window. Standing on the sidewalk buried under a crust of ice, Abel will catch a snowflake on his tongue and start walking beneath windows where eyes appear and then dissolve along with the snow. He will walk the streets with his mind blank and a sad feminine fragrance clinging to his clothes, watching the cars inaugurate the morning with their steaming hieroglyphs, whistling fragments of Kurt Weill, patting the pencil that grows warm in the inside pocket of his suit jacket. He will see, as if it were part of a faraway dream, a beggar dragging a bag full of naked dolls behind him, a mass of bodies jumbled inside a plastic womb that only partly protects them from the inclement weather, and that image of peculiar fragility will accompany him until he reaches the diner which he will enter, followed by the jingling of the bell above the door.

He will study the place, where four or five customers battle their lethargy, steaming cups in front of them. After breathing in the aroma of tobacco and closed-in night that hangs in the air, he will decide to sit down at the counter, a few stools away from the youth wearing a woolen sweater and beret and flipping through a newspaper without paying it much mind, his gaze fixed at regular intervals on the front window of the diner, a cigarette burning down in the ashtray near his elbow. Aware of the grumbling coming from his intestines, Abel will examine the menu and order breakfast from the man who comes up to him from behind the counter and then shoots him a perplexed look before disappearing into the kitchen.

Hours later, bent over a dissection table, a forensic doctor will dictate into a microphone the following stomach contents: remnants of ginger nut biscuits, fried eggs, blackberry pie.

Thinking for some reason of a final request, Abel will finish eating and ask to borrow a cigarette from the youth reading the paper, who will light it for him with hesitant complicity. The first drag will give him a coughing fit that will die down beneath an avalanche of fragmentary memories: an adolescence become a cloud out of which the features of a few friends emerge, the patio of a high school at twilight, books sitting on a desk that smells of pencils, a one-eyed dog, a flash of motherly fingers engaged in a seamstress' labor, stitches unraveled by death, the fatherly delirium—something about having been a lookout in a desert tower—accumulated over an alcoholic, solitary widower's life. Abel will stub out his cigarette as if wanting to reduce his memory to ashes and observe the tabloid left on the counter by the youth, who now focuses his full attention out the window of the diner, following the example of the other customers who are also dressed—Abel only now notices—in dark berets and sweaters. Among the front-page headlines, after the photos of the burial of the policeman who died at the rally, he will sense a signal—hair whipped by wind, voices that call out to him from an inky gloom: A-bel, A-bel, A-bel.

The next day, in that same newspaper, the statements from those who witnessed the demonstration against the oldest pencil-manufacturing company in the city will agree on one point: the unknown man who came out from the crowd had a feverish gaze and nodded his head as if he were receiving orders from a voice that only he could hear. "The voice of God, our Lord and Demiurge," one old woman, who refused to give her name, will suggest. "The call, right, the call of madness. How awful about the vandals," one of the company's accountants will comment to a radio news announcer, and then he will elaborate: "Ever since I was first introduced to him I knew there was something strange about him. The eyes, right, the eyes don't lie. No, he wasn't a friend of mine. I barely talked to him, right, just at lunchtime."

Two cups of coffee later, Abel will interrupt his contemplation of the jellos displayed like multicolored organs in a case behind the counter. He will turn toward the youth with the newspaper and discover him tensed, a spring ready to leap from the mechanism that imprisons him. He will spin in his seat and see the other customers: each in his chair, gazes magnetized by the clock above the door of the diner, threads awaiting the tapestry to which they belong. The smell of tobacco and closed-in night will have been covered over by an almost electric anxiety, an energy that will make the cashier leave his spot beside the register to go out into the street.

Abel will take refuge in his cup just as it begins to vibrate, a series of concentric waves beginning to disturb what remains of his coffee, the tremor spreading to the jellos in the case, to the napkin holders on the counter, to all the windows in the place. "Earthquake," he will tell himself, imagining the city run through with seismic rattles that will be silenced when the first thread in the crowd, the head of the hydra that slips always toward the origin of the snow, appears outside the window: a man wearing a beret and a dark sweater wielding a placard proclaiming "Writing in Winter is forbidden." Others, with diverse demands, will be added to that placard—"Death to the pencil industry," "The trees belong in our fireplaces," "End the graphite oppression," "More heat, less writing"—and the earthquake will become a stampede of boots that the customers in the diner will join, knocking the cashier down as they rush out.

Abel will feel the tugging in his gut, the first bubbles as his blood starts to boil, and he will hear quite clearly the tribe's clamor: A-bel, A-bel, A-bel. He will see lips opening and closing to chant his name, teeth chewing it like a black banner that will wave in the white air—A-bel, A-bel—and he will understand that the moment has come, that the queen of all tresses awaits him at the beginning or the end of that sea of sweaters and berets, that the face stained with blue numbers that appears in the doorway of the diner only to melt back into the mass that vomited it out could be nothing more than the face of rage, that the boy running beside his father isn't a ghost but a demand and perhaps the print of a child's shoe, that the eyes that come to rest on his even if only for a second are actually hands that push him toward the street, toward the uproar: A-bel, A-bel, A-bel, A-bel.

And suddenly he will be assimilated into the crowd that has invoked him from the depths of time and dreams and the two will form one entity, an invincible body that will snake through alleys and avenues, between cars caught in a paralysis of steam and honking and pedestrians who will move aside with a fluttering of overcoats, past shop windows that will shatter in a rain of glass as they yield to the attack of iron pipes, beneath bus windows behind which the din of another mob will pound, A-bel, A-bel, A-bel. Little by little he will recognize the features of a number of his colleagues: a pair of glasses that retain the numerical sheen of an accounting book, a set of cheekbones that sink into the shadows of the dining room at lunch, a nose that climbs toward its forehead like a gloomy staircase and once again that face stained with blue numbers, there on the corner that the multitude will turn with an obsessive syllabic rhythm shared by hundreds of feet that will synchronize with the growing din, A-bel, A-bel, a term split in two, a word exploding with biblical fury against walls and passersby who will intone it with their gazes lost on the horizon, A-bel, four letters flung out to the four cardinal points, A-bel, key to all locks, candle of twilight, comfort for windows, relief for thresholds, shelter for dust, healing for broken dolls, tower of cotton, tower of bones, tower in the middle of the desert, foundational pencil, name of names, hand that lifts up the old man fallen in a vertigo of boot heels, hat snatched by a rush of air, overcoat trampled in the stampede of berets, suit jacket that waves like a runaway flag, breath transformed into ephemeral scribbles, sweaty features, gaze fixed always ahead, lips that open to join the cosmic outcry, A-bel, wake-up, A-bel, wake-the-hell-up.

His voice just a scratch in his throat, Abel will understand that the crowd—his body, his spirit—is indeed heading toward the origin of the snow: the brick mass that has silenced his steps and his life, that number-populated gloom where he's been hibernating for the past ten years. He will identify the street on which so many times before he's wanted to see the furrows made by his footsteps, the portico that has unceremoniously devoured him every day, the phone booth on the corner as it's overturned by a group of youths, and he will smile: a nostalgic grimace rising up between clouds of breath that someone will remember later, raising their glass of rum in a toast.

Motionless in the sea of berets stopped in front of the company's administrative offices, he will raise his eyes and see, black against white in the depths of the sky, the circles traced by a raven. He will think he can make out the flapping of a mane of long hair and a child's shoe left to its destiny when Mr. Kane's capillary blaze appears in the entryway of the building to greet the car surrounded by the masses, out of which will emerge a bald pate radiating the hard brightness of a fist, a face across which slithers—from one side to the other—a thin scar, a glass eye that flashes with barely contained rage in the direction of A-bel, A-bel, A-bel, who will take advantage of that pause in his name as it's chanted by a million voices to open a path among the people, listening to the slogans clouded by an avalanche of sirens, scrutinizing with a fevered gaze the placards become an ocean of crosses in the midst of the whiteness, nodding his head to make out more clearly the outcry rising up from history's entrails, A-bel, A-bel, A-bel. The sensation of another mob behind him, the first howls of pain and the thud of clubs against flesh, will accompany him as he approaches the threshold of the building where the company director remains paralyzed between three men in suits who attempt in vain to obey Mr. Kane's orders, Mr. Kane's shouts which dilute like a bird's cawing amid the din of voices clamoring for A-bel, A-bel, who will move his hand to the inside pocket of his suit jacket while through his memory flashes his entire life registered in accounting books, his biography in mathematical code.

He will understand, as he extricates himself from the crowd and hurls himself upon Mr. Kane, that without the masses the individual is nothing: a thread in search of its tapestry, a tiny speck at the center of a desolate drawing. Just as his pencil finds Mr. Kane's left eye and sinks down into it with viscous diligence; just as the alarm leaves his supervisor's face, only to be replaced by an almost ridiculous astonishment that will soon be stained with red and gray numbers and out of which will gush one last sentence, a belch that sounds something like "Where is the jawbone, o brother?"; just as Mr. Kane's body falls to the ground like a pile of disused clothes; just as the butt of the gun held by one of the three men in suits smashes down against the face of his watch, stopping time forever, Abel will turn toward the left, only to be blinded by the flash of a camera.

He will understand, in the midst of a cyclone of luminous points, that the photograph that will be on the front page of the next day's newspaper seals his betrayal of the crowd, that the price for recovering his individuality has been very high, that his portrait will never hold a place of honor in the album of a collector of multitudes. He will know, when he sees the pencil buried deep in Mr. Kane's eye, while the company director fades away into the gloom with a twinkling of glass and a couple of police officers hurries toward him, clubs held high, why writing—true, unique writing—has been practiced with blood since its origins and will continue being practiced thus for centuries upon centuries. Before he turns toward the cops to face the first of the blows that will make him commune with the shadows, he will contemplate the street for a moment. He will think that now, more than ever, the snow seems like dandruff shaken from a mane of dark hair that awaits him beneath a tumult of pages dated December 31st.

May this vision, he will say to himself then, be my final report.

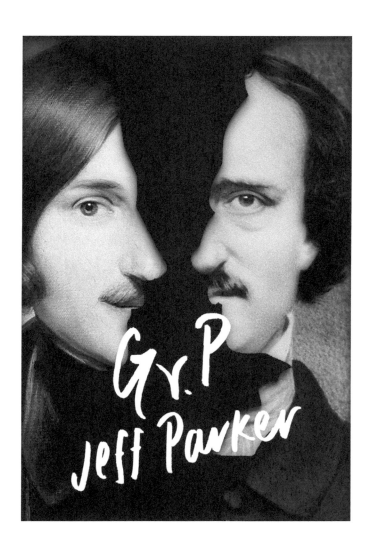

G v. P

Jeff Parker

1.

The rain fell in trochees: DUM-da DUM-da DUM-da DUM-da DUM-da DUM-da DUM-da DUM-da. The tripping rhythm, our species' ideal metric tone. The sound of the human heart.

For fact, was it the rain rapping against the stone of the ditch and the hollow of his cheek, or was it his heartbeat? His internal and external sensations were all mixed up. The ringing in his ears rang louder than ever, or was that a steam whistle?

No matter—he was alive. After all they put him through, he was alive.

P's mind said, *Turn to the side, you. Draw breath, you.* His body—DUM-da—did not answer. *Get up and crawl from this ditch*, he thought. Some tether or tendril or ligature or link had gone missing. A new fear gripped him. His bowels released. The rain splashed—DUM-da.

Okay, good. *Blink*, he thought. And he blinked. *Splutter*, he thought. He heard himself splutter. Some tendril remained. If he could blink and splutter then they wouldn't bury him alive. He might drown here in some ditch but then he'd be dead—DUM-da—when they buried him, and he would rather be dead than entombed down there with only the DUM-da of his heart to keep him company.

A hopeful notion: Maybe this was death? The mind went on but the tether or tendril or ligature or link to the body released, the mind freed to float the universe until a tether or tendril or ligature or link to another body caught.

His abdomen cramped. No, no. More likely, a switch goes off and absolutely everything about you, everything except your de-animated flesh and bone, stops.

How many days had the ratbags had him? Through how many precincts had they run him? How many changes of clothes with how many other unlucky bastards, showing each other their inexpressibles?

With how much laudanum had they pumped him? If it wore off before the ditch filled up, before the rats got over their fear of the rain and his turning . . . the connections might re-tether, and he could tell his body to stand and get out of the ditch, and his body would listen.

What a sorry twist of fate. If they hadn't snatched him, who knows, maybe he'd be married by now. Elmira was game again . . . *Elmira*—the beginning and end for him. She would be worrying over him. And the world—how would the world cope with the loss of a talent such as he? Children fantasized their own deaths in order to feel the satisfaction of their parents' heartbreak and regret. No parent ever much gave a shit about P, but he could feel that satisfaction now at the public's sadness and regret, the posthumous coronation his work would receive—we never appreciated him, we never bought enough of his books, we never showed him our proper affections, the great writer . . . the great great writer . . .

The rats' eyes zig-zagged.

What color ballot had been for whom? And did whoever he was for win? P pled that the guttersnipe did not win.

A vision danced before him. Might this be what they always meant about one's life flashing before one's eyes? If so, where was his mother? Virginia? Poor Virginia. Sarah? Henry, his long-dead brother. No, not them. Rather, the vision was of G, his insufferable journey with the insufferable G.

G, the hopsnot rapscallion, the only one besides maybe Hoffman who might hold a candle to him and then only if he wasn't such a joker. Before all the bad stuff, all the blunders and shit luck . . .

The meter of the rainfall accelerated. Dactyls now, alien rhythms . . .

The black blobs writhed across G's face. G's body was like a taut wire that kept getting plucked by the grimy appendage of some external force. His teeth chattered and he felt sure they were loosening. He stared straight up, straight through the writhing black blobs to the geometric patterns on the ceiling.

"How much longer?" G asked the bloodletter.

The bloodletter didn't answer.

One of the black blobs inched along the pointy ridge of his nose. Might be cute if it wasn't after his blood. It reared up and smelled the air. G had the dreaded sense that it would dive into his eye. The bloodletter pinched it off before it could dive into his eye or latch onto his schnozz again. He pinched off all the rest of the leeches, sliding his fingernail under the jaws to detach those still sucking.

Oh, the hunger at the pit of him.

The other bloodletter sliced into his leg. The external force plucked his body and his teeth chattered but he didn't even feel the cuts anymore. How much had they drained out of him? He felt cold, weak, sick, but the bloodletters would save him. They had saved him before and they would save him again.

They loosened the tethers on his arms and left the room. One of them lay a hand on his sweat-soaked brow in what was meant as an affectionate gesture, but G recoiled at human touch. The bloodletters left the room. He swung his smeared legs off the bed, covered them with the gown, and picked up his satchel. Inside were pages and pages, tattered and yellow. His scrawl covered them. He held a page to the candlelight.

Drivel. A decade of work and every line drivel. What had become of him? He read silently, drops of blood from the bites on his nose fell on the manuscript.

In truth, he did not remember writing this farce, this fraud. The public would read it and laugh at him like they laughed at his first book. It would spoil the legacy of the only good work he'd done. No, this could not be known.

G remembered what K had said. He'd be damned for this work, K said. This work was sin incarnate, he said.

He collapsed before the blue tile fireplace, the manuscript spilling across the floor. He gathered pages and whipped them into the fire. They curled and blackened, letting out smoke that smelled of mushrooms. The flame grew, the smoke spinning off in little pigs' tails.

P's voice played in his head. As the pages burned, he thought of that time when he was young and calm and clear-sighted. He thought of when he used to burn his manuscripts with joy just to rewrite them better. *Fire*, P had said. *Fire is a great refiner.* The line came to him as if from a million miles away, from a different lifetime. P, the son of a bitch.

G put his hand to his nose. The leeches' anticoagulant was wearing off, and the blood was congealing. He experienced a moment, just one singular moment of peace, hardly a second, before his heart dropped and he realized it: A trick! He'd been tricked! The devil!

2.

P flipped the pages of the pamphlet, staring at the impenetrable lines.

Trying to read a language you didn't know was one thing, but he loved how traveling reduced everything to the senses, reduced everything to just what it was. Ordering a cup of coffee or discerning the simple convention of walking down the street might render you helpless, a child.

He kind of got it in other places, say Greece, but nothing like here. Here was something beyond his ken. Further, the aesthetic allure—those onion domes, the ladies' dresses, the manner of being—his kind of place . . .

A man appeared, snatching up all remaining copies from the shelf of the very pamphlet P was holding and spilling them in front of the proprietor.

"I wish to buy these," the man said to the proprietor.

"You wish to buy these, sir?"

"All of these. I wish to buy them."

"Sir, you yourself sold them here several days ago."

"There's been an unfortunate, er, error! They all have to go back."

P did not understand any of this other than that the interaction was odd for both interlocutors. The man looked over his shoulder and only then did P get a load of the schnozz on him. The man's face was a boat and the nose was its sail. The man noticed that P was holding a copy of the book and approached him, making what P interpreted as formal greetings.

"English," P said, "American." G looked taken aback before collecting himself and speaking in a stilted and nasal but interpretable English.

"Sir, this is rather inopportune . . . er, ah, the matter is. I'm speaking here about the book in your hand there. There's been a . . . what some might call a mistake or problem—an error of sorts. A printing error, yes! I've been obliged to, like your cowboys with the cattle, round them up, so to say. If you'd not mind, you see, I've no choice in the matter. Deep apologies. I am sorry."

"I can't read it anyway," P said.

"It's better that way in all truth . . . it's, er, my gratitude to you."

The sight of the man's nose put P into a state of reverie. G's hand was outstretched and yet P held onto the book. It made a slight hook to one side, but like those paintings in which the eyes follow you wherever you stand, the nose seemed to hook toward P no matter the direction the man turned his head.

"Of course. Of course. Printing errors of magnitude should not be countenanced. Disrespect to the reader and of course to the writer."

G's pained face transformed as he took the book. Relief washed over him. "I see you're a man of culture," G said. He bowed. G gave the proprietor some bills and he left, arms full of the books.

P could not say why but he followed him outside where G bumped into an old lady who called him something that P could not understand but that sounded vile, and he scrambled to pick up the books. P knelt to help.

"Let me give you a hand," P said.

"Don't touch!" the man said. "Don't touch them."

"My apologies. I wanted to help."

The man's body sagged and he went to all fours. Passersby made their way around them, leaving footprints on the books.

"Might you wish, um, what I'm saying is . . . well, I haven't been a very good host on behalf of my nation. Where are you from?" G said.

"Richmond," P said.

"Hm, might we, if you'd wish we could, let's say, repair to a local hostelry," G said.

"I thought you'd never ask."

They collected all the copies and dipped into a little jaunt. They stacked the books on the table. G ordered heated goat milk with a shot of rum, a piece of white bread, and chocolate. P said, "I'd had in mind the local nepenthe, but make it another heated goat milk with rum. Hold the white bread, double chocolate." G did his best to translate this and then removed a newspaper from his coat pocket. He turned a few pages and opened it in front of P.

P could not read it, but he could smell a bad review a mile away.

"You won't believe what they're saying."

"Quote me one line."

G cleared his throat. "After reading this drivel, it is unclear why, as the publisher states in his introductory note, the man is proud to introduce to the public this young new 'poet.'"

"Who's the publisher?"

"That'd be me."

"And the poet?"

"Moi."

They held up their glasses of heated goat milk and rum, nodded at each other, and sipped. G bit off a corner of his square of chocolate, and P bit off a corner of his square of chocolate. G took out another newspaper and set it down on the table. P made out that the mast read, *Moscow Telegraph*.

"This one's even worse," G said. He pinched some bread out of the slice and rolled it between his thumb and pointer.

"So there wasn't any printing error is what you're saying?"

"Rather, um—how would you say?—*disposing of the evidence?* Unfortunately, they're deposited at every bookstore in the city."

"Slam that goat milk," P said. "You and me are going to round up these puppies. Can you hire a carriage?"

In several hours the majority of the print run covered the muddy carriage floor. Despite the fact that G groped at his heart every time they discovered a copy or two sold before they arrived, he was in better spirits now.

"And now to the Neva," G said, "where these embarrassments will sleep forever with the fishes!"

"No, no, my friend," said P. "Fire. Fire is the great refiner!"

A spark lit in G's eye. "Yes," he said. "Yes, you're right. Fire. Coachman, to the square near the Kalinkin bridge."

In the course of this endeavor a rapid acquaintanceship took place between the two men. G learned that P was also a poet and taleteller, and they bonded over a shared love of the Prussian with his mouse kings and sandmen.

In the square they pitched the copies into a nice pile. Though it was still light out, there was a candle on in a sentry box at the far end of the square. G handed the coachman some bills. "Go negotiate with the sentry. We'll have a quick burn and we'll be on our way. No need for any hubbub." The coachman set off for the sentry box.

P found himself transfixed by the city and would spontaneously rave, "Magisterial. Decadent. It's older than my entire nation." Their errand had amounted to a fine introduction for P to the city, the canals, the river, the Hay Market, the churches and cathedrals, the Italian facades, and the Gostiny Dvor.

G said, "It's built by a tyrant genius and one hundred thousand serfs, whose bones are rotting in the swamp beneath our feet. A bonafide ghost town if ever there was one."

A lamplighter passed by, and they borrowed his flame. G tore the cover from one of his books and rolled it to make a little torch, which he touched to the lamplighter's flame and then touched to the pile. It smoldered black, caught, and burned. The lamplighter went on, looking back over his shoulder at the sight of two strange men burning a pile of books in the square.

"Feeling better?" P asked.

"Always a relief it is, disposing of the evidence."

P appreciated the man's smile. It lit up his face. At the same time, G, flush with joy, considered P. They were born in the same year and yet P looked twenty years older than he did. He had no nose to speak of, just a rugged little *kusochik* of cartilage in the center of his beet-red face.

"You've done me a great service. I cannot repay you."

"Nothing I like better than a good book burn," P said.

They assumed footsteps behind them meant the coachman's return, but it turned out to be two ruffians. They were all shoulders and heads, knees and boots. They got right into G's and P's faces, and their breath smelled of pickles and liquor.

"You gents have your fire so's you won't be needing these," said one of them, seizing hold of their collars. G was about to shout, "Watch," when the second man thrust a fist about the size of a human head into his mouth, muttering, "Now scream!"

The men stripped off P's and G's coats and kneed them in their backs. They fell before the fire of G's books, curling ashes wafting about.

As fast as they appeared, the ruffians disappeared.

The men stood and brushed themselves off.

"Were it winter, we'd be fucked," G said.

"And we have fire, the warmth of the light from your early attempts. The best, my friend, is yet to come!" G felt overcome by a sense of endearment toward the man.

"I leave tomorrow for my home. Join me."

"I don't have any money. Honestly, I don't know how I may get home."

"Then it's settled. This is how I shall repay you."

3.

P gave G a copy of his book, and G read it on the carriage ride to Ukraine.

"Why didn't you put your name on it?" G, who had used a pseudonym on his own book, asked.

"Why didn't you put your name on yours, Mr. V?" P said.

"The reviewers knew. Everyone knew. Correction—everyone would have known if not for, well, if not for your kind assistance in disposing of the evidence."

"Mine was discernible, given the right inquiries."

"'A Bostonian' it says? I thought you said you were from Richmond."

"Richmond but born in Boston so, well, technically."

G felt it must be the case that P had left his name off the book so as to potentially distance himself from a juvenile work. It was clear that P knew little of the historical figure he based the poem on, and in any event the figure was immaterial. Any powerful or successful figure from any epoch might have served just as well. He was put there for the reader to recognize only that for all the power he'd amassed, it came at the expense of love.

But who was he to judge? G thought. And then he promptly answered that thought: he was someone who had had the sense to burn every extant copy of his juvenile work. He puffed up and let his head totter with the bumps of the carriage.

P presumed that G had found the book so good as to put his own to utter shame. He felt for the man, who must have taken it with a mix of jealousy and admiration. He who had been forced to burn his own first book had borne witness to the real deal. P was a little sorry for G and quite pleased with himself and sat in satisfaction watching the birch forests through which they passed.

4.

G's mother ran out to greet her boy as he leapt from the carriage into her arms. P cried watching her cradle and rock him like a babe. Then he introduced himself with a bow. She touched his cheek. Maria Ivanovna reminded P of his aunt who was also named Maria.

For P, the visit to Poltava was a blur of sights and sounds and impressions. The Triumphal Arche dedicated to Alexander I, covered in copper decorations that all the locals believe to be gold. A black and white cow chained to the side of the road. Whole seas of sunflowers and fields of rye and buckwheat. And two churches, the first surrounded by rowan trees and orange berries and to which G's mother had gone to pray to St. Nicholas for a child after her stillbirths. G confessed to P that every time he passed the second church, the one with the golden spire, that he hallucinated a painting of the devil on the side.

G's family estate was the highlight, though. It was like the home that P never had.

G and P spent the majority of their time there eating and walking. In fact, P watched in fascination as G consumed delicacy after delicacy and meal after meal. One night he polished off zakuski and a dozen blini dipped in butter before they headed to a tavern and he ordered suckling pig with horseradish and sour cream.

A typical day of eating for his new friend: coffee, lard biscuits, poppy-seed pies, salted mushrooms, vodka, dried fish, various porridges, savory stews, watermelon, pears, fruit dumplings with berries, more lard biscuits, truffle-infused risotto, duck confit, and molten chocolate lava cake. On some days they had marinade with black-currant leaf, wild thyme, or cloves and walnuts. They wrapped honey-drenched poppy seeds in soft bread and chased vodka with pickled saffron milk cap mushrooms.

When not eating, P and G walked the estate. G utilized his shiny black cane with the goose-head handle. It was too short for him now but he used it anyway, though there was nothing visibly wrong with his gait. G told P about how his father had led him around the estate as a boy handing him stones to throw. Wherever the stones landed, his father planted G's favorite trees, linden and oak, which trees now dotted the estate.

His father liked to sit in the grotto, and so G sat in there too whenever he was home. There was a rock in front of the grotto that he asked P to sit on rather than inside, out of respect for the sanctity of the grotto and his father's memory.

P honored this request and sat on the rock outside, desiring for himself a grotto and a father who'd erected a grotto and left it for him, his son, that P might ask others to not trespass thereunto out of respect for the sanctity of his father's memory.

As they sat silently, P wondered whether the G family crest was horseshoe-shaped because of the pond or whether the pond was horseshoe-shaped because of the crest. The latter would suggest they had a lot more coin than he presumed.

One evening, after P retired, he heard G and Maria Ivanovna talking. G begged her for money for their trip. They spoke English. Why? P could not say. Maybe, it occurred to him later, it was precisely so that he might overhear them. G described P to his mother as an "exalted being," a "god slightly clothed in human passions." Such fancy had nothing on the bullshit that P had told his loved ones to get money, but he appreciated these phrasings.

In the morning, G said, "She's springing for it. We're going to America!"

They celebrated their last day with fishing, an idea his mother thought they would enjoy, and though neither of them was into it, neither fisherman per se, they felt the need to put on a good show of it if only to honor her kindness. One of the servants arrived with poles and tackle and a bucket of freshwater shrimp, formidable, thumpy ones.

The servant seemed to understand that neither man had fished.

He said something to G and G translated, "He asks if we know how to hook the shrimp."

"We do not know how to hook the shrimp," P said.

"He says if you put it in their brains they die straightaway."

"Don't we want to put them out of their misery?"

"Apparently we want to extend their misery as long as possible."

The servant inserted the hook through the creature's exoskeleton sideways.

"He says to tuck it in gently just behind the horn."

"Tuck it in where?"

"Behind the horn."

"The horn?"

"The horn."

P and G nodded. The servant looked amused. He handed the pole with the baited hook to G.

P held a shrimp by the legs and ran his finger along its smooth back. Then he took the hook from the end of his line and gouged it, as instructed, behind the horn. He cast and the shrimp flew off the hook, plooshing into the surf quite far away from where P's line lay across the water.

"Oopsie," P said.

The servant, recognizing the men's hopelessness, took leave of them.

P gouged another shrimp, gently, behind the horn, or what he believed to be the horn, which, left to his own devices, he would have called a *spike*.

It bucked when he punctured it, and then he cast, plunking it into the surf.

"That's where all the big ones are," G said, and as if he were some kind of prophet, the line went taut. It yanked the pole out of his hand. G snagged it and brought it back to him, reeling hard, the pole bending.

After some time and effort, P reeled in a fish. It flopped in the sand. It was hefty but short and had a mouth big enough to swallow a bottle of vodka.

The fish's mouth was bleeding. G asked P how he was going to get the hook out. "I'm not," he said. He cut the line with a knife and kicked the fish into the pond.

"Shame," said G. "We could have made four-cornered fish pie out of him."

But the whole fishing business was gruesome, G thought. He set his pole down and drank his beer. It warmed his stomach and made him want to pee. He kicked over the shrimp bucket and all the shrimp spilled out. G felt good about kicking over the shrimp bucket.

They sat out there until the sunset.

"We're a little early in the season. I'd have liked to take you to find the fern flower. It blooms on the night of Ivan Kupala."

"Fern flower? You mean fiddleheads?"

"A rare sight. The blooms are ordinarily yellow, but on Ivan Kupala night, they're red. A witch appears when you pick it, but she'd probably require a blood sacrifice."

"We might have given the witch fish blood."

"I don't believe witches accept fish blood," G said. "I'm turning in. Long days of travel ahead."

They brought the poles and tackle inside for the servant to collect the next day, and they retired to their quarters.

P awoke shortly thereafter. He often awoke at night. P could hear G snoring through several doors. P hated waking at night. It was the most awful time to be awake. He flipped on his side, and that is when he heard something else.

P guessed at first that it was his own heart. He placed his fingers on his pulse and listened to the slow heartbeat, perfectly counting seconds. But this sound was not the trochee of a heartbeat. Rather, a hard, pulsing *thwock*. *Thwock* followed by a cavernous echo.

P stood. He shivered and then froze in the middle of the room. The sound was deafening. No, it was not possible—the whole house should wake up if it was real. But no one stirred. The sound could not be real. The sound must be in his mind. Had something broken in his mind?

P went into the hall. With every step the sound rang out. *Thwock*. And then the cacophonous punctuation. If this sound was a bird it would be a cormorant. If this sound was a verb it would mean to beat your loved ones.

As he stood in the bathroom, the sound ceased to be external to P. It was inside of him. The *thwock* ricocheted off the inside of his skull and his whole head vibrated. P put his hands to his head and felt the vibrations.

P plunged into a deep fear. Nausea overcame him and a coldness washed down his chest. Flashes of light twinkled around him and then . . . calmth. He was a young man and Frances Allan was stroking the back of his head, petting him like a little dog, saying, "There there, my sweet. There there, my little boy." P came to on the floor. He pushed himself up. There was a small blotch of red on the hardwood. He touched his forehead, dabbed blood.

The *thwock* again. And that's when he saw the bucket move in concert with the sound. What was this?

He creeped toward the bucket, peered in. And there was the culprit.

One of the shrimp had managed to hang on after G kicked over the bucket. This whole time it had been trying to hop out, thwacking its body against the steel of the bucket. P's mind had tuned into the shrimp's desperation and fear. He had a connection to a crustacean.

P scooped up the little fella and walked outside. The shrimp thwacked and jabbed in his cupped hands. It was an athletic shrimp. He would like to see it in a thwacking/jabbing contest.

Outside, the moon was nowhere to be found. A moonless sky always made him sad. He walked down to the horseshoe-shaped pond and held his hands open. The shrimp thwacked out and splashed somewhere into the dark water.

5.

A truly strange event occurred within the borders of the territory of Italy—a series of carriages transported them from Ukraine to the Western Edge of Europe, along, it must be said, a circuitous route. Neither could explain the experience and neither ever felt comfortable discussing it with anyone. It returned to them in flashbacks from time to time, particularly later in life, but for the most part the episode, and its attendant hauntings, lay buried in the closets of their souls.

It might be described as a shared hallucination, if indeed it was a hallucination. A collective pit stop in an alternative spatiotemporality.

It began when G noticed a gelatinous bubble or cloud in the roadway up ahead.

"What is it?" G asked.

"It's road," the driver answered, seeming oblivious to the bubble.

But as they approached and then entered into the bubble—P thought he could see sets of yellow eyes refracted in water, G saw a geometric pattern—they found themselves no longer in the coach but standing in something resembling a ballroom. Their dusty clothes from the carriage were gone, and they were instead done up in the most fashionable habiliment. Music played from a piano somewhere, and dignified personages from both of their worlds fluttered about on the dance floor. They thought that they recognized some, but it was a little hard to tell because everyone, including them, they realized, to their surprise, was wearing facial coverings that looked like duckbills. The duckbills were white and had straps that wrapped around the backs of the wearers' heads.

G and P looked at each other. The duckbill had changed G's face considerably. The size of the schnozz did not register as it would without it. It was untenable that the schnozz fit under the mask, distorting, as it did, the topography of his mug, but it seemed to, or maybe it was all just a trick of the light.

A man approached them and hovering beside him was a red balloon of human size and shape, curvaceously feminine shape to be precise. The balloon also had a duckbill mask on its face but no discernible eyes or ears, just smooth balloon skin where everything should be.

"I would like to introduce you to your wife, sir," the man said to G. G chuckled. For all his neuroses, he had a good sense of humor. "Call me L," the man said.

"Good day, L," P said. "May I ask you to repeat yourself. Did you just say that you'd like to introduce my friend to his own wife?"

"This is his wife, according to future perception. This is how he'll be known, as the womanless friend who married a red balloon."

The smile disappeared from G's face. He looked with some horror at the man and then at the red balloon standing arm in arm beside him. "You will be such an indiscernible laughingstock; this is what they'll say about you. About your best work, you'll be glorified—movies, fame, grandeur. But they'll say about you only that you consummated love with a synthetic ball of air."

The music stopped. A door slammed. Everyone turned.

P recognized then his Aunt Maria. She was in a cauldron. She was being boiled in a cauldron and someone was cutting her legs off.

A new man had crashed into the hall. He took a dramatic pose. He wore the duckbill mask, only his was red, the exact color of the red balloon with L. The man removed the mask and fell into a coughing and sneezing fit, kneeling and then keeling over onto his side where he choked and spasmed. Everyone took small steps away from the spasming man. He rolled onto his back and heaved.

"We have to get him out of the hall," someone shouted.

"He'll infect us all," another.

Everyone was transfixed by the spectacle except G, who, finding himself standing next to the balloon, lowered his mask and then reached for the mask on the red balloon and slid it over the top of her head. He pressed his face against the smooth place where, if the red balloon had a mouth, its mouth would be. P saw then that the nose was a major impediment to affectionate interaction for his friend. The balloon did not even have a nose to counter G's with, but G's nose extended far enough that it was difficult for him to kiss the place where her mouth should be. His chin rose up, and the top of his head went way back. P could not be sure the kiss was consummated, but the cries of the crowd drowned out the pop—.

Then G and P were back in the carriage, the long open road ahead of them. They looked at each other, at each other's face absent the duckbill masks. They looked behind them and saw the other side of the gelatinous bubble they had passed through.

"Lunch is nigh," the coachman said.

"A little further please, down the road," P said. "We'd like to eat lunch a little further down the road if you will."

G's fingers fished in his mouth for a second, and then he drew out a shriveled red noodle that he held in the air between the two men. With the exception of this episode the trip was monotonous and uneventful, and P and G worked when they could but mostly lay in reverie contemplating this episode.

6.

As they waited to board the ship, G considered turning back. His stomach was doing weird things. And the relations between the two men had begun to sour. What had he called P to his mother? An exalted being? An exalted idiot perhaps. P kept giving G stupid puzzles to solve and asking him to come up with substitution ciphers—"Stump me!" P implored—and spouting off puns.

"Why does a lady in tight corsets never need comfort?" P had asked him. "Because she's so laced!" He died laughing and then calmly explained the joke to G. A corset so laced. Solaced.

In the night P cried out, something about a cauldron, waking G. Because of this he hadn't slept and he wouldn't sleep the longer they were bunked up.

G abhorred puzzles and ciphers and cryptograms and made his feelings known. P would not let up.

What was he doing going to America with this waste of protoplasm? What was he doing going to America? He was up for a teaching post in St. Petersburg. And if that didn't work out, well, he didn't want to be in America. Italy seemed nice. Maybe Italy? He stared at himself in the mirror, stared at his hideous nose in the mirror. Some vision took hold: he saw black blobs crawling around his face and sucking blood from his nose. In the distance, a rickety ladder. There was a story his grandmother used to tell about a ladder that carried people's souls to heaven. The black blobs leapt from his face and sprinted to the ladder. They descended it. He screamed and felt the urge to flee.

He can't say what eventually calmed him. Certainly, to some degree, the notion that maybe he should at least see the new world while he had a guide, a friend, one might say, with him. And anyway, he was a free Cossack after all.

P had had his doubts about the trip too. G's admiration of him was problematic, unreciprocated as it was. Trouble awaited him in Boston. Why go back there? He had lived with Frances and Mr. Allan in London ten years ago during a time that was maybe the only truly happy period of his life. There were connections there he could seek out. No creditors were after him there. But the draw of home is sometimes too much, and he felt a sense of responsibility to return the favor to G, who needed him if he was going to get by there.

7.

Fuck the devil, G thought with glee. *Gleefully fuck the devil.* He'd devised a brilliant plan upon realizing who had tricked him into destroying his genius, and now he would have his revenge. He would starve himself.

The prospect of starving himself to death did not bother him. He was likely already halfway there. His only concern had to do with the later stages of starvation. What was that like? Might he, at his weakest, lose consciousness and be mistaken for dead? He had stipulated in his will that he should not be buried until the obvious signs of decomposition appear. But who would heed his wishes? The bloodletters? They seemed to G as ready to be done with him as he was to be done with himself. Their leeches were thirsty for something more viscous than G's thin blood. They'd want him in the ground first thing. And already there had been times over the course of his illness when his entire body went numb, and his heart all but stopped, when they could pack him inside a coffin and plant him underground, the repellent smell of wood and earth assaulting him.

In any event, certainly death by starvation was more definitive than death by whatever his condition was. He came to believe it likely that, given his condition, he'd be interred during one of his episodes. Most coffins were not going to be deep enough to contain his nose. Some hungover day laborer wouldn't hesitate to smash it whilst nailing on the coffin lid. He could see himself lying there, the slightest protrusion of his schnozz in the warping ply, drowning on his own blood before blessedly, at exhaustive length, asphyxiating.

He had of course requested a deeper coffin. But no one bothers after the wishes of the dead. They simply go through the motions, sweeping the dust under the rug.

Along with their love of Hoffman, G and P shared this fear, one central to their lives and practice. Yes others bond over chess or religion, dice or sport, drink or women, hobby or quest. P and G bonded over the fear of being buried alive.

It's funny, the trek on the ship was bleary and clouded in memory. Not a single definitive moment stood out. But as soon as they disembarked P got squirrely and it all came into sharp relief.

There were shifty faces all over the Boston shipyards. P couldn't know who would be looking for him. They navigated through the streets and came eventually to a station where a strange train waited. This train was not a regular train of the day. It had the curvaceous and shiny spirit of future. While steam, it had closed carriages and inside something like book sleeves stacked vertically for passengers to sleep in. G did not know why P was squirrelly and how he had obtained two tickets for them on a train that should not exist, but he was now totally and completely in the madman's land and to a large extent, at his mercy. They settled into their coupe and the train left the station. In no time at all they entered forests and mountains.

"That Germanist Irving would set one of his plagiarized fairy tales there." P pointed his stubby finger out the window. "I steal, but I only steal from myself."

"Thievery is thievery."

"It is and it isn't."

"Your country smells like a chocolate bar," G said.

"Your country smells like nutmeg. Heady."

"Touché."

Except for the brief time at the G estate, they had been in a state of forward motion together since they had met. But this was the best version of forward motion. It was comfortable and fast but not too fast, and the ride was tranquil.

Despite the pleasantness, in a kind of harbinger of the fear and loathing to come, conversation sometimes petered out between them. It just flowed right out like liquid through a funnel. And they both sought their solitude, writing and sulking in each other's company.

The first night G readied himself for bed, got into his gown, tended to his toilet. Back in the car he climbed into the book sleeve. The clackety-clack, clackety-clack kept him awake for some time, but eventually he lapsed into a half-sleep, and in his half-sleep he saw himself lying in the pine-board coffin that he often saw himself in. He sweated and his bowels contracted. He slid out and breathed deep, then tended to his toilet once again.

He wandered the empty train, finding himself in the dining car where, to his surprise, P sat before a glass of scotch, his eyes bewildered, dancing in their sockets.

"I thought you were still sleeping like a baby."

"I should have told you, G, I am a taphephobe. I may never sleep in these human book sleeves they've concocted."

"You too? I have dreamt myself in the coffin more times than I can count. Always, the coffin is not deep enough for my schnozz."

"Your schnozz is not that bad, G. You're on about it too much. Let it ride. You keep obsessing like that and who knows what it will do to you, your work."

"Generous of you to say, sir. One cannot know one's strengths without knowing one's weaknesses."

"Once immured your schnozz will be the least of your worries."

"The truth is," G said, "that immurement as a punishment is cruel and terrible, but it is not equivalent to being buried alive. In immurement the victim dies of dehydration or starvation. When buried alive, one dies of asphyxiation."

"Shouldn't coffins come standard with a bell pull connected to an above-ground dinger?"

"They absolutely should. And a breathing apparatus."

"Do you imagine horrors—do you imagine them to the degree that you, you know, experience them?"

"True wretchedness. It is true wretchedness."

"But the object of our journey is the opposite of being buried alive. We should remember that. We are here to live!"

P, spirits lifted, switched subjects.

"I have concocted for you a simple cryptogram. I know they are not your thing, but if you'd do this one I'd never ask you again."

G felt they were having a tender moment, and he assented. P reached into his pocket where he had the cryptogram ready:

W hxp qmr ag yki lb rzglr
Tbva hxp qmr lbi ayi
Tlsllcgajpl
Lktqle

"I will do my best," G said.

"So there's this one about a cat," P said, offering to G for the first time the germ of an idea. "Or rather it is about a man, a cruel alcoholic. His relationship with his cat goes through several stages. He tortures it, as we do animals, and then feels guilty and then slowly gets over his guilt and tortures it again. Soon he has gouged out its eyes and strung it up. A lookalike cat appears with a gallows on its chest. The man is losing his mind by now. In an instant of rage he goes to kill the cat but instead kills his wife, who cannot abide animal murder. He encases the body in the wall with . . . wait for it . . . wait for it . . . the cat! Incessant meowing ensues. He cannot detect wherefrom. The mewling completes his madness and eventually gives him up to the authorities."

G made no sound and did not move his face or body other than to blink.

"Something along those lines," P said.

"The premise is a bit predictable."

"Aha, predictable but True."

"Perhaps."

"The cat was immured," P said.

"What?" G said. "What?"

"Immured. The cat was immured. But your sympathies will not be with the feline, will they?"

"My sympathies may lie only with the immured cat. But that is not the point of the story."

"Of course that is not the point of the story. You are a special man if your sympathies lie with the immured cat. Have you had a cat? You do not seem like a cat man."

"I am not a cat man; I am a grotto man. When I inherit my parents' estate, I shall sit alone in my father's for all of time and if I must be buried let me be buried there, in the grotto."

P did not rightly understand this reaction.

"Might it sit better were the cat drowned?" G asked.

"How's that?"

"Did you think of having the fine fellow drown the cat rather than hang it? Like in a pool or pond for instance."

"I need the hanging for a special little detail, an effigy in fire and smoke, an echo of the gallows in the white mark on the lookalike beast."

"I see."

P sensed something off and tried to change the subject. "Have you heard, my dear G—'Le Refus' by Pierre-Jean de Béranger. 'His heart is a suspended lute, as soon as it is touched, it resounds . . .'"

"Overwrought," said G. "My god, you Americans are sentimental sops."

"He's French."

"I'm talking about you. You. Now, allow me to recollect a melancholy incident that transformed forever the life of a peaceful nook in the Ukrainian countryside. Two peasants, a man and woman. Their home has singing doors. No one can say why the doors sing, whether it is because of rusty hinges or because someone had installed some mechanism. No one knows. One makes a tinkle, one makes a bass, another says, 'Oh, I'm so cold.' And so on. But here comes the cat. The woman loves the cat, the man tolerates it but does not see its value. The cat disappears and when found again it seems to have turned feral. The woman is distraught. It comes inside to eat but if not feral, it is . . . different somehow. She sees it as a harbinger of death and indeed she soon falls ill and dies. Soon after the man dies. Someone else takes over the estate, and it falls into disrepair under the stewardship of some cheap Moscow bastard. And so on like that. These things do happen."

"And you said we are the sentimental sops. Nice touch with that feral cat."

Upon his deathbed, G felt himself slipping. Shame and guilt choked his heart. G had not thought of the cat, the one that P's story had reminded him of from his childhood. Had he really drowned it? Had he been the one to throw it again and again? Who was that boy who had done that and what relation did he have to the man G was, the young man on the train and the man who lay there on his deathbed? A terrifying notion kicked up: the cat was waiting for G on the other side, at the bottom of the ladder, the real cat that he had drowned as a boy and that feral cat from the countryside and maybe the black cat that the cruel alcoholic hanged and the lookalike with the gallows on its chest.

P eventually wrote his story and sent it to G some years ago, but G never could bring himself to read it.

On the train, in the human book sleeve, G wanted to sleep, but his eye . . . try as he might, his right eye would not close.

8.

The rat looked at P. P knew what it wanted. The vermin might as well be translucent as clearly as he could see through to its heart. It was waiting for him to drown in the ditch. But frankly he had a greater concern. When would the laudanum clear his system?

P thought, Suppose I made it through the night without drowning only to be found by some of the marauders' consorts in the morning. They might rush me to the coffin, and what then? I'm under the laudanum, they get me in the coffin, pound in the nails, lower me down and cover it quick with dirt. Claim I'm some bum, some street hoodlum, anything but what I am, indisputably, this country's greatest living writer. Once down there there's not much recourse. Resort to long slow breaths and pounding on the lid. You can't pound too hard, overexert, just a TAP-ah-TAP-ah-TAP-ah-TAP-ah. There is maybe seven hours of air down there. If they bury you in the morning you have a bit more cause for hope, someone might hear, TAP-ah-TAP-ah-TAP-ah-TAP-ah. If night falls you're as good as gone.

What I need do is not be face down in this ditch, P thought. I need to turn myself over. If I can do it then I can avoid drowning. Will I lose sight of the rat? I will. But I am going to have to live with that. The rat is going to do what the rat is going to do. It has lived its life. It has grievances with people no doubt. I could understand any number of revenge scenarios circulating through its mind right this moment, driven by hunger or maybe even some sense of comeuppance.

And suddenly, I am on my back, looking at what is left of the night sky, at the rain falling. I see an elderly bearded man dressed in robes and with wings. He glares at me and then he moves. And what is that he is holding? A scythe swinging over my chest. It is my own mind working against me here.

No, P told himself, you were not mistaken for a homeless person at the bar and conscripted into a zombie voting scheme. You were not changed into the clothes of true homeless people and left in a ditch. You are not now lying on your back in the water of a rapidly rising ditch. And maybe it was not such a great idea to be on your back after all. Maybe all that effort and exertion building on blinks and sputters was a stupid idea. What a metaphor for my life!

Where is my valise? P thought. I'm going to need my lectures. If I'm getting up out of this ditch, I'm going to need my lectures . . .

The rat stands atop his head. It has summoned the bravery to make of him an island. And it, the rat whose yellow eyes he's been staring into all this time he's been in the ditch, has brought a population with it. They scatter and bite up and down P's body. P wants to laugh. The rats are now crawling under him. They are smart. Now they will eat him from underneath to keep their fur dry. But what is this? They are not staying out of the rain, they are writhing and huddling together. They form a mass and nudge him up. He exhales on a pillow of rats while they sacrifice themselves, drowning underneath his head, giving him just the reprieve he needs, before they are washed away down the ditch.

9.

The trains sometimes dead-ended. When the trains dead-ended, G and P mounted carriages to take them to the next station. The carriages sometimes dead-ended. When the carriages dead-ended, G and P walked.

Once, walking across Georgia or North Carolina or Virginia or Tennessee, the two men came by several roadside stands. At the first stand, a toothless man sold boiled peanuts.

"What precisely is going on here?" P asked.

"Not much going on, beyond boiling peanuts."

P and G looked at each other.

"Why, sir, may I ask, would you boil peanuts?" G asked.

"Ain't nothing, and I mean nothing, better than boiled peanuts. Everyone around here knows that. Ain't nothing I like better. Do I take correct by your manner of speeching that you are not from around here?"

"You take it correct, sir," G said.

"People from all over the world come through here and had my boiled peanuts. But I have not heard an accent like yours'n."

"I'm from Ukraine."

"Yucraint? I have never heard of Yucraint. That is a country? What do y'all boil if you do not boil peanuts in Yucraint?"

"We boil beets, potatoes, cabbages, carrots and . . . hm."

"Boiled beets!"

"We boil lots of things, sir. Soups we boil a great deal. Not nuts though."

"I am going to change your world, Mr. Yucraint." The man ladled several peanuts onto a stump. Boiling water ran along the grain and down the bark of the stump. The peanuts were dark grey. An earthy smell rose up from them. "You should appreciate that the peanut is a ground nut now, as opposed to a tree nut. There will be no boiling of tree nuts on my watch. Unnatural. Take it. Go on."

G took the boiled peanut. It felt like brain tissue from a still-warm corpse.

"Pop it wholesale in your piehole and then work the nugs out. You can spit the shell anywhere."

G did as the man instructed. For P, it was fulfilling to see G having such a moment with one of his countrymen. The peanut flooded his mouth with salt. He sucked the warm water, and then his tongue unwrapped the nuts. He chewed them a little. They squished and he spit the shell into a bush. This, he thought, is the taste of death. He might throw up, he thought.

"Now what do you think? Be honest with me now."

"Unspeakable," he said, gagging.

"You can have the rest there." G would never eat another boiled peanut. Not now and not ever. G moved along.

P stood at the adjacent stand with a toothless man selling oranges.

"Shall we have an orange?" P asked G.

"An orange sounds like a good idea." G glanced back and the toothless man at the boiled peanut stand was watching him.

"I cannot recollect the last time that I had an orange."

"I had an orange once. For Christmas."

"Take a few," the toothless man selling oranges said. "Wards off scurvy. You both look scurvy."

They each picked an orange. The toothless man with the boiled peanuts shook his head and made an outraged face when G placed a couple coins in the hand of the toothless man selling oranges.

G and P sat on some boards near the third stall, where a toothless man was selling wooden ducks.

"Do you have a knife?" P asked.

"I have a pen."

"Excuse us, sir, is there a technique you would recommend for getting into these oranges?"

"Use your nail," the toothless orange seller said. He snarled up his face and wiggled his thumb.

P and G gouged the oranges with their thumbs. G did not manage to pierce the orange flesh.

"The smell is exquisite," P said.

"A rich, tropical perfume," G said. "A fine antidote to the boiled peanuts. I would call this smell: life."

"Sunshine."

"Sunshine—even better."

"Ow," P said. "Ow, fuck." P got up and started jumping around, shaking his hand. The orange fell and rolled through the sand. "It burns. The peel's stuck under my nail. Give me that pen!"

G gave P his pen, and P dug the orange peel from under his thumbnail. He walked down to a nearby stream and submerged his hands.

G fiddled with his own orange and as he did so turned to examine the wooden ducks. "These are fine ducks, sir," G said. "I want one." G had managed to get through the peel part, but the fibrous white stuff was impenetrable. He decided just to eat it. He split the orange in two, watching the sinews of the fibrous stuff stretch and break. Juice spilled onto his shoes and onto the boards of the wooden duck stall. He felt proud that he had gotten the orange open. He popped a piece into his mouth.

"You can pick any one that you like. They're all for sale."

Let me see. G wandered the stall, popping orange pieces into his mouth and dripping juice down his chin and onto the boards.

G used his pant leg to buff the juice from the orange into his shoe. G made sure the toothless boiled peanut seller could hear and said, "I'd like one of the most expensive, one that cost you the most time."

"That's not how it works. Sometimes you work long and hard on one, and it's shit. Sometimes inspiration strikes and you hammer something out, and it's shit. And sometimes vice versa. I sell based on quality not on investment or material. The cost is one-hundred-percent divination. I don't charge for raw product."

G perused the shelves. The range of wooden ducks was stunning. It could not be said that the man did not have an identifiable aesthetic. It was an aesthetic similar to that which G felt defined most of his own body of work. It was folksy, yes. It was filled with love for the people wherefrom he had come. His skill in several areas was incomparable while there were flaws of basic technique in others. (While his beaks sucked, his feathers were remarkably lifelike. Running your fingers across his feathers you'd expect them to be soft and light and when it registered hard wood, you were taken aback.) The intent of the ducks reached beyond the plane of ordinary wooden duck whittling. He was an innovator who had tradition in mind and who had refined his craft. His ducks, also, were very very funny.

There were the realistic ducks with their green heads and blue highlights. There were the cartoonish ducks. There were the fantastic ducks. And there was a section of ducks that were not ducks at all. That last category was a bit much. Who wanted a duck that looked more like a turnip or a mongoose or a steamship than a duck? G appreciated the paean to the agrarians, the exotic animal lovers, and the tech aficionados. It was smart marketing, but the man had such a gift. It felt a shame that he stooped to market demand. If left to his own devices, if told that he need not subsist on his wooden-duck proceeds, that his subsistence would be taken care of and he need focus strictly on his artistry, what then would this man be capable of doing with wooden ducks?

"Fascinating," G said.

"You want to know the secret, young fellow?" the man said.

"Yes, I want to know the secret."

"Burn the early attempts, protoducks, models—you know. Let me just tell you. Sometimes they get ugly and no matter what you do to them, file, carve, whittle, smooth, you can't get that ugly out of them. Now there's good ugly and bad ugly and here I'm talking bad ugly. When there's one that's got that bad ugly in it, I burn it. Believe you me. There are wrong roads you go down in life and art, and some of those roads there ain't no coming back from. Shit the bed."

G swooned. "I have more in common with duck whittlers than scholars."

P returned, sullen and sans orange.

"What is it you gentlemen do?" the toothless wooden duck purveyor said.

"I am the greatest writer who has ever lived," G said.

"I am the greatest writer who has ever lived." P said.

"Writers?"

The toothless boiled peanut purveyor appeared behind them. "This un told me he don't have money, Clyde. That other one threw Zeke's perfectly good orange into the river. I seen him."

G lit up: "I told you I don't have money for your fucking peanuts. Boiling peanuts is unnatural, whereas carving ducks is a beatific craft. Your peanuts are not fit to adorn the most commercial of these ducks' backs. This man, Clyde the duck whittler, is an artisan. His work, as we say, is such that, well, a mosquito will not sharpen his nose!"

P worried that they might have to fistfight the toothless purveyor of boiled peanuts, and possibly, depending on the nature of their relationship, they might have to fistfight the toothless purveyor of boiled peanuts and Clyde, the toothless purveyor of wooden ducks, but after fronting another moment or two, the toothless purveyor of peanuts buggered off.

"This is the one that you want," Clyde said, handing G a gray duck with red eyes. G looked at it and decided that it was the very embodiment of evil. It was satanic. The eyes were clearly the eyes of a devil, black and red.

And while it was satanic, its plumage gave the impression that if a pillow was stuffed with it, that pillow would be the finest, softest pillow, upon which one would sleep the sweetest sleep. The feathers gave the impression that if they poofed up a pillow, you might fall into it as if into a cloud.

G held it under his arm like future little boys cuddle footballs.

The man handed a second wooden duck to P.

"This is supposed to be a duck?" P said. "Honestly, it doesn't look much like a duck."

"It's a duck. They're all ducks. They're all me. I am a duck."

G and P sensed that the three toothless purveyors might be dangerous and that they might have overstayed their welcome.

"It has some qualities of a crow or raven but I see its duckishness now," P said.

"Can I give you some advice?" the man said as they were walking off. "In life, you need to be pert humble and pert shit-don't-stink. Check ye selves, before ye wreck ye selves."

10.

G and P walked for some time before they got to the next train stop. The special train was there waiting like it always was. Back in their coupe, chugging across the land, G churned butter from milk that he acquired from farmers at stops and the two men ate it smeared on bread. Whenever they found someone selling jam, G bought as many jars as he could. He entertained P by showing how his gluttonous friends in Poltava ate jam. "Wait, I'd better show you how a friend of mine eats it, look, like this, and another friend of mine eats it like that," and so on. And while P laughed at his imitations, G emptied jar after jar.

Invariably the train line ended again, and there would be carriages in their future and nights in strange towns before they would find it again, waiting for them at some other station like a miracle.

In one such strange town they took a room.

They huddled together in a shared hotel bed. In the middle of the night, P announced, "There is a lyric that I would like to share with you my dear friend, G. When I am in mood it's one that brings me good cheer."

P sang:

On top of spaghetti
All Covered with cheese
I lost my poor meatball
when somebody sneezed.

The ballad of a meatball propelled across the table by the hero's sneeze was inventive, thought G. After rolling out the door, passing through the garden and under a bush, the meatball turned to mush. But then inexplicably it rose from its emulsified state and grew into a meatball tree, which without so much as pollination produced the next generation of meatballs.

G felt touched. A single tear manifested in his eye and rode the steep angle of his nose to the very tip.

Their legs bumped. G was horrified at the feel of P's leg, a warm cactus. P slid his scratchy leg across G's shin.

"*Freakadelki*," G said.

"Come again," P said.

"Meatballs in my tongue: Freakadelki!"

G dozed. P rolled over. G dreamed of meatballs. For his part P could not sleep. He drank a pint of coffee before bed. The moonlight was shining into the room and cast a white glow over everything. He was startled by a shadow in the corner of the ceiling, a bird gazing down at the bed. He got up for a closer look. He thought there must be a bird sitting outside the window and the moonlight was casting its shadow on the wall, but it turned out not to be the case. The culprit was the wooden duck that the toothless wooden duck whittler had given P, the one that looked like a raven or crow. But who had placed it atop the bust of Pallas, god of war?

G shouted, "They're rolling over me!"

"G, G, wake up," P said. "You're dreaming of meatballs. Wake up! G, did you put the duck on Pallas?"

"What?"

"Did you put the wooden duck—did you put it on Pallas?"

G slowly raised his head. "Yes, yes I put the duck on Pallas!"

"Phew," P said. "Scared the shit out of me. Was starting to think it flew up there its own self."

"Wooden ducks don't fly," G said. "On top of Old Pallas, all covered with cheese . . ."

This invention, said in G's thick accent, made P laugh.

"That is the funniest you've ever been."

"You want to hear something funny? My name means wood duck. But the kids in school always called me 'mysterious dwarf.'"

The two men laughed uproariously. The landlady barged in. "It's the middle of the night!" she screamed. "Why is that wooden duck on my bust of Pallas? By dawn I'll have you out of my establishment and off my property!" She slammed the door.

"Wait, G means 'wooden duck' in your tongue?"

"Wood duck, a type. The most colorful of waterfowl. Not to be confused with a Bofflehead. I had hoped to find one at the wooden duck purveyor's. It's compact with a growth on the head. Cute."

"What do they have to do with wood?"

"I don't know what they have to do with wood. Maybe they live near wood, or in it?"

The two men lay together looking at the statue of the duck perched atop the bust of Pallas. The shadow brought both the bust and the duck to life.

"That wooden duck's shadow looks even less like a duck than the wooden duck itself."

"Drop it. Don't think about it, nevermore. We've got a long walk to the train tomorrow. We need us some shut-eye."

11.

G tasted the boiled peanuts now. The room had gone cold. The manuscript was burnt. The bloodletters were gone. The boiled peanuts' taste and the boiled peanuts' smell had traveled through some crack in the walls between space and time. His beliefs were being held to account. Did he really feel that when he passed he would be shepherded into the arms of some benevolent God? It was all too silly. But here presented another possibility, one more terrible than even the fires of hell: To die meant to smell that earthy stench of boiled peanuts for all eternity.

The bloodletters appeared. They again sliced into G. They sopped up his blood with rags and squeezed it into porcelain cups. The dripping sound made him feel weak and feeling weak made him feel good. Weakness was the sensation that he appreciated the most. Strength suggested that he was coming back, and how exhausting to come back. Better would be to see how far one can fall into weakness. Weakness had always seemed a never-ending sea in which one flattens and diffuses until—until what exactly? He wanted to pool in the bottom of the cup of human weakness like his blood pooled in the bottom of the porcelain bloodletter cups.

One of the bloodletters held G's leg up and sliced into the place behind his knee.

It dawned on G that his offering was incomplete. G had offered up the second part of his masterwork, but his brain was failing him. Had he another copy somewhere? If he had offered up his masterwork as an offering and was even unintentionally holding onto a copy somewhere, what kind of offering was it? He needed to recollect where the manuscripts were, but it was becoming impossible to think. Oh, now they're soaking me in cold water again, he thought.

"Am I not cold enough?"

"It will slow the bleeding, sir," one of the bloodletters said.

"Not cutting me anymore will slow the bleeding."

"Yes, sir," the bloodletter said, making another incision in his side.

12.

There was no more ludicrous American region than the West. Old Pushkie would have appreciated it. Pushkie would have spent his whole exile there, stealing people's wives and blustering his way into and out of duels. G owed Pushkie everything. He had provided the seed for two of his greatest works, but ultimately he was a ludicrous man, well made for a ludicrous region like this.

G and P had decided to hike in the desert. Their guide told them not to touch anything. That everything in the desert was designed to hurt, kill, or just plain terrify you. They crested one hill and a poisonous Gila monster sunned on a boulder. At the bottom of a valley, a tarantula the size of P's head crossed the path in front of them.

In some ways it reminded G of the countryside back home. It was absolutely different in every way, the fauna, the flora, the smell, the dry heat. It gave him the sensation of being on a different planet, but it also gave him the sensation of being at home. It was the only other landscape he had ever encountered, besides his home, in which he wished to wander, in which he thought he might find himself and other recognizable devils.

G should have heeded the guide's admonition. To say that G was a space case was putting it mildly. A cluster of spiky balls around a spaghettish plant caught his attention. The spiky balls seemed to be the offspring of the spaghettish plant. They were brown and orange at the bottom and a pale yellow at the top. The spiky balls looked like creatures, babies gathered around their mama. G picked up a spiky ball. He felt that he was in a children's story about a man on another planet who finds a spiky ball that is alive. In this vision the ball has big eyes and a pink nose. When it rolls it sniffs.

G lowered his hand to release the creature. But it did not want to go. It loved him. It wanted to stay with him. It would not leave. G used his other hand to nudge it away and now this hand stuck to the spiky ball. A shiver of panic. He wiggled his fingers, the pointer, middle, and thumb of his right hand and the pointer of his left. It was like being stuck in Chinese handcuffs except every time he moved, the spikes burrowed deeper into him.

"P, I'm sorry but I've found myself in a bit of a pickle here."

"Is that cacti?" P said.

"Jumping cholla got you," the guide said. "What did I say?"

"He said, 'Don't touch anything,'" P confirmed.

"Yes, yes. He did say that," G said.

G put his hands on the ground where P used the toe of his shoe to press down on the spiky ball. "Now pull your hands away," P said.

G yanked his hands away and P's shoe crushed the spiky ball. The spikes stuck in G's hands and fingers. G bit them out. He bit out one, then took it from his mouth and looked at it. The microscopic hook had a small bit of meat from inside his finger on it.

He bit out the next one. The ends, G deduced, were alive. And they burrowed into any surface they contacted.

"What did you call this thing?" G asked the guide.

"The jumping cholla."

"It didn't jump," G said. "I picked it up."

"That was neither smart nor in accord with my directive," the guide said.

"Give me that one," P said. "Watch this." G handed P one of the cholla spikes. P tucked the spike between his lips like a toothpick, and then he opened his mouth and made it do cartwheels, closing his mouth again and wiggling his eyebrows. He opened his mouth again, presumably to present it again, and grimaced. The spike had latched onto his tongue. He stuck out his tongue with the spike sticking out of it and laughed.

"I'm in a bit of a pickle here," P said, imitating his friend's accent.

Each of G's fingers had a globule of blood where the spike had come out. G pinched the spike in P's tongue. It was wet with his saliva, and G could not find purchase. P flinched, and that was just what the spike wanted. It worked itself deeper. "Fuck it," G said, pushed P's tongue down and grapped his lower jaw and plucked the spike out. P's tongue was scarred and rough, like he'd bitten it many times, almost bitten it off.

P giggled.

"What is wrong with your friend?" the guide whispered to G as they scaled the next mountain.

G sucked his fingers. "Many things are wrong with my friend," G said. "But many things are right with him too."

"I don't know. That trick with the cholla spike. That was some weird business. He won't last too long in the desert. You neither."

"This is not our natural habitat."

"Where are you from?"

"Ukraine."

"He Russian too?"

"He's American as apple pie."

"Apples don't grow out here. Sidewinder pie maybe. You like sidewinder pie?"

They forded a creek the color of rust. They crested a mountain upon which there was snow in summer. They stood under a natural white arch of rock.

13.

"Kansas City, Kansas City," P sang. "You got some pretty little women, and I sure want to get 'er done."

"Quiet this singing. I haven't slept in states thanks to your snoring and your nightmares."

"Ah, I'm sorry, G. Is it the cauldron again? Must be the schnapps. I hit the schnapps and nightmares all night long, when I can sleep at all that is. Say, you never told me, you got a girl back home?"

"Of course. You don't think that red thing with the mask was—love interests aplenty . . ."

"Sounds serious."

"Very."

P took a cluster of letters from his valise. He flipped through them and removed one. "Read this line right here," P said. G took the letter. It smelled faintly of perfume. *I can only say to you that had I youth and health and beauty, I would live for you and die with you.*

"A girl uses the conditional tense, you know it's real love."

The train pulled into the station and the men got out.

"Kansas smells of meat," G announced.

"Ain't Kansas. It's Missouri."

"Didn't it say *Kansas City*?"

"That it did."

"And Kansas City is not in Kansas?"

"Give the Russian writer a cookie."

"Ukrainian writer."

"Give the Ukrainian writer a cookie."

After finding a boarding house, they made for a restaurant in a trolley barn across the street.

"Are they cooking meat everywhere here?" G asked. "Why does it smell like meat?"

They sat at the bar and ordered drinks. There was no heated goat milk with rum. Instead they drank Horsefeathers.

P angled his head funny, but G could tell he was eavesdropping on the convo at the end of the bar. P had excellent hearing.

"Watch this," P said, "play along."

"Along with what?"

"Barkeep!" P shouted. "Barkeep, can we speak to you please. Yes, yes, I know that you've been expecting us. We're the sanitary inspectors."

"The sanitary inspectors? Weren't we told they were women? Weren't we told next week?"

"We're men, and we're here now, and we intend to sanitary inspect!"

"Come along then," the barkeep said.

They entered the kitchen. "This is it," G said. "This is the source of the meat smell."

"Sir, do you know why my associate here is a sanitary inspector? Do you notice anything about him."

"Accent?"

"Anything else?"

"He's dressed funny."

P leaned into the fellow's ear. "Check out the schnozz," he whispered. "Guy's a human bloodhound."

Here G turned it on. He steeled himself to do something that he rarely did, that is, follow his own schnozz. He put his nose in the air. He went left, right, spun in circles, and ended up on the trail of a mustardy quality. When he opened his eyes he found himself before a vat atop a large fire, P and the barkeep following behind him. He lifted the lid on a giant pot.

G leaned his schnozz over the pot. The humidity from the steam melted right through his sinuses. "Yes, mustard," he said. "Mustard seed, molasses, cumin, the usual suspects of course and yet, yet, what's this? Bird droppings, mouse parts, human finger."

"We are not pseudo-scientists," P said. "We don't believe in little invisible creatures okay. But you can't go selling folks mustard sauce with rat and human fingernail in it. That is not sanitary. And we are the sanitary inspectors. Our job is to find that which is not sanitary."

G followed his nose to a smoker made with bricks. He sniffed down the line, past charred husk after charred husk.

"Beef and pork," the fellow said. "Them's chickens."

G pirouetted. "Dog, cat. Them's rats."

The man stared in wonder at G's nose. It was eerie to him what G could detect nose alone.

"Times are hard. We're all of us barely getting by. Perhaps we can make an arrangement."

"Perhaps," P said.

"Might the arrangement include some pro bono plates?"

"You mean, you know what it is and wish to eat it?"

"Not like it's boiled peanuts."

"My man has quite the appetite," P said. "His tastes map to his olfactories, you know."

"What can I get you, sir?"

"A side each of dog and cat, two rats, and please cover it all in that mustard/molasses/mouse-part/human fingernail sauce."

G polished it off while P negotiated with the barmen. Two women came in and sat in the chairs next to G and P. P's head swiveled.

"Ladies, my colleague and I would wish to buy your drinks."

"Not necessary, gentlemen. We occupy a certain station."

It took P half a second to process what this could mean, and that was precisely the amount of time that it took for the lady closest him to announce to the barkeep that they were the sanitary inspectors, at which his associates looked at each other and removed large sticks from under the bar. G and P, reading the writing on the wall, bolted, the men in hot pursuit through the greater downtown area of the meat-smelling metropolis.

Once they had eluded the men they doubled back to the boarding house and crept inside. They climbed into their shared bed and G propped his leg on P's rough shins.

"Those babes could have been ours," P said.

14.

G would soon return to Boston. Word from his mother was that they wanted him for the teaching position in St. Petersburg. His ticket for his ship left in just ten days. He worried about missing it. He would lose the position and then what would there be for him?

His mother would be heartbroken. She wouldn't understand. She didn't understand what he was doing right now, traveling across a strange country with a strange man. And all because of what? Because of their shared love of Hoffman, a dead Prussian fairy-tale writer? Because they were both terrified of being buried alive? Upon his return she would assume him infested with every manner of venereal disease imaginable.

He couldn't help but writing to her and expressing his anguish, *Mother dear*, he wrote. *Save your poor son! Drop a tear on his aching heart. See how he is tormented! Press to your bosom the orphan! There is no place for him in this world! Pity on your ailing child!*

P was proving more and more unreliable. His unreliability correlated with his drinking. He proved more and more drunk. When they sat down in the dining car, they made a copacetic pairing: G ate everything in sight and P drank everything in sight.

G also understood that something moved inside of him when he woke up now to P's face and his sour breath and the sharp prick of his legs. He understood that this would lead nowhere good. He would share no more boarding-house beds with him. It would be only book sleeves on the magic train until he could take leave of him for good.

It was difficult for G to understand his own emotions. His hemorrhoidal illness spread to his stomach. It never left him in peace and interfered with his work. He spent much of their travels in various bathrooms and hidden behind trees.

They were on a stretch of track through Ohio when G's demoralized sense tipped toward despondency. He was not himself. This was not him. He no longer wished to be G, the wood duck, the mysterious dwarf. He wished to be someone forceful, someone healthy, someone conniving, someone who could one-up P at all his tricks.

He wished to go home.

For his part, P drank himself silly because as much as he loathed his traveling partner and his obscene schnozz, he could not shake a great fear: the man was a better writer than he was. The stuff he had put down on their trip was next level. And there was something about him that made P feel like a fake. P would never admit this to anyone, but there it was, wrapped up tight with all his self-loathing and his fear of death and all the other parts of him that he would just keep secret for as long as he lived.

The thing was that G brought a high comedic flourish to everything. P was not funny. G was funny without even trying. The role that he had played in Kansas City was beyond the pale. P was totally and completely unprepared for this life. How had he lived this long? Why were his thoughts so muddled? He was young. He wasn't old and demented.

"G," P said. "G, I'm done. I need to go home."

"Go home?" G said. Though this had been precisely what G had been thinking, he felt outraged and rejected by P. "What do you need to go home for? This whole thing was your idea."

"I don't think it's very healthy for the two of us to be together anymore."

"Nothing is healthy. Living is not healthy. Drinking yourself to oblivion is not healthy."

"This is not good. It's got to end."

Hearing these words, G felt there was only one recourse. He wanted to go lie in his coffinlike bunk. He wanted to feel the sensation that life had passed and he was confined to a box that he could not get out of and in which he'd be buried alive. "Well, go on then—go with God," G said. "What are you standing there for?" The two men retired to their book sleeves, each embittered at the other.

15.

In this train car, the train car car that would return them to Boston and to G's waiting ship, there hung two lifelike portraits on the wall. They had been nailed to the wall paneling so that they would not wobble off or, presumably, be stolen. One of them was a portrait of a girl and the other the portrait of a man.

"Go ahead. Tell the story, go," P said. From time to time, such a proposal had become their equivalent of a duel.

G took the portrait of a man and recounted at exhausting length the tale of a young painter who finds the beautiful and realistic portrait in a shop. He takes it home where it comes to life and offers to endow the mediocre painter with skill and powers far beyond his ken. He accepts and much success and superficial happiness come his way for some time until he stumbles across a painting by another painter, and it's possessed of such beauty, beauty beyond anything he has ever made with or without the magical painting's gifts. He falls into a fever and dies.

P yawned, nodded his head, and began to tell a short tale of a husband, a painter, and his young wife. Upon their marriage the husband has the wife sit for a painting. He aims to capture her as wholly as possible, to replicate her true form, which he adores. The endeavor takes a long time, but the young beautiful saint that is his devoted wife sits and takes it, looking otherworldly and magnificent to the very moment he is finished, after which she keels over and dies.

The train slowed as it pulled into the station.

"I have to admit, G, there have been times I have thought you better than I. But if there is one thing that I can say that may help you, it's that, this painter, all these villagers of yours, they're amusing, but the only stuff worth pursuing is the devil business. You're a one-trick pony and in prose only, I'm afraid. The true music of literature is in poetry."

"You, my friend," G said, "are immured in juvenlia. Is there any way for you to get off of this death-of-a-beautiful-woman stuff? If so, you might just write something of consequence one day."

Both men went silent. They felt a mixture of shame and guilt. Each had lied, in a way. Each felt the other the flip side of the coin that was himself, but neither would admit or express this. And each felt possessed to make a different kind of confession.

"My life has been a longing for solitude," P said.

"I am a riddle to everyone," G said. "No one is in a position to know my mind."

Each felt that he could have said what the other had just said.

They took last looks at the portraits, seemed to record something about them. They walked past the book sleeves that they had slept in so many nights through their travels. They stepped out of the train.

"Did you ever solve the cryptogram?"

"My brain doesn't work that way. I tried my best."

"No matter," P said.

P directed G toward the boatyards and without a handshake or an embrace, barely without looking at one another, they parted ways.

16.

The rats that so valiantly collectivized in order to save him had long ago washed away. P felt the water rising around him and stared at the moon and a nearby star, pink and bright. He felt the cobblestones under his neck. This was not how he'd pictured his death. While the water would soon drown him, it was refreshing. The sky was open. The air was clear.

And then a shadow blocked the moon and the pink star. And how annoying this was for him. He wished now only to lie there and watch the moon and the pink star and to feel the water rushing over him until he was drowned. The shadow said something, shouted something, and P could not understand, wanted only to be left to this agreeable death.

The shadow lifted him up out of the rising water in the ditch and dragged him. The heels of the scuffed and heavy boots that were not his scraped against the street. The figure dragged him all the way to a hospital and this is where it would happen. P could tell. They would mistake his laudanum-induced paralysis for death and he would be buried alive like he knew he always would be. They would take him for a pauper, a homeless person, a drunk, an addict, a pervert. Deep down, he appreciated that the truth was that he was all these things. If only someone might recognize him, though. If someone might recognize him he could go on perhaps for some time continuing to ride the razor's edge he had ridden his whole life, the edge between being an orphan and being someone's son, the edge between being a real writer and being a hack writer, the edge between being in love and being loved.

And then it was happening. It was happening.

"Do you know who this is?" someone was saying.

"No," said another.

"Can't be," said others.

A young doctor shined a light into his eyes. "Mr. P," he said. "Mr. P, is that you? Can you hear us? We love your work, Mr. P. Come back to us now."

He sat up. Where on earth had his lectures gone? Where were his clothes? Whose fucking clothes were these?

"Get me out of here," P cried. "I have to find my lectures." P cast the young doctor aside and leapt up from the gurney. "My lectures! They're in the ditch. I'm sure of it. The rats will eat them. They'll drown. I have to find my lectures!"

The young doctor scrambled quickly to his feet and pounced on P, bringing him to the ground. A group of nurses joined him. Someone stuck him with something and he felt the world go woozy once more.

"It's okay, Mr. P. We're going to take care of you."

"Can I get his autograph?" one of the nurses said.

"Wait until he comes to. We dosed the hell out of him. He's strong as an ox."

When he regained something like consciousness, a line of figures stood before him. He could not draw a breath except with intense agony.

A radiant figure, too bright to look at, directed questions to P. A figure resembling Virginia asked what right had he to live when so many better than he had died. P answered with uncertainty that we are all separate souls. Another figure reminded him of Elmira. She asked whether his word was a true word, and he answered, more confidently, "My lie is a true lie." Then there was the cauldron of boiling liquid and a demonic voice ordered that P be lifted by his hair and dipped into the hot liquid up to his lips. As the directive was given, a sense of calm permeated P. He thought again of G. While he had neither spoken nor heard from him in twenty years, it occurred to him that the demons, all those devils he wrote about in his stories, they would have gotten the best of him by now, or soon, too.

"G, my friend, help," P said. "Help my poor soul!"

17.

G woke from his episodes with a burst. He heaved forward, but his nose crunched against something hard. It was darker than any dark he'd ever seen. He felt around to the sides and to the top and to the space behind his head. He moved his feet and felt the board there. He knocked and he could tell by the dull thud that the wooden box he was in was buried underground. There was supposed to be a space there right above his head with the bell pull in it, but of course it was not there. He had made a down payment on the coffin with the bell pull but he was not surprised.

In a weird way, it came as something of a relief. There would be no more ice baths over his head, no more incisions made in his body, and most blessedly no more leeches affixed to his nose. He wondered what his old friend P would say if he could see him now. He would write a good story about this.

There was one thing he wished he'd told P. G had, after much struggle and after consulting an Italian code breaker—G's brain really did not work that way—solved the cryptogram: *We are all of them, they are all of us. Streetlights. People.*

G spent his life hating people, insulting them for the quality of cream they brought for coffee, celebrating God and Dante and Pushkie. The devil had fully taken him over. He lied to his mother who loved him beyond all else, and he didn't properly take care of his family estate. What he wouldn't give to be sitting in his father's grotto right now rather than lying in this coffin like some impotent vampire. He remembered the cat that he had drowned. How could he have done it? What was it after all, in the heart of man? There was a question he hadn't been able to answer. G drew in his arms and legs and scooched. His shoulders were not broad, but it was difficult for him to turn over in the coffin. When he finally managed, it was considerably more comfortable prone. He would maximize his breath this way. There was no cause for hope, and yet he could not help thinking of the one thing that might save him, the one thing that might save any of us.

"The ladder," G spoke, "quickly, bring me the ladder!"

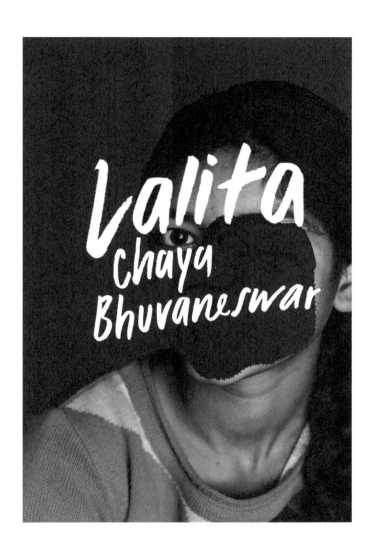

Lalita

CHAYA BHUVANESWAR

1.

One cool, daring night the weekend before spring break, while she was singing with Chrissie Hynde, *I'm special, so special / Gotta have some of your attention / Give it to me*, Lalita decided she was going to lose her virginity to her high-school friend Noah. They were at college now, both sophomores, and he lived four blocks away. She sat down at her desk and put on her shoes before she changed her mind.

Noah was white. He didn't have to be the man. She'd always thought she'd give her virginity to an Indian man, or a Black one, just definitely not a man the same color as the boys who had called her "ugly Hindoo" in elementary school. She could still wait. Tomorrow evening she could go up to one of the good-looking Black men who had the habit of approaching her on York Street near the Yale Co-op and saying, "Hey baby, how you doin' today?" They were older men with slack, exhausted faces but frank compliments. Some of them worked at Yale, maintaining the Art Library or the Peabody Museum. Others had jobs at United Illuminating before it had gone out of business the year before. Those men had always made Lalita wonder what it would be like to press against one of them, dancing. Wearing a new red dress and white gardenia like Billie Holliday's, her lover stroking her hair and the flower with one hand, kissing her neck with dry kisses like he was saving the wetness of his mouth for when they were alone.

She got up from her desk and put on her new denim jacket. So, Noah. Why him? He was just an acquaintance. And there was one other thing. He'd just broken up with Lucy, Lalita's freshman year roommate and sometime good friend. Before that he would come to their room whenever Lucy went out with somebody else. He'd flirt with Lalita. Not that surprisingly, Lucy had been the one to end it, so there was no reason for Lalita to feel guilty for sleeping with Noah now. Before Lalita knew it, she was out the back gate of the residential college she lived in, crossing Wall Street, walking past the little grocery store.

What if Noah said no? She was already outside his house on Temple Street. Her mouth went dry and she couldn't reach out to ring the bell. From somebody's window, snatches of music . . . A lyric from The Pretenders, about how she'll make you notice her. Same station on the radio. A fellow fan of Chrissie Hynde. But Noah liked opera, not that skinny singer from Ohio with her black eyeliner and fierce androgyny. Lalita remembered how the one time she came home with him—they hadn't done anything, just laid down next to each other in his bed—Noah played her a Lucia Popp CD. "She's good, but no one's better than Joan Sutherland," he'd said, his breath smelling of pickles and cigarettes, reedy against her ear. Expectant.

Lalita walked past Noah's house until she reached a storefront about a block away that had steps leading down to the street. She stood across from a bank building with a reflective sheen that would be a brilliant gold when the sun rose. But that night sitting in the dark on the steps she thought: yes, fine, why not, it would be Noah, but she would get herself ready first. There was so much to do, a simple shower wouldn't be enough to get really clean. She worried about the feel of her hair and skin, her smell, the look of her underwear.

Lalita planned everything out as she walked home, and when she got to her room, she called Noah. He was at home too, trying to read. He didn't seem to know that she had nearly rung his bell. He agreed to meet her when he went to Rego Park to visit his parents for the holidays the following week and have generous helpings of blintzes and kreplach his mother made for Passover. She got excited talking to him, listening to him laugh. She touched herself and almost came a few times before she fell asleep that night, much closer than she'd been before. Close enough so she could believe she would with him. It would be all right. She would do it with Noah in her bed at home with her parents safely away, and then she would know that they didn't have such a hold on her after all. She told herself, before she went to sleep, that nothing her parents had done, no matter how many times, could stop her from being normal, doing the normal thing and having sex with someone she wanted. No matter how many years she'd woken up in her mother's bed, shirt half off and trapped in her sticky, triumphant embrace; her lips, her eyes, her chest the sight of her mother's intensely possessive scrutiny, the shame of her leg draped in sleep over her mother's ankles, her walk self-conscious from the knowledge that her mother might slap or caress her buttocks suddenly, even at age fifteen, sixteen, nineteen; because no one, just looking at Lalita, whistling from a car, playing with her hair like Noah did, flirting with her over the phone, could possibly know how her mother had started following her to bed whenever Lalita came home from college. No one could tell. No one would find out.

A few mornings later, Lalita stood packing a small bag for New York. Her mother had called and left five messages in the space of two days, which Lalita had still to return. She had borrowed a CD from Noah, Lucia Popp singing Schubert lieder, and was enjoying the round tones, the ripe phrases, thinking over her next move and playing *Der Jager* over and over. The hunter.

Noah, on the phone the night before: "So are you really going to have an arranged marriage? Is that true? There was this rumor in high school that you were already engaged to someone by the seventh grade."

"Is that why you didn't ask me out?"

He laughed.

"Well, everyone got it wrong," Lalita said. "You see, my parents sold me to their friend's son when I was still in the crib. So, there's like, no way out of it. He's not too bad looking, if you don't count the limp from one leg being shorter than the other, the fact that he's five two and at least two hundred pounds, the skin rashes, the man-breasts."

"Eew," Noah said, and kept on laughing.

Lalita remembered with a sliver of fear how her mother had once pointed out such a man, someone she'd never consider, the simpering son of someone they knew from the temple, and said that man might very well be the only one left to marry in ten years, no one could know, and who was to say he would make such a bad husband after all?

The memory had just strengthened Lalita's resolve while she was on the phone, made her voice honey, husky, even though she was talking in real time to Noah and not just practicing.

"Aren't you glad—I mean, isn't it convenient, I'm not going to have an arranged marriage?" she asked. "Isn't it good that I'm free to do . . . whatever I want?"

"Oh yeah," Noah said, catching on quickly. "That's something I look forward to."

And it went from there, better than she had expected, easier with the distance of the phone call. Noah even telling her to pack the black halter top she'd gotten brave enough to wear to a "Nearly Naked" party in the dorm the year before, so they could go dancing in New York. Noah, well-practiced, ended their conversation in whispers.

But just this morning as she was setting out her clothes, a wrinkle appeared in the plan Lalita had made to seduce Noah. Not that Lalita ought to be surprised by wrinkles—she had never been particularly good at ironing, her mother said, stalking her around the house, picking up her clothes and predicting that she was too much of a slob for anyone to marry her. Her mother's favorite joke was that Lalita could never have a baby, like normal people did, because the child would get smothered in all her mess.

In a tone of exquisite, pretended disgust her mother would say, "The baby might cry but you won't even hear it under all the piles and stacks of dirty clothes, books, papers, plates and mugs everywhere," and on and on, long after she had shame-facedly cleaned her room, her mother laughing until the tears came.

"There'll be a little hand sticking up through all the piles of dirt in your house, but no one will see it because it's too small, and your husband will be frightened away," her mother choked out, between laughs.

Even when she had been too young to give the bad feelings a name, Lalita suspected that her mother's disgust at the idea of Lalita as an adult, living in filth was really joy, masquerading. She was a witch in a mother's costume. She had stolen her from her real mother, a mysterious and solitary woman who'd been left somewhere to grieve for Lalita.

At times, it seemed her witch mother's pleasure came from having a sense of exuberant, cackling control over Lalita, beyond the boundaries of age, propriety, even the boundary imposed by others' revulsion.

"But why would you want a husband? What you don't realize is that it's more trouble than it's worth. Why be so close to some dirty old macho man? Just do cozy-cozy with me," she said, her arms suddenly clasping Lalita around her waist, bringing Lalita's body flush against hers and then reaching up to stroke her hair.

The unwanted intimacy continued when Lalita fled to college—over the phone, her mother ranting and convinced that no one outside the family could ever be counted on or told "the truth"—about men and their innate infidelities, their dirty desires, about women and their inevitable envy, how no one understood that it was good for Lalita to trade beds with her father, so that the big bed in her house was occupied by mother and daughter, while husband and father slept alone, that "dirty man," as her mother called him.

Lalita wouldn't be deterred from normalcy. She vowed not to return her mother's calls, no matter how many messages she left, until she had figured out how to seduce Noah.

But now, it was Lucy, half-Kenyan, glamorous, beauty-queen Lucy whose mother was normal, who might prove an obstacle.

The wrinkle in Lalita's plan to set herself free of her mother had come in the form of a call from Lucy just yesterday. Lucy's parents were going to be late coming back from their trip to see her grandparents in Kenya; their train had been delayed, they'd missed their connection. The house in Oregon would be empty, and Lucy's mother had suggested that she stay with a friend over break, go out and have some fun instead of waiting alone for them to return. So—could Lucy maybe come home for the spring holidays, with her ex-roomie Lalita?

"Of course," Lalita said, changing her plans without a pause. It would be Lucy's first time in New York.

Even picturing Lucy's beautiful face as it expressed wonder, as her radiant skin shone in the dark of New York streets, as she smiled and was charmed by New York's novelty, its absolute difference from Boring, Oregon—even hearing, in her head, the sound of Lucy's seductive laughter, her eyes capturing Noah's—Lalita committed to staying the course.

Lalita needed Noah now; Lucy didn't. There was nothing anymore between Noah and Lucy; and Lalita's parents would be gone. If Lalita were determined enough, it wouldn't matter that Lucy was there; and if she lost her nerve, she didn't deserve freedom after all, she told herself, going to answer a knock at the door that must be Lucy herself, bold and unmistakable, setting Lalita, by inspiration, down a path that could lead to becoming someone different—Lalita was sure of it.

So far so good, Lalita thought, still anxious about what was to come.

Lalita's parents had left about four hundred dollars, carefully divided between Lalita's top dresser and her purse, along detailed instructions about how to entertain Lucy, whose visit they approved, "because she's not *completely* Black."

Lalita's mother delivered this reassurance along with the warning that Lalita must call her every single night—or else she'd come home early and "see to" things.

Then Lalita's mother and father went to stay with one of her 'aunties' who was reluctantly going through a divorce. The woman's engineer husband decided to stay on in the Gulf, where he traveled for his job and had met another woman. There were no kids, so a divorce. It's "such a shame," her mother said, looking incredibly intrigued, Lalita thought, by someone else's shame. Her parents' trip to New Jersey was to comfort this aunty, who was no blood relation of theirs, helping her sort through the logistics, and most hospitably of all, preventing her from killing herself, which, her father correctly predicted, the woman would surely think about doing at least once before Lalita's parents left.

With Lalita's parents' indifferent blessing: Lucy and Lalita, alone now in Lalita's great house, sleeping in beds that Lalita's mother had lined up across from each other in the big guest room, reminiscent of how they'd been arranged the year before in freshman dorm. Bored again by Long Island, Lalita had fallen fast asleep right after eating Chinese take-out with Lucy. They'd been too tired to do more than watch TV, finding the movie *Dangerous Liaisons* by what struck Lalita as an auspicious coincidence. Giggling, they repeatedly replayed the Uma Thurman-John Malkovich nipple-kissing scene, till Lalita was giddy, her breasts warm.

In the middle of the night, Lucy's cell phone rang. She grabbed it from her purse without turning on the light and spoke in a hush for nearly half an hour, words Lalita couldn't quite make out, then cautiously inquired into the darkness of the room:

"Lalita?"

"Yeah?"

"Sorry that woke you honey," Lucy said. Lucy using terms like "honey" sounded like the way Lalita imagined beauty contestants, in pageants in the South, spoke to each other.

"No sweat," Lalita said, playing it cool.

Lucy laughed delightedly. "Can you believe my Mom?"

Lalita didn't speak.

"She called from Heathrow somehow, in the ten minutes they ended up having between flights, just to say hi and to make sure I was okay. God alone knows how much it cost her."

"That's really sweet."

"She said the next time she wanted to hear all about my new boyfriend Max, you know, the scoop—where he grew up, his dreams, everything that makes him tick. Every award he's won as an artist. But what's so amazing is, she doesn't care what his parents do or how much money he'll be making next year or not. My mom couldn't care less about anything like that. She wants to know things like whether he's a good kisser! My mom . . ."

The sound of Lucy's voice was embracing.

"But Lucy, what about your Dad," Lalita found herself saying, mainly because he was the parent Lucy usually complained about. "I mean, he's a provider and all. He'd want to see you settled in life, like reasonably secure, right? I mean, wouldn't it bother him just a little bit that Max makes Jackson Pollock-type abstract art, writes screenplays for films that no one wants, and lives with his cousin in a studio? And that he's twenty-eight, and like, so old?" Lalita paused, holding her breath. Rather than answering right away, Lucy had turned to face her in the dark; now Lalita could feel Lucy's large eyes piercing the distance between them with amusement, compassion.

"Well, alright Miss Know-It-All. You've got my dad's number, he'd hate Max. Ergo, he doesn't know anything about him, and he's not going to unless and until it gets straight up serious."

"How do you keep a secret like that? That you're in love with someone, that you're even sleeping with him Lucy, my gosh . . ."

Lucy laughed a tinkling, charmed laugh.

"Go to sleep Miss Moffett, we'll have a lesson in the art of healthy deception in the morning. I knew there was a reason you'd invited me."

Lalita laughed politely, but turned away muttering, "Goddamn."

"What'd you say honey?"

"Nothing, I'm going back to sleep."

" 'Night Lalita."

"Night."

This morning, leaning against the door of her bedroom, listening to the music that Lucy had picked out—it was Lalita's one and only rap CD, Salt 'n Pepa's *Very Necessary*—Lalita felt nearly as vulnerable as she had when they first met, as if she'd never be dark-skinned or Third World enough to count as a person of color in her eyes, as if she'd never be as skillful as Lucy at standing up for anything or anyone, least of all herself. On the first day of freshman year at Yale, when the two of them were still moving their things into the room, Lucy unfurled a huge, forbidding poster of Malcolm X and smoothed it down over their entire front door without even asking permission. A few weeks into the semester, Lucy could be seen in front of an anti-apartheid shanty, serene behind designer sunglasses in the midday heat. Then Lucy sat on the ground with her gorgeously bare legs stretched out, watching other Black students give speeches and shout out slogans to passing cars and faculty on Beinecke Plaza.

After a few months of getting used to living with Lucy, when the fear of saying or doing something unknowingly or accidentally racist had become at most a subliminal awareness, an occasional vigilance, because Lucy cared about her, Lalita was sure of it—Lalita would run home from her classes and talk about everyone she felt attracted to or wanted to gossip about or on the down-low might have *fucked*. If given the opportunity. If given ... the right setting. If she could be sure her body looked okay. Lucy would laugh, commenting gently, "You have a lot of conditions! But when it's someone great, you won't think about that." And this made Lalita, just for those sweet moments, feel hope.

Now watching Lucy putting on mauve lipstick and combing her hair delicately, Lalita couldn't quite bring herself to confide "the Noah plan." When she tried to think of why, she couldn't get past the difference between them. Lucy had pride. Not misplaced vanity, not arrogance, but simple pride in what she did and how she looked. Pride in her origins. There was the picture of her father on her desk at school, handsome and stern with pitch-black skin—an engineer from Nairobi who'd won a big scholarship. And Lucy's mother, blond and waifish, a soft voice on the phone. A doctor's receptionist who never had a chipped nail, always had dinner on the table by seven, and was going to night school for her bachelor's degree, Lucy liked to tell people.

Lalita could almost hear her own mother answering Lucy. Her mother's lectures sounded if her mother were talking only to herself, and not to a daughter who would lie awake afterward, wondering if anyone would marry her.

"Well, a man *would* like that of course," her mother would've said, if she had heard about Lucy's mother. "Some little blond, like Lucy's mother.

A doll. A woman less educated, less threatening. Too bad for you your mother wasn't just some anonymous housewife. Too bad for your father, that I'm—oh, nothing much. Just an MD doctor. While he's a bookkeeper. That is all."

There really was nothing to say in response to her mother, Lalita felt. No argument against the kind of rage that made up its mind to be right no matter what. Rage that would always have its way.

"I'm finished," Lucy said, opening the door wider so Lalita could take her turn. "Oh, you're using it. I hope it's good," she beamed at her, noticing that Lalita held the mango and citrus bubble bath Lucy had brought her as a gift.

When Lalita came into the bedroom after showering, loving the fresh scent of her clean skin, she found Lucy reading a magazine and listening to Enya, wearing a white silk mini-robe they had seen in a lingerie catalog a few months before and lounging on the bed.

Lalita was truly clean, at last. No evidence of her mother's touch on her body.

At last, she was clean. She could be ready for Noah.

Lucy looked up and smiled at her in kind admiration. "Let me do your hair," she offered, making room for Lalita, touching her arm quickly, not seeming to notice that Lalita flinched.

Lucy wasn't embarrassed about touching Lalita or any woman-friend; she did it all the time. They could be talking about women's tennis or the governor's race in Connecticut that year, and suddenly Lucy might say something like, "I wish my breasts were shaped more like yours. Yours are rounder," reaching out as if to stroke the side of Lalita's breast but then pulling back, laughing at the shocked look on her face.

Lucy seemed to love being shocking to Lalita specifically—versus the rest of the world, where she was usually composed and out of the reach of most people who desired her. At Yale, there had been many nights when Lalita peered out from under the covers, listening with rapt attention as Lucy sat on the edge of her bed, just like now, and described how she drank champagne from a boyfriend's mouth, modeled lingerie once for a catalog, was stopped by a man painting portraits outside the Yale Museum, near Atticus, and offered hundreds of dollars to pose nude, yet managed to say no tactfully.

"Now I think I should've maybe said yes. I might've let him at least go down on me, just to assess the talent," Lucy admitted, sly, but before the whole narration could be completed, Lalita would blush, held her hands up to her burning face and say, "Stop! Enough!"

Undeterred, and somewhat ideologically, Lucy would laugh and tell her more, relentless, calling this verbal porno "feminist praxis" from the Women's Studies course they both were taking. It made Lalita feel like she was playing the game Red Rover in a school yard, one person facing the wall alone, heart beating a bit faster, unable to see what the kids behind her are doing, hearing their voices, conscious of how they must be coming closer and closer until her back tingles, they must have reached her, they can touch her now, grasp any part of her. Lalita shuddered at this memory. Aware of how much she didn't know about real sex.

"What is it?" Lucy hadn't finished combing Lalita's hair. "Would you be still?"

Bending her head forward now, obeying Lucy's instructions over the soft buzz of the hair dryer, Lalita thought of another story she has never told, a more secret story than any of Lucy's discreet adventures. Once Lucy asked her, putting on a serious face, if she ever had an orgasm; if she knew that a good man could be trained to give her multiple orgasms. "And multiple kinds in the same night. Clit, vagina, G-spot, even A. Don't let him off the hook—that is his *job*," she said, still serious. Lalita couldn't help giggling at Lucy's solemnity.

But also, she'd giggled at one of the few secrets she sometimes thought of with pleasure. How Lalita did know about all that, or some of it at least—that is, being pleasured; she had her first orgasm when she was fourteen, at the very beginning of the journey that she planned to end tonight, in bed with Noah. As if nothing else had happened to her, in between.

Eleanor Fish was the one responsible—girl who was also fourteen at the time. They were both in the eighth grade, but by then Lalita was already an "early developer" and made a point of taking her showers alone, before sunrise at the summer camp where she met Eleanor. Lalita didn't want anyone to see her and point to her rounded belly, her breasts that by twelve were already like a camp counselor's, her calves that were already hairy by middle school unless she shaved them, her thighs that were still unfashionably full, though strong. During the day, when other campers tanned or positioned themselves strategically so that the cutest boys would notice them, Lalita would hide behind a cheap paperback version of her latest thrilling library discovery—*Portnoy's Complaint, The Rubyfruit Jungle, Oranges Are Not the Only Fruit.*

Mornings at camp were always more difficult and exposed than any other time, all the girls jostling to get ready. Hoping to evade them, Lalita started her shower. Eleanor walked in alone, brushing her teeth and sitting on a stool right outside the stall where Lalita stood. There were no curtains. Lalita positioned herself carefully so that her back was to the other girl, but she could feel her staring. "Do you have a staring problem?" Lalita almost said, repeating what other girls in camp would say whenever they caught her looking at them longingly, wondering what they were whispering and laughing about, but also thrilled by the sight of their bodies. But Lalita stayed silent—even now she couldn't say why no words had come that day—and finally turned around, letting water run over her arms and thighs, covering herself with a washcloth, but Eleanor was still watching, seeking eye contact. Lalita refused to look directly at her face, turning around again, like a cat circling on a ledge. She turned off the water. To get to her towel, Lalita would have to move past Eleanor and grab it from a hook on the wall. There was less than a foot of space between Eleanor's stool and the wall and the girl showed no sign of moving out of the way. "Excuse me," Lalita mumbled as she moved past, feeling Eleanor's hot breath on her skin, the wetness of her tongue at her belly button, fingers plucking first at her hip. Then the warm wetness on Lalita's mound, caressing it. There was a moment of direct, searching eye contact between this Eleanor girl and Lalita, but Lalita continued moving away, grabbing the towel, wrapping it around herself without drying off first, and then running the several yards to her cabin without a word, not even "No."

She hadn't wanted to say no. But what if someone had walked in on them? The other girls were still asleep in the dark room, so Lalita crept back into bed under the sheets, still wearing only the towel. Experimentally she slipped it off, imagining her body as that of Eleanor's—smooth, pale, white, hairless, and most importantly, slender. The kind of body that looked good in designer clothes, or saris, for that matter. She rubbed her body—Eleanor's naked body—against the sheet and touched herself, first with her palm, then with her fingers, moving from her stomach to that place which always tingled whenever she had to urinate or was truly embarrassed, watching someone handsome on TV, and brought herself to that first disciplined, hardly moving orgasm of her life. The shame she felt was from the memory of the first time a woman had touched her body without permission, the shame at how the touch was distressingly, unavoidably similar to this strange girl Eleanor's, even though Lalita tried and tried to think of only the stranger's exploring touch. Only the thrill of Eleanor's bright and alert eyes.

"I didn't do anything wrong," Lalita could hear her mother say, about how Lalita's mother had touched the sides of Lalita's breasts, her neck, her belly, always through her clothes, always so quickly and lightly she could have slept through it as if it never happened, as if she weren't supposed to know. "I just wanted to love you, my baby. I just wanted to have you all to myself. But don't tell other people about cozy-cozy. They would make something out of it. You just love your mother the best, that's all. You just don't need to be anywhere else."

When the solitary wave of that orgasm, gifted to her by a stranger named Eleanor, had subsided, Lalita got out from under the sheets, still holding the towel around herself and quickly pulling on her clothes, then sitting back on the bed somewhat abruptly to eat all four bags of cookies and pretzels her mother had packed for the week, until her next trip upstate to visit Lalita at the camp. She crammed them into her mouth in one huge, nauseating, self-punishing breakfast. "God, Hindoo, you're gross!" someone called out from the bunk across the room. It was one of her chief tormentors, an older girl who was a local swimming star, lissome and cruel and beautiful.

Lalita's heart quickened.

"You fucking cow. I can't believe you ate all that," the girl had said, to Lalita's great relief.

Sophomore year of college now; spring break; the here and now, no parents here, the house all safe, and Lalita and her friend Lucy were the lissome, beautiful ones now, Lalita tried reminding herself.

They were the ones with the power, she and Lucy. They could choose, name and humiliate—or favor with touch. Lalita felt eyes longing for them, tongues wishing to taste their skin, as she and Lucy moved through the half-full subway train.

Without haste, Lalita and Lucy made their way into the city. Finally, they reached Central Park, and she and Lucy sat down, alone, under a tree just a few yards away from the Model Boathouse and Conservatory Water. Two children were throwing a bright pink beach ball up in the air and running after it, running all around, almost into the pond, then panting and laughing, trying to tag each other as they ran back to their mother. A thin, frizzy haired woman sat under a cherry tree near the statue of Alice in Wonderland, leaning against the trunk and smoking a cigarette. Both she and the children had skin the color of heavily diluted Darjeeling, one part tea to three parts milk. A chocolate-skinned Black man, possibly Cuban, wearing just an undershirt above his jeans lay on the grass close to the woman, arms folded across his chest, a soft beige cotton summer hat resting on his face so that only his mouth showed. Lucy sat silently watching them. In the Oregon town where Lucy grew up, her family was the only inter-racial family for miles, and she was the only Black student in her high school. It didn't stop her from being home coming queen, class valedictorian, 4H leader, debate team captain—facts Lalita knows not from Lucy herself, but from Noah, who went home to Boring, Oregon, with her one long weekend while they were still dating and witnessed her celebrity.

Lucy, while trusting Lalita with many details of her dating life, has never shared what it was like growing up where she did. In this, they match, Lalita thought. Quiet about what really hurt.

A cool breeze came through the long grass around the pond and rippled the water. Lalita shivered in pleasure at the feel of it, thinking of a line from *The Tempest*—or is it *Hamlet*? *Hamlet*. Ophelia. *I know a bank where the wild thyme blows/ Where oxlips and the nodding violet grows/ Quite o'ercanopied with luscious woodbine/ With sweet musk roses and eglantine.*

No, it's Oberon. About the place Titania takes her asinine lover, initiating him into the pleasures of her flesh. Ass-anine: a taxonomic word, like canine, or just an insult? Lalita opened her eyes wide and inspected her arms and hands. She should have worn sun-screen, she had to guard against a burn.

She looked down at her wrists and noticed how narrow they were. So delicate, one of her TA's had said, in a Directed Studies seminar, during the spring term of last year. Tom Sarchassian, fourth year Literature graduate student, only twenty-five years old. She hadn't told Lucy about him. She had told no one.

On her Descartes paper, Tom wrote that her philosophical sensibility was "highly developed"; that her thoughts were often "articulately provocative," and that he'd be more than happy to meet her to talk about further work in philosophy. Meet her after class.

He'd understood then, what she'd been trying to do in her paper, Lalita realized. Walk through the Cartesian catalogue of doubts; then ask whether Descartes is convincing when he argues against them to prove his faith.

Lalita enjoyed writing that paper. For him. Even more: she enjoyed the idea that faith could be elastic, testable. All through her last class with Tom, their last formal meeting, she flirted with the idea of majoring in philosophy and even dared to flirt a little with him, staring at the black hair on his wrists, the dark traces of stubble on his cheeks and the sultry shadows under his eyes. She shook her head. His lips were pale and soft pink. She tuned out most of whatever else was said in class, thinking of what she would do if he asked her out. Was she supposed to tell him no? Would it be more effective to act indifferent? Once they had kissed, would he expect her to know what to do in bed? What if he demanded a blow job, and she couldn't breathe? She got so flustered that when the end of class finally arrived, she could barely stand up and follow everyone else in putting chairs back into place, lifting up a bench and moving it back under a tree just opposite the stone fountain that stood in the center of the courtyard. She lifted one end of a bench tentatively, waiting for one of her classmates to help her with the other end. But then Tom was suddenly standing next to her, brushing her bare forearm with his hand, grasping the bench firmly and dragging it. "You're so delicate!" he said, smiling down at her.

And then something unusual happened. Lalita became too excited to be nervous. She followed him to his office, they'd been talking about Heidegger's essay on a pair of shoes painted by Van Gogh and the text *Hippolyte on Consciousness* in his bookshelf, other texts he'd promised to show her. She was leaning against the window, and he had one arm braced against the wall, positioned well to look into her face as they talked and to lean forward and kiss her. But she didn't let him do it first. She could feel his breath on her face; she fumbled for his hand and put it flat on her breast, making him rub it awkwardly. He laughed, and she almost stopped, embarrassed, but having gone that far, she reached out again for him and cupped his crotch. "We're standing here in front of the window," he whispered, looking at her with heavy-lidded eyes and not moving. "No room in here." But she persisted, grasping anyway, shaping the soft cloth of his trousers around his erection with both hands, rubbing the shaft back and forth as if she would never stop. He looked tortured but didn't say to stop. "What are you trying to do?" he gasped, gripping her shoulder. "Not here." He finally pushed her away. "Let's go right now." He grabbed his jacket from a chair and touched the small of her back. "Let's go." He pecked her on the lips and turned off the light. "You first," he cautioned. "It shouldn't seem like we're leaving together."

Of course, the panic hit before she reached his apartment, a little studio two blocks away from his office. Tom drew her inside, kissing her on the mouth and unbuttoning her shirt, pressing his erection against her. Making her need it. She ground herself against him, suddenly ashamed because it felt too good. "You're my TA," she blurted out, afraid of not stopping him.

"Oh Jesus," he said, sounding surprised but not angry.

"Lalita?" Lucy asked, breaking up her thoughts. The two small children they were watching have gone back to play near their mother. They were dancing around her and chanting, "Todo juntos," singing a song from Sesame Street. The woman gathered up their things into a large plastic shopping bag and then shook her husband's arm. So ordinary, but Lalita watched as if she couldn't get enough. "You just have to accept that you may not have a family of your own," Lalita heard her mother saying, as she has so many times, so matter of fact. "For an educated, Indian Brahmin girl to find someone suitable . . . it's very hard. What you have to accept is—he may not be attractive. He may be short, overweight. But he could still be kind to you," her mother said, pretending encouragement, patting Lalita's arm in just the way the woman in the park is touching her husband—a knowing, steady palm pressed against his skin, saying *this is mine*. Except not having to insist, because her touch was what the man wanted.

Lucy's eyes were looking into hers, concerned. She smiled only when Lalita did.

"Lalita, we're meeting Noah, right? Let's go."

They were at least forty minutes late. She pictured Noah pacing on the Number Seven platform at Grand Central where she'd asked him to wait for them in front of the news stand. He would have taken the E train and threaded his way through the crowd of travelers pushing into Port Authority or walking up to the station, startled and scared, if they were coming off a bus from somewhere far—Idaho, even Oregon. Noah would wait, tapping his foot. Maybe he'd have the thought that Lucy had stopped to call her new boyfriend; maybe he tormented himself by imagining their conversation. Lucy clomped ahead of Lalita at a rapid pace, unconcerned by the number of men staring though Lalita felt a moment of sadness. Maybe because Lalita moved with such uncertainty now that they were almost with Noah, the men didn't seem to notice her behind Lucy, following along.

"You're both looking great," were Noah's first words to them. As he hugged Lucy, his eyes met Lalita's and he winked.

"And Lalie, you just get better looking every time I see you."

No mention of their phone call or "the sweet time" he had promised her. Noah was suave, except his hands gave him away. They fiddled with the broken zipper on his leather jacket, touched Lucy on the shoulder unnecessarily, brushed against Lalita's fingers as she stood trying to decide where they should all go for dinner. When Lucy interrupted, "Hey, do you guys want to go hear live jazz instead of just going to some movie afterwards?" all Noah could manage was to laugh nervously and look at her.

Live jazz at a bar. John Lee Hooker covers by a knowing, patient woman with cleavage, and experience. Add alcohol to Noah's mild confusion, and somehow organize a cab ride home with just herself and him.

That was the plan—Lalita had the money for it too. "Who's going to pay for that?" her mother always said. "My daughter isn't going to be a waitress or a glorified secretary," she said, dismissing the term-time jobs Lalita came up with as a way to have her own spending money. Money Lalita could use to live at school instead of coming home for breaks. "Nothing's too good for my daughter," Lalita's mother whispered—then hours later, screamed, "Ungrateful wretch. Unbelievably lazy," over some infraction, like leaving an empty glass on top of the TV set in the family room. "Unbelievable! Disgusting," she spat.

Imagining the cab ride home with Noah, Lalita's plan seemed feasible. *I should put the plan on PowerPoint*, she thought, trying not to laugh. Also, she had the fleeting, delicious urge to do something terrible to Noah, whom she didn't love, and who clearly wasn't all that into her either. All she wanted was to tie him up in the cab after he'd made her come, go down on him, spend him, then just leave him there with his underwear pulled down around his thighs, helpless and passed out, vulnerable. No permanent damage, right? Just a little fun, to pay him back for ignoring her now. To show that even after everything, she could be playful about sex. But Lalita felt as far from doing that as she was from even kissing him, and as she watched him whisper into Lucy's ear, she realized there was almost no hope of bridging the distance between her trashy daydreams and reality.

No hope of living a normal life, like everyone, inspired by fantasies from porn.

Could it really have been as long ago as last year that Tom Sarchassian, Tom the teaching assistant with the irresistible hard-on and little walk up on Park Street, had almost slept with her? Had even found her seductive?

"You're my TA," she'd blurted out, secretly hoping this reminder wouldn't stop him.

"Oh God," he said. Gasping and sweating, he'd pushed her away and, after a few seconds, gone into his tiny kitchen to get a glass of water from the tap. "Okay. You should go home," he said, drinking it quickly and not looking at her. Lalita buttoned her shirt and leaned against the door.

"Can't we talk about this?"

Tom laughed. Lalita's eyes smarted with tears. He stopped laughing.

"You want some water? Hey, are you okay?" He put his glass down and came near the door as if he were about to gently show her out. But her panties were still wet and without meaning to she stepped closer to him, taking his hand and placing it where she wanted him.

"I want to," Lalita said, stroking his crotch before he could move away. "I do."

"I know," he said, with a compassion that, in that moment, struck her as completely hateful.

"What happened to you?" he asked. "Did something happen?" He stroked her hair. "Listen, I'm not going to sleep with you, even though you are very pretty." He kissed her cheek.

"Why do I have to go?" she heard herself pleading. "Can't I just sleep next to you?" she asked. "We don't even have to talk, if you don't want."

He shook his head, stroking her face. "It's not a good idea. You should go home."

She shrugged, deciding not to cry in front of him. "You know, I won't tell anyone."

"I know you won't." He smiled at her before closing his door. She stood outside for a moment, listening, hearing the lock slide shut.

What happened to you? Did something happen?

She wouldn't have told Tom anyway. She wouldn't have even stayed the night, most likely, but it would have been so lovely to lay down with him.

She started regretting now, that she had never told Lucy of her one, single, sexual adventure—with Tom, when she was a freshman—because at least that way, she could have relived it.

He'd kissed her over a year ago, but Lalita could still remember how he smelled.

About a month ago, one day this past fall, sophomore year, Lalita had seen him walking on Chapel Street in New Haven, outside of Phelps Gate, holding hands with a woman she recognized as a graduate student in English. Shakespeare TA, beautiful breasts, long blond pre-Raphaelite hair. They looked happy, or at least for the moment absorbed in each other, much to Lalita's relief, she told herself. It saved her the embarrassment of Tom noticing her when she was twenty yards away. No way would she have exposed herself that much to begin with, by staying to talk to him once he'd made it clear that he wasn't going to kiss or hold her again under any conditions. That day if he had let her stay in his bed, hold him, kiss him while she was lying down and feeling safe . . . maybe. Probably she would have told him about her mother then.

How could Tom stand to look at her after that, though? He wouldn't.

What was it that he'd said once, at one of those seminar meetings where half the class hadn't shown up, and it was only Lalita and two guys in baseball caps who looked bored and made polite eye contact at best, never raising their hand or indicating in any way that they'd done the readings or cared about the summary Tom had not only written up beforehand but printed out and handed around earnestly, like a political pamphlet?

"People misinterpret Kant's categorical imperative as the Golden Rule, but it's so much more than that. It's about living by your own principles."

"Life on your own terms," Lalita supplied.

"Well yes," he said. "Not just following rules, but internalizing rules that Kant thought were just sort of objectively out there for everyone to see, like stars in the sky, and then creating your life to be exemplary."

"It's like you answer to some higher authority than what anybody says. So, if some ruler, some dictator tries to tell you what to do, you're not anti-authority for resisting it. You're just being moved by a higher law," she went on.

"I mean, you're not doing anything wrong at all. You're just doing what you have some inherent, divine right to do. What no one has the right to take away. No one."

"Autonomy," Tom said, turning to smile at her. "Beautifully and capably summarized—thank you, Lalita."

Baseball cap boy number one tittered at the word "beautifully" but she and Tom didn't look away from each other for a few seconds. In that class, Tom had been sitting next to her, and when he smiled, she felt the weight of his body in his chair, his hips, the way his pants fit over his thighs, felt a hot blush come over her face that she hoped he wouldn't notice. But he had.

In the end, it had been good that she hadn't opened herself to Tom by telling him anything personal even when they were alone. She hadn't even known him, after all. The promise of sex, the possibility of kissing in bed was in its own way confusing. Memories of being in bed with her mother were what she would have wanted to erase by telling him.

It would have been too much to ask, but she still felt a twinge when he walked by with his haughty blond girlfriend. She found herself walking faster once they were gone, pulling up her coat against the cold and thinking ahead to when she would have a different life, in that distant time her parents used to refer to as "when you graduate," before she'd started going to college, with graduation a specific day in the future. Now her parents used the phrase "when you're all grown up" as substitute, with its erasure of a point in time.

At some point during the movie she was watching with Noah and Lucy on either side of her, the money in Lalita's coat pocket went missing. Years later she would wonder if this moment was the important one, her true "graduation." She didn't know exactly when it happened, because she was too busy trying to keep track of all the Krystof Kieslowski references decorating the indie film that she'd persuaded Noah would be good. But this was no Decalogue, with its raw murders, tender penitence, icy cold waters, father's grief. Honestly it wasn't that straightforward to tell what the movie was even about.

Lucy looked bored; Lalita felt a pang of remorse for being such a bad hostess to her friend, and for the futile quest to get Noah, whose heart Lucy still seemed to hold captive.

During the summer after their freshman year, Lucy had written Lalita a letter about going out to dinner with her friends from high school, driving around late at night with Donna Summer blaring and "getting drunk on being young and happy and in love with each other."

Lalita saved the letter, the only letter Lucy ever wrote her, and read it more than once in bed, because she couldn't imagine what it would have been like, to ever be that young.

When she herself came home late a few times in high school, testing the waters by going out to dinner with the other girls on track team, Lalita's mother would stay vigilant no matter how many times Lalita had called to say she was fine and on her way. Her mother would wait downstairs with the light on even though she had to get up by five-thirty in the morning to make it to her job on time. If she were going to make a sacrifice, she wouldn't wait long to make Lalita pay for it. At one or two a.m. her mother would scream and scream when Lalita came home, even when she was dropped off by the track team coach and escorted to the door—screaming with a terrifying, wrathful certainty reinforced by a hard grip on Lalita's shoulders or a sudden ruthless crack! on her arm—that she was wrong for wanting to be separate, wrong for going out with people, wrong for waking up some mornings and wishing her mother were dead.

On nights when Lalita did stay home, she used her books and papers as barricades. After Amma had watched her TV shows, yelled at her to turn off the light and go to sleep, come to her room two or three times to see "if she was okay," and finally, complaining about the lack of space in Lalita's bed and how "disorganized" her papers were, she would go back to her own room at last. Her mother would stand at her dresser in the dark, cursing at Lalita and agreeing with her father who said loudly enough for Lalita to hear that she was "headed for a fall"—but it was worth the price of the cursing and the threats, for only with her mother gone could Lalita get up and turn off the light, close the door and push the books on the floor so that they'd make a noise if her mother came back in, then finally falling into the free space of her very own empty bed as if it were a new start, a state of grace.

The movie wasn't terrible, even Lucy thought the second half was better than the first, but Lalita's wad of her parents' cash was gone. Lucy and Noah were whispering and laughing, standing in front of the ATM just around the corner from the huge theater on 34th Street, with its escalators and neon lights both inside and out, when Lalita put her hand in her pocket and realized there was a hole in the bottom. She shook her head. Not sure how to say what had happened, she looked at the two of them—Lucy laughing uproariously at something Noah said and leaning her head against his shoulder, smiling at Lalita until she realized something was wrong.

"My money's gone."

They looked at her. "All that cash? My God."

"I've got more than enough to get you home," Noah told them, but he was looking at Lucy.

"Let's go back and look for it," Lucy said, taking Lalita's arm. "If it just fell out of your pocket, it could be there. Like under a seat."

Noah snorted. "Hello. This is New York . . ."

"Shut up, Noah. Let's go."

There was no sign of the money anywhere as Lalita lifted up seats and talked to the manager with signs of increasing desperation, because she thought, as she was looking for it, that this was it, the limits of what she could endure—she felt so sickened by the prospect of once again being completely dependent on her parents, no money of her own, that she wasn't going to go back to their house, her mother's house. She'd find the money and buy herself a ticket out of here, take out loans and find somewhere else to live. If she were on her own, she wouldn't even have to give her parents the number. What mattered now was just finding the money; proving to her father, though she wouldn't ever talk to him again, that he was wrong. Making all the wrong choices, reading books and writing instead of studying finance or engineering—getting overeducated so no one would want to marry her, letting herself get fat every summer so she became unattractive as well; she was a worthless daughter, *nashamapovay, deerdram, shanyangal*, she would come to nothing in spite of all the money they had sacrificed and spent on her, in spite of her blessings. She would ruin her own life. The whole litany—the ranting prayer on her father's part, as if by saying she would fail in life, he could make it so—could only be answered with the money back in her pocket.

Lucy put a hand on her shoulder but Lalita shrugged it off, looking under every seat in each row, starting in the back. Lucy and Noah stood and waited patiently.

"Four hundred bucks, a lot of money to lose. I'm real sorry about that," the usher who had turned on the lights said to no one in particular. "Tough break."

"Do you have a flashlight?" Lalita asked. He shook his head. She carried on. In her peripheral vision, she could see Noah and Lucy whispering, concerned. Why did it always come to this? People standing away from her, distancing themselves from what she knew was a wrong way of acting, trying too hard, needing.

Since they didn't have money for a cab all the way back to Long Island, they took the train home from Penn Station. Lucy and Noah sat in a double seat across from her, talking and laughing. Lalita pretended to read the newspaper she'd found on the seat. Once when she looked up at them, she she saw Lucy and Noah kissing. Noah caught her looking and pulled back. "For old times sake," he said, looking affectionate and happy.

"Don't feel bad about the money, shit happens," Lucy said, running her hand through Noah's hair.

The sight of them, too much. Suddenly Lalita knew she wasn't going to be able to stand it anymore. Not Noah and Lucy, not what they did, toward which she was more or less indifferent, benevolent—so Noah wasn't going to be the star of her very own "Tie Me Up, Tie Me Down," that she had planned. They were only two of millions of people, millions of men and women drawn to each other. There could be others, drawn to Lalita instead, except, frozen, she couldn't touch them back.

It was her own life Lalita couldn't stand. That she was repelled by. She didn't want to be a virgin anymore—not this kind of virgin, at least. She chafed with self-knowledge, wondering what to do first, feeling aroused by the sight of Lucy placing a hand, deliberately, on Noah's thigh while his hands trembled. She'd never have seen it if she'd stayed in the house with her mother, afraid. *Go on*, she heard her voice taunting, her mother's voice. "I will," she thought. "I will go right now." Reminding herself of the urgency with which she'd once managed to go with Tom, alone, and touch him in his apartment.

Now Lalita put the paper down and stood up, holding on to the pole and leaning over them.

"I need your help," she confided finally, in Noah and Lucy, because they were there.

Her jacket felt lighter and more stylish without the wad of money weighing it down, and without the big set of house-keys Lalita had thankfully kept in the other pocket, the one without the hole. She had given the house-keys to Lucy after they'd all gotten off the train together. They'd all three sat close together on a bench, planning things out loud, instead of Lalita trying to make plans only in her head.

Noah showed Lalita where the train was to take her back to Times Square, then Grand Central.

The train platform through the big archway, opposite the Information Booth and clock, was where Lalita stood now waiting for the Metro-North back to Yale. Her friends had made it so she'd never have to return to her parents' again.

While Lalita prepared to take the train to New Haven, Noah was busy taking Lucy to Lalita's house by LIRR again: they would pick up all of Lucy's things and some of Lalita's as well, especially her journals and books, and traveler's checks her parents had left in their master bedroom. Lucy had urged her to take the checks, plus whatever other cash lay visible, just to have more support in her new life, though Lalita didn't want to accept any more money from her parents, and didn't want to steal. She was already stealing her own life. But Noah too said she should take all the checks they'd left for her, that he knew a place in the city where they could be exchanged for cash, where Lalita couldn't be traced by her parents.

Before leaving with Lucy, Noah had called his mom, had told her everything. Noah's mother would be meeting Lucy and Noah at the train station in Kensington, take them to Lalita's house, to retrieve Lucy's things, then drive both Lucy and Noah back to his childhood house out in Jamaica Estates afterwards, where they would sleep, exhausted but at peace. Noah and Lucy could have taken the LIRR back to Rego Park as well, but Noah's mother insisted on helping.

Noah had bought Lalita's ticket back to New Haven on his mother's credit card number and loaned her some cash for the cab-ride from the train station back to her dorm at Yale.

What surprised Lalita most was how they hadn't demanded an explanation. Maybe they'd be more curious later. Yet they acted like they already knew. She'd just said it wasn't safe for her to go back home; that she was leaving her parents. She'd expected them to try to talk her out of it, but Lucy had known her for a year when they'd lived together as freshman room-mates. Lucy had heard some of the messages her father left on their answering machine. Lucy had whispered something in Noah's ear. Without making Lalita convince them, Lucy and Noah took over.

Her parents were still far away at their friend's house, grumpy at being awakened when Lalita called the, just to make sure they weren't back in Kensington. Her father told her they were planning to stay put for at least another two days. Her mother was too fast asleep to even come to the phone. Thank God, Lalita's mother truly used sleep as a drug.

Once her father had called Lalita a "rival" for her mother's affections and advised her to "just stay out of their lives." Once he had raised a glass bottle to throw at Lalita's head when she got in between him and her mother having an argument. She watched him uncomprehendingly as he came at her without stopping, until she recognized the rage in his eyes and ran for her life. He was her father, flesh and blood. He sent her out barefoot, running down the street. When she came back there was a wooden splinter in her foot. "Serves her right," he said from the next room, as she heard her mother soothing him, saying something beyond her reach as she braced herself and teased out the splinter with the knife she put under her bed afterwards, when she turned out the light and hoped her mother would not come.

Talking to her father, remembering all that, Lalita found it easy to keep her voice dispassionate without feeling guilty for the lies she told her parents about her plans, her whereabouts. Her parents would soon try to look for her, find her—Lalita knew that. But what they would actually do to bring her back might be limited by their own fear of embarrassment. Of exposure.

At last Lalita stood there with some confidence, waiting for the train and praying that her parents would leave her alone. It was an unrealistic hope. They wouldn't let go . . . and yet, part of the punishment for leaving them might be ignoring her, at least for a little while.

And in that space of being thankfully ignored, who could know what was possible?

The newspaper bins weren't empty yet, so she fished out a copy of the previous week's *New York Review of Books* for the one-hour ride. Lalita's new plans were all she could think of, shaped by her talk with Noah and Lucy. People they knew who lived in a house where she would finally be safe; the phone number of the girl renting out rooms in a co-op near the water at Longwharf that only asked for $300 a month as long as she did some kitchen work. She might have to tell all the people in the house so they would know not to admit over the phone to anyone that she lived there. She would have to get a car—she would have to learn to drive. She wouldn't get her parents' money anymore—she'd have to ask for loans and work-study to pay for the rest of the college. Lucy was doing it; it was hard, how would she do it suddenly, starting in the middle of the academic year? Nothing came free.

When the train came Lalita got on, the next to last car that stopped right near the escalator in the New Haven station. Afterwards she'd take a cab, back to the dorm, and Lucy and Noah would come back tomorrow—they'd agreed to meet for dinner as soon as they were all back at school. Both of them had given her parting hugs. Their touch felt good.

After that, what? She didn't know. She found herself sobbing with pangs of sadness over Tom Sarchassian of all people, because she realized suddenly that in addition to the sex, he could have fallen in love with her. Like Noah had fallen for Lucy. The next time . . . maybe a kiss, slowly deepening; no memories, no fears. Safe in bed the next time. She had no choice but to search for it. Return to Tom. Or someone new. Try.

How she would get there, she didn't know, but the train was moving forward now, moving in the night, so fast it made her feel that she had not lost any time.

2.

It was still warm outside on a late September afternoon, the sun dazzling on the Maya Lin fountain in the library walkway, but Lalita was curled up in a large brown leather chair in the L&B room at Sterling Memorial Library, trying to write an overdue term paper on an Adrienne Rich poem. Her notebook was blank even though the poem had plenty to say. It was about a woman is moving furtively, high above the street, reaching the other side of a great distance without being seen, and it was dedicated to another woman poet, Denise Levertov, translator of Indian erotic poetry.

That was what Lalita wanted to become—a thinker, a roof-walker, someone who could navigate uncertainty with deftness and a poised silence. But other people's questions stopped her in her tracks. And unlike a stranger might have done, her mother posed these questions like stern prophecies in her letters, like the one she'd sent a few weeks ago.

Lalita's father was alive and well; it appeared he had given over letter writing duty to her mother for now and there was no more direct mention of suicide. For that matter, in all the letters, no direct mention of anything that ever happened between the three of them. Her mother never asked why their daughter left.

But her mother didn't have to ask, Lalita thought. Like Luther nailing his theses to a wooden door, Ma always already knew what everything meant.

This time she'd clipped and sent an advice column where someone had written, "Dear Abby, my fiancé hates his parents, and I admit I don't fully understand the reasons, but frankly it's hard for me to care anymore. He blames them for everything that's ever gone wrong in his life, even though some of the struggles he's had must have been his fault, and I think are probably due to his problems in getting along with other people. I'm thinking seriously of not marrying this man—his bitterness drives everyone away, and even though he's good looking and talented enough to get many opportunities, he always blows it because he's so mired in the past." Like anyone she knew? Aren't you afraid of ruining your life the same way, ending up alone?

Plain and precise—no matter what Lalita did, how many offerings in her parents' name at the Hindu temple in Branford, where she went every few months to pray for answers, no matter how many letters she wrote her parents trying to forgive, the facts were the facts, and she, Lalita, daughter of her parents and refugee from her mother's bed, could not be alright. She would be damaged by what happened after all, no one would want her. *Nashamapovay*, Lalita could hear in her head, translated loosely as "you'll be ruined." Clip, clip, went her mother's shears around the crisp newspaper page.

Like one of the Fates, snipping a lifeline.

Tom said to throw the article away. They'd been traveling by train from New York to New Haven, back from a conference he'd had to go to on some topic in comparative medieval literature, something about Parsifal and a tragic love story about which she could understand nothing because the papers were all in French and Italian. They were sitting close to each other, reading.

"Look what my mother sent," Lalita said, and something in her voice made him look up.

His face was angry as he scanned the page, then bland. "Well, she has a right to her opinion. We don't care," he said, giving her a quick kiss.

"Do you think I should throw it away?" Lalita asked.

"You definitely should." This time his kiss was longer, inviting. She wiped her tears, then got up to discard the packed envelope from her mother, with its furious writing and sharply folded newspaper clipping, in the bin outside the lavatory where she washed her face.

Lalita's now-best friend Lucy was the one who'd eventually convinced her to call Tom that first time, soon after Lalita settled into the house in West Haven. They were at Lucy's house, talking and making food. The house was on Whitney Avenue just off Science Hill and Lucy was only renting it. She had offered it to Lalita for the coming year, since she herself was getting ready to take a year abroad in Italy, her dream.

This is the happiest I've ever been, Lalita thought. She had been standing in Lucy's living room that July, which she would have as her own until the next June for a still-reasonable rent. All she had to do was clean the house and help take care of the landlord's pets—a red mynah in a cage, a black and white kitten that had most likely been abused or neglected, the way it fought invisible enemies with surprisingly sharp claws, etching its battles into the hardwood floors, and a large, imperturbable poodle with tragic, inky eyes and a speckling of dirty gray hairs throughout its fluff. The landlady, Ann, was a retired Chemistry teacher from a New Haven high school whose husband had been an astronomer at Yale. "There's the meteorite named after our daughter Isabel," she said, pointing to a picture taken with a telephoto lens. Her eyes as they took Lalita in were kind and keen in a face aged by a vigorous life.

Ann was a volunteer with the alumni association and, every year, rented part of her house to a female student at a low rate in exchange for the light cleaning "and the company," she said. Right now, Ann was off in Taos, New Mexico, visiting her second daughter, a painter and sculptor. She would be back and forth throughout the year. Lucy was upstairs packing her suitcases in the tiny room that would be Lalita's own—cool with a white eyelet bedspread that Ann had carefully washed and dried before her departure, made up with blue and lavender sheets that were faded but clean. Lalita was pleasantly awed by Ann's house—the large bowls, many that she had made herself at a potter's studio, usually spilling over with flowers or fruit like you would see in a display.

Each piece of furniture was carved by one of Ann's Norwegian relatives, an uncle who still had a carpentry workshop and sent her hand made tables and chairs when she'd gotten married over forty years before. More than the beauty of the house—never immaculate, usually clean enough despite the dog and cat, but never House Beautiful—the love was what you noticed first, the love for her daughters, neither of whom had gotten married before the age of twenty-nine, which Lalita's father had always considered the hopeless age (when marrying even a white man might be tolerable for an Indian girl, so that she wouldn't be unmarried at least, but only just). Love spilling out in loose abundance, safe enough to welcome the daughters back from their travels whenever they could manage it but cool and capacious enough, like the house itself, to never demand their return or to exact a more passionate and entwined loyalty.

It was the end of May, and Lucy and Lalita were making dinner together. Strips of grilled chicken and tofu, bright red peppers on Ann's white cutting board, tortillas on an earthenware plate made by her daughter in New Mexico.

"Hey, who do you want to invite?" Lucy called out, one hand over the receiver. It was Noah on the line, asking how much wine and dessert he should bring.

Lalita thought of Tom Sarchassian, whose picture had been in the *Yale Daily News* that week because of some teaching prize he'd won.

"Lucy, you invite someone for me. I don't know that many people well enough."

"You will." Lucy smiled from across the kitchen and went back to talking to Noah.

Noah brought over a flamenco album he'd been listening to lately, one that his sophisticated new girlfriend had bought him as a present from a Romani vendor selling CDs outside the Alhambra. Lucy outlined her itinerary as they ate. She'd spoken to her new boyfriend Raymond that morning—he'd gone to Paris ahead of time for a conference on the rights of undocumented *sans papiers* North African immigrants, getting ready to meet her there and then make their connection together from Charles de Gaulle to the country of Burkina Faso. Then Lucy would do her year abroad in Italy, with Raymond coming for visits. Lucy's other boyfriends, filmmakers, law students, an MBA or two, all had receded into insignificance. Raymond was her sun and stars. Raymond her ray of light.

Enjoying the dinner, Lalita also enjoyed watching Lucy's face. Excited, beautiful, in love, she thought. Noah looked happy for Lucy. His own girlfriend Celene was five years older, a French beauty who was lively enough to draw Noah out but was no longer interested in sleeping around, wanting the productive lull of domesticity. She was at a conference but back soon.

After dinner, while they were sitting on the porch and drinking the excellent Riojas Noah had brought, also picked out by Celene before she left, the whole story about Tom and Lalita—minus the scene in his office—slipped out when they pressed her for details about why she wasn't dating anyone.

Lucy was insistent that she call; Noah was cautious.

"You don't know if he's still seeing that blond Shakespeare TA. They could be married. She could even be pregnant by now. Or else he could have decided never to date students after what happened."

"Well, first of all, Lalita's not his student anymore. And if he's married, he'll say so. But what if he's sitting alone in some carrel at Sterling, blowing the dust off some boring manuscript and just wishing . . . I don't know."

"That someone would come along and give him a blow-job?" Noah finished.

"She should still call him, smarty pants."

They finished another half-bottle of wine. Lucy soon retreated upstairs to take a long-distance phone call from Raymond. After Noah said goodbye to them, Lalita found herself alone on the fold-out in Ann's living room, putting antiseptic cream on a new scratch the kitten had made on one of her feet when she had been sitting at the kitchen table, that kitten another one of Ann's rescue projects.

Unguarded, Lalita thought of Tom Sarchassian, remembering his hands. Still Lalita waited; she went to Sterling Library a few times that month without telling anyone, after Lucy had left for the summer, hoping to catch a glimpse of him—no luck.

Burkina Faso was a small country famous because of the 1980s famines and a tragic coup, destroying the life and promising leadership of Thomas Sankara, a handsome and charismatic man who had a cabinet full of articulate women and mostly honest men. Sankara gave meaning to the name of the country, "Land of Incorruptibles." He was unseated by the unscrupulous and mercenary military leader, Campaore, who, first thing after installing himself into power, bought himself a jet like John Travolta's Scientology showpiece, disbanded the Ministry of Child Welfare and the Vaccination Initiative. Because of his CIA-backed, unmitigated corruption, and reluctance to invest any foreign aid in the infrastructure required to distribute food, thousands of bags of wheat and millet donated by the World Bank for famine relief in rural areas had succumbed to mold or been eaten by rats. Lalita knew these details from some of Lucy's enthusiastic tirades, which had become more frequent in the months just before she was leaving, as her fiancé Raymond, now a full-fledged crackerjack human rights lawyer who worked against police brutality in between writing critical theory articles on race, brought her deeper into a life of fucking, laughing and taking political action with him.

Lalita wondered if the two of them would last—over distance, Raymond's career, Lucy's unabashed desire for money and glamour. But look at the photo from the tiny airport in Ouagadagou that Lucy had sent with her letter, beaming from under her head wrap. Lucy had, as planned, gone to visit him there, before her junior year in Italy.

By the time the postcard from Lucy arrived, Lalita felt fully settled into Ann's bright house—a house she would have chosen for herself. There was an Ansel Adams print of the moon over Death Valley, where Lalita planned to go one day—maybe drive a rented car from the Las Vegas airport, stay in a cheap little motel and watch a soft porn flick, go out to the dunes in the middle of the night and contemplate "the nothing that is not there, and the nothing that is."

Pottery she'd made in a class at the Arts Space off Orange Street was stacked in the kitchen; she'd leave them in the house after Lucy came back, as talismans of the good fortune that had come to both her and Lucy under its roof, where Lucy had relaxed with Raymond and Lalita relaxed into herself.

Lalita constructed rituals: going to a café to read after a long run to East Rock Park and back; biking to Nica's Market on a rusty boy's cycle with a little wicker basket that Ann had bought second-hand for when her grandchildren were visiting.

Lalita was having tea at Atticus with a book of poetry by Marianne Moore opened up to the poem about marriage, when she felt someone staring at her. Lalita had just been wishing she could be as reserved, self-sufficient and fucking *elegant* as Moore, when she looked up to meet a man's eyes–of course it wouldn't be Tom, and it wasn't, just some other moderately-attractive grad student who wanted to know if he could buy her another cup of tea or something to eat.

Lalita nodded, sure, glad she had become slightly more comfortable when men flirted with her. But as the grad student started talking, asking questions about the book, Tom Sarchassian came into the cafe and, since he knew the guy apparently, ended up sitting down with the two of them.

Tom spoke to Lalita politely, as if they only knew each other from philosophy class, and her shame the night she left his apartment came back to her in full force.

But she was so far now from that miserable, short night. Tom had switched to talking to his friend, sitting at their table, giving her a chance to be normal with him. He wasn't wearing a wedding ring; he'd come alone. He didn't even seem uncomfortable, for which she was grateful.

She might learn something, knowing him. Even if he didn't fall in love with her.

And Lalita loved to learn. Suddenly she was bold enough to look directly at him, blinking obsidian eyes and moistening her lips.

"Are you still seeing Rena?" his grad student friend asked. "What's that little Swedish princess doing this summer?"

"I don't even know," Tom said, not explaining what he meant.

Soon after, Tom left Atticus, giving Lalita one brief speculative look she would have missed if she hadn't been watching so closely, and when she looked down into her teacup and smiled, the clueless graduate student asked her, "What?"

"No frigging way that Tom Sarchassian could want me," Lalita wrote that night in a letter to Lucy, thrilled by the suspicion that he did. "It would probably be a terrible idea to call him."

"Call him today," Lucy wrote, all in capitals on the postcard that arrived a few weeks later, otherwise covered by colorful stamps. Lalita smiled; by then she had.

At first, Tom was cautious, asking "if this was about philosophy" and saying, before she could answer, that "he wasn't going to be able to be an advisor to any more students."

"It's not anything to do with school," she said. "And I'm not in any course in your department, by the way."

A pause. "What is it then?" Tom asked.

"I was wondering if you'd like to have coffee with me."

"I shouldn't do that."

"Do you want to take my number in case?" Lalita felt a strange, delicious calm.

"There's no need. You're in the directory, aren't you? I mean if I wanted the number."

She was ready to hang up, ashamed, but then he spoke again.

"Well, maybe I'll call you. If you're sure."

"I really want you to," she whispered, beyond shame. "Please."

"I'll call you tomorrow," he promised, and did.

It took another week, but soon enough, around July Fourth, they were relaxing in Ann's house, kissing in bed with their clothes on. He was glad she didn't have any roommates; he wanted them to be discreet. In case. He was about to start a teaching job in New York City, in August, many miles from Long Island, a world away, Lalita kept reassuring herself. Once he had started his new, hard-to-get job, and wasn't teaching any Yale students anymore, they could do what they liked, whoever saw.

"I mean, that is, if you still want me then," Tom said, attractive for how he didn't assume she still would.

By the September of her junior year at Yale, Lalita found herself on the train showing Tom, who was officially her boyfriend by then, her mother's letter with the *Dear Abby* clipping. Even the way it had reached her had been uncomfortable.

Lalita had written a letter to her parents—one of her customary, once-a-week missives, like a military bulletin, a duty—explaining that she would be returning to the city for a day and asking if they would like her to collect the rest of her things. She had only another year to go before she'd graduate from Yale.

Her mother Kamini had been demanding that she collect her things anyway, writing a letter nearly every month since her departure to Lalita's post office box, saying the least she could do for her parents, however ungrateful she may have become, was to "take away all her junk" because it was "cluttering their house."

Her mother's reply to Lalita's polite but admittedly impersonal letter was prompt. Her parents were about to go on vacation to Florida, just the two of them. Would she like them to leave her things with a neighbor, since she did not have any way to get into "*their* house"?

When Lalita arrived at Mrs. Johanssen's house two doors down from her parents,' in Kensington, Long Island—the neighbor's house she used to go to nearly every day to eat Toll House cookies and escape the occasionally nagging, usually indifferent babysitters her mother was forced to hire in order to continue practicing pediatrics while Lalita was still in elementary school—she found her mother had not lied about what they'd left Lalita.

The suitcases Kamini left were literally full of junk. Old debate team trophies from high school, post-it notes from books her mother had gone through and excised of her presence before deciding to keep. Mismatched and often dirty socks. A sweatshirt from the third grade that was too stained and bedraggled after all these years for her mother to be possibly hoping that Lalita would pass it on to her own daughters.

Lalita took the suitcases without comment, giving Mrs. Johanssen a bouquet of pink carnations and wondering what it would have been like to be part of her sweet and proper, wryly humored Swedish family instead.

"But then you would have been blond, and I have a bad history with blonds," Tom said to her, when she told him her wish, making her laugh.

The letter from Lalita's mother had been tucked into the front zipper of one of the suitcases—the one stuffed to overflowing with more of the silky Indian clothes Lalita had gone through the phase of wearing early in freshman year, soon after she'd lost her baby fat from high school and flirted with an exotic glamour. But the attention had been too much, the stares too frequent and prolonged—mostly admiring, a little frightening when they came from her middle-aged English professors, some of her classmates' fathers, the strong and seductive dyke waitress at the Daily Caffe, so she switched back to jeans and anonymity.

She might be ready to try wearing those Indian clothes again, she thought, feeling a rush of warmth toward her mother. Including the clothes meant that she wanted Lalita to be beautiful to others, didn't it?

That was when she found the letter. She thought about her mother's message for a long time after she had cried and discarded the papers, wondering if the prophecies it contained would come true, and she would end up alone, full of resentment at having squandered all her opportunities, obscured her gifts with bitterness. In her religion class at the temple—a weekly ordeal until she was thirteen and thankfully excused so she could go to SAT prep instead, only slightly less painful—it was taught that Hindu prophecy was inexorable, story after story showing not just the futility, but the arrogance of trying to escape your fate. Your future was written on your forehead by a divine hand; so close, so much a part of you—impossible for you to read, yet thankfully so—for who can change what is written?

For the same reason, Lalita took comfort in a prophecy her mother had told her when she got her first menses at the age of eleven—that the astrologer in India who had done her horoscope when she was born had predicted a long and happy marriage.

The horoscope was the one thing she didn't tell Tom, for fear of scaring him. Yet he had coped well with the rest, and he was the one who said he loved her first. She could tell that he was unsure what the future held, that it surprised him to say it. He had just given her an orgasm when the words slipped out of his mouth in the dark, and she didn't respond. Then predictably, for her, she cried, told him that she loved him too. What it was like when she thought there was no chance, that he was gone. When she said she loved him too, what she loved best was the embrace, the fact that they were close enough to at least think they were in love. "It's like a thaw," she wrote in a letter to Lucy. "I thought it would be so painful not to be frozen anymore, but it's warmer than anything."

They had the number, Lalita divined. Looking at her father's face, the flat surface of it, smugly composed for once instead of explosive with rage, Lalita was sure of it. Her parents had had her telephone number in West Haven all along. They'd known exactly where she was. She pictured the "family room," as they called the small room behind the living room, in front of the kitchen. There was a darkened yellow easy chair, moved out of sight when anyone came over, the only one in the house not covered with plastic, so anyone talking on the phone could sink down in oblivion, rubbing their bare feet against the pelt of that chair as if they were sitting on an easy-going, long-suffering dog. The phone was on the wall just above the chair, and next to it were scribbled pieces of paper, cardboards with columns of numbers, like lists of ghetto residents. Taped to the phone was her number, maybe her address, secure, everything they knew and had known, she suspected, soon after she thought she'd moved out of their reach.

Having her undoing taped up there was enough for them. They wouldn't have even needed to look at it. She thought back to her most recent conversation with her mother. Now it was nearly a year after she'd left. Her mother had just sent her the book, "Forgive Your Parents, Heal Your Life," full of stories of repentant, newly evangelical adults who, like lottery winners, had prospered suddenly once they'd gambled on reuniting with an alcoholic dad, a vitriolic mother they hadn't spoken to in years. The best way to move forward was to forgive. She couldn't imagine what that meant. Or—she could imagine but couldn't distinguish between the various possibilities that presented themselves at odd moments in the day or the first thing in the morning. Did forgiveness mean getting married to Tom, having his children and then once they were safely born and sheltered by his side of the family, allowing her parents to see them? Not alone of course. Did it mean calling her parents every week? Giving them her number and allowing them to call her? Allowing them (as she knew with a singular certainty) to slide right back into behaving the way they always had. They would find reasons for her leaving that would put them in the best light. "You were unstable then but thank God, you're much better now." "God be praised, you lost your weight, Daddy was beginning to worry that nobody would marry you." "I think college was too stressful for you—you couldn't handle it at first, you took it out on us." "Generation gap. A lot of Indian families have problems because of the whole immigration, what can you do." She heard them saying these things so clearly because, through the years, when her angry, clear sadness had led to the inevitable confrontations at home, not tolerating the touching or the hitting and threats, at least for a time, these had been the words they'd found to defend their lives against hers. To silence her.

But what did forgiveness mean? Did it mean forgetting *who said what you did you smacked you cruel hate cut my hand!* How *bastard said it was my fault Thatha had a stroke because I talked back, even though I loved him too, you bastard, stupid,* Lalita thought, hating her father for how he blamed her for whatever misfortune he was ruminating on that day.

Despite their intensity, whenever her hot feelings of rage coalesced into words, they cooled and became redundant, crumbling like volcanic rocks. And she in turn felt cool and nearly indifferent, her attention turning to the present. How she felt after a good run up Science Hill. Dishes from the Provence cookbook in Ann's kitchen that she wanted to try making for Tom. Flowers to buy and put in a vase she'd made on the third try in pottery class and painted. Studying, the term papers she had to write now that she'd chosen to be an English major focusing on poetry. Her part time job as a research assistant for an Economics professor who studied the Grameen Bank in Bangladesh, and who invited her to dinner every now and then in case one of his sons should take a liking to her despite her mentioning Tom. Shamed by her anger, by her good fortune, Lalita had tried to move on, tried shaking off the heavy guilt.

But all this time, while Lalita was thinking about her parents, often when she didn't even want to, forcing herself into reflective moods that felt like contrition—they hadn't even cared. Power was what they were after, and when they got her number (from where? Friends who lived in Connecticut and had children who read it off a poster somewhere?) her parents had their power again and were too content to bother to grasp at her anymore. They could have called at odd hours, when they knew she was unlikely to be home, just to hear her voice on the answering machine, echoing off the walls of an apartment they could locate at any time. In fact, she knew almost without a doubt that they'd been making such calls all along.

Why hadn't it occurred to her before? What did it change? Part of her was still thinking: Maybe I'm not important enough, maybe they don't care and that's why they let me go so easily. I'm not even worth their letters anymore. I'm not worth their rage.

Lalita shivered. Her mother could still harangue her in dreams, especially when Lalita was in bed with Tom.

In dreams that came when he was by her side, she was back in her parents' house alone, like she'd never met him. All of it the same, as if she'd never left. In one dream, Lalita was at the top of the stairs, a door separating her from Amma, who leaned against the wall at the bottom of the stairs, shouting at the top of her lungs like she would never be pacified, no matter what. And that was the point of it, Lalita understood. To pacify, to be commanded to pacify. The screaming wasn't instructive; it didn't change anything Lalita did or had the power to change. But it was her job to pacify. And it was Amma's power—to turn Lalita from a reverie, the contemplation of whether to buy a new shirt, of whether or not to cut her hair, or from the ending of *Little Women* or *Crime and Punishment* or *Wide Sargasso Sea*. To turn Lalita into someone desperate, unable to sustain any other wishes, but to make the screaming stop.

Instead, Lalita had to make the peace; come down from the shelter of her room, confront Amma, scream back if possible so that her nerves were frayed, lose control in a panic of disgust and resentment over the woman's insistence on disrupting her peace, on screaming about something, something, what?

Sometimes Amma herself admitted she had no reason and simply insisted on her human right to scream. "Pretend I'm talking to the wall," she said furiously. "Don't I even have the right to scream? Not that you or your father would listen."

But Lalita herself losing control was the key her mother was seeking by screaming. A switch. Then Amma was fairy mother again, calming, controlled. "Alright now, calm down. It's all going to be alright," and so on, an hour passed and Lalita no longer breathing hard but disgusted with herself, confused, repulsed but passive as Amma kissed and caressed her.

Yes, physical affection was normal between mother and daughter, she replied to Amma's voice in her head. But not sleeping and touching in a bed like married couples do. And not after that kind of staged screaming match, Amma. When you needed me to lose control so you could feel in control again; when you couldn't stand my having peace of mind, and the freedom of not being an adult yet and your house not being my house to run, your husband not being my husband to put up with. When you mistook my body for a thing you could call yours.

One day later that spring, nearly a year since Lalita had left home, when Tom was away and she was trying to sort out forgiveness, she called her parents' number on an impulse.

Her mother picked up the phone and said, "Hello."

Lalita answering sobbingly, "Hi, Ma."

Her mother had been startled at first, then had responded with cunning. Well of course Dad was still a problem. Yes, sometimes he had his rages. And how was Lalita? Did she, by any chance, know a good therapist for Dad? Lalita, herself startled into action, a suggestion of change, family again? found herself promising to find someone.

It was only afterward that she realized how strange it was for her, having been cut with a knife and attacked with a bottle by this man, called a slut since she was twelve, told she was going to come to ruin, promised that no one but her mother would want her, slapped, hit and given concussions, and had her mind turned, over the years, from fairly contented and benign to vengeful and brooding—well of course she had to be the one to find her father a therapist. Why else have a daughter? she thought again, looking at her parents sitting across from her now in the Manhattan restaurant to which she'd ill-advisedly invited them, about two weeks after that call.

This was the sort of restaurant her father would never have come to willingly. Run by Black Muslims, "so-called Muslims," her father said sneeringly, crammed onto a street in Morningside Heights, the place was humble but known for good food, a favorite of Columbia students.

The Black man at the counter had brightened, answered, "Alaikum al salam" in response to Lalita's polite greeting, "Salaam." As perfect strangers, she and the man could wish each other peace, Lalita thought.

And I shall have some peace there;

For peace comes dropping slow—

Her parents were already sitting at a table by the time she arrived, looking prim. Their water glasses were untouched, her father's elbows rested on the table. They both had a few more gray hairs and her father had put on some more weight, but otherwise looked the same, their frowns identical behind thick spectacles.

She sat down, drawing her chair slightly away from them, thankful that her mother didn't reach out to touch her right away.

"So," her mother said, gathering steam. But Lalita interrupted her.

"I wanted to say I forgive you," she began. "I mean, not that I'm the only one who needs to forgive. I'm sure I did things that angered you."

"I'm very glad you realize that," her father said, supercilious. "So thankful you're aware you have at least a few faults, Lalita."

The world was simple when she hated them too. Why the fuck did she take this on, again? Thankfully the waiter came. He was "from Pakistan," he said.

"So, you are all from India?" he said, smiling, taking note of her mother's bindi. She noticed his embroidered cap. "India hasn't been so kind to Muslims, but good health to you!" he said smilingly, not reacting to Amma's cold stare.

"You take us to a dirty Muslim place?" Amma whispered. "Is this how you treat your parents? Better you should just pretend we're dead."

Appa closed his eyes and massaged the sides of his forehead. "*Anayum pitayum munari daivum*," he said, his eyes still closed.

"Your mother and your father are your first gods," Lalita said. "Is that what it means?"

"You tell us," Lalita's mother said.

"I don't know what *you* mean by it," Lalita answered, in the monotone she'd practiced in the train, *sotto voce*. "But if you had been my first gods, I would've had to let you kill me eventually, or keep me with you for the rest of my life—one of those two. I had to leave for my safety. For my basic sanity. The cozy-cozy had to end sometime."

She sounded reasonable, even to herself, and this time she wasn't crying. So many times, over the kitchen table she'd told them tearfully that what Appa had done had threatened her safety, that it wasn't normal to grab a knife and go after your daughter when you were having an argument, even if you claimed afterward that you never would have used it, even if that same scenario repeated almost every week. And this time, like all the times in the past, she expected him to sneer at her again and imitate how she said the word "safety," as if it were a concept only spoiled brats or cowards ever appealed to. Or a hoity-toity word, he said. Arrogant, American—as if safety were something everyone was entitled to, regardless of means.

"She thinks her safety is threatened," her father had often said, in a hard voice of contempt.

"Who puts food on the table for you every night?" he would start. "Who sent you to college in the first place? Who works day and night to make sure you never go hungry or homeless, like I was hungry when I was a boy? I. Am. Your. FATHER," he would shout, nearly apoplectic, stabbing his finger near her face. "Say whatever you want, you *deerdram*, but you cannot change that fact, and don't you forget it."

They were in a public place now. The sharpest thing near Appa (she'd already checked) was a blunt knife on the butter plate, and she took that in her hand, meaning to lay it down out of his reach.

Her father saw. "Look at that," he said wearily. "Will you look at that, Amma? She thinks her own father wants nothing more than to grab a knife and go after her, in a public place. Do you want to see your father in jail? Is that what you want? You're a clever girl, Lalie," he said, changing tactics when she sat stiffly unmoving, her fingers still grasping the knife. "A very clever girl. You have the brains to twist things around. Alright. Okay. Very soon you're going to find that you have no one at all. Very soon, my girl. You're headed for a fall. God is watching you."

She was tempted to say, "How do you know God's not watching YOU, Appa," but held back.

Later that night, when Lalita was in the flat that Tom was subletting uptown, he wanted to know why she hadn't said the words out loud, to her father.

She shook her head, unable to communicate the dread she felt—however unlikely its object—about suffering some retribution for what she was doing. She was living in sin, not just because she was having sex with Tom, but because she had stolen her life like a golden apple from her parents, taken something they'd polished and always meant to have, and pushed it with all her might out of their reach. How could she think the gods were on her side?

Soon after Thanksgiving, when Lalita had been with Tom well into her senior year at Yale, but never once stopped looking over her shoulder, an

Indian woman she didn't know was raped on campus. When she'd stopped asking herself, "Why her, not me," Lalita had the chance to see what her classmates were doing. After the rape were the shouting matches, intimidation episodes in front of Linsley Chittenden and in the Stiles courtyard, the newspaper editorials by students who didn't even know anyone involved. Not because the concept of "date rape" was new in 1995—the annual Take Back the Night rally had been started a decade ago, and Lalita herself wore a purple button from the most recent rally on her denim jacket every day.

Never anonymous, the rape victim was nonetheless an unknown quantity—not an outspoken feminist or someone any of the newspapers had ever interviewed for anything, but the apparent opposite: a petite and voluptuous, exotically sexy girl from south India who kept to herself a fair amount, was never seen without full make-up and bangles and gauzy tight-fitting clothing, never spoke up in class, headed for an arranged marriage though she never said as much. She told the police that she'd been raped by four of the best-looking, top performing and best-connected basketball players on the team. The men refused to discuss the case, but they had so many friends and hangers-on in the fraternities and sororities that they didn't have to. You'd have to ask yourself why they would have even noticed her, and almost everyone on campus did ask—not just in private and contemptuous conversations, but in flyers they taped to the kiosks outside Morse and Stiles college, the Daily Caffe, the Yale Co-op. The girl's accusations—the accusations attributed to her, though she was not the one who told the police—were nothing more than fabrications to cover what had really happened. Her loser, backward Indian boyfriend had raped her, she was too ashamed to tell the truth, and there they were, four solid guys who had been drinking a little too much and maybe, at the most, touched her casually or made a suggestive remark—and there went their promising futures, their lives, down the drain because of her lies and her shame. The guys were all good guys, well known. The girl? A nobody with a name you couldn't pronounce, some girl with no money who'd gotten an abortion the year before according to the rumors about her. Her injuries were from domestic violence. Her broken, dislocated arm, the fractured collarbone, large bruises on her face, legs and torso, could all be explained by some jealous Indian boyfriend, punishing her for killing their baby. The two of them never should have been accepted to Yale, the rapists' friends and fraternity brothers concluded.

When Lalita saw the posters a few weeks later on one of the kiosks outside the Yale Co-op, she was making her way through the passage between Morse College and Mory's. She stopped to read the whole thing because it bore an Indian girl's name.

There was Jayanti, the rape victim's, picture. Lalita recognized her from one of the Diwali festival shows where she had danced in a line of other beautiful, anonymous Indian debutantes. Lalita tore the insulting poster down and hurried on around the corner with it balled up in her fist, down York Street, past the post office, into the Women's Center next to Durfee's Sweet Shoppe. Lalita used the payphone in the lobby to make her call; she had to wait for several minutes as the hospital operator paged Lalita's psychiatrist aunt Shama to the line. She found herself brushing away tears while she waited.

Shama Aunty, who was a friend of the victim, who'd even bought some of her art, said she'd been helping Jayanti, who thankfully had left the Yale campus before seeing or hearing about any of the posters, which only went up the morning after she had gone.

The Xeroxed posters featured Jayanti's picture from the freshman face book and the caption, "Liar" in block print; on top of this, on the poster Lalita had taken down, was hand-scribbled "SLUT" in black marker. Dave's friends from Morse had put the posters everywhere. They'd held a meeting to talk about how to support him and the other athletes involved once the trial date had been set. It was a college-based hearing—not in formal court, but a hearing by the academic senate, where Deans presided. The boys who were accused had chosen this over a criminal trial, although years later, Jayanti would wish she had listened to Shama and hired a lawyer to press a formal suit. Expulsion from Yale didn't seem like enough punishment; they'd go to a different school, a Colgate or Oral Roberts or Sweet Briar or Southern Baptist or Colby College, some school dominated by families who had gone there for generations, not as much a symbol of meritocracy and class mobility as Yale still seemed to be to Jayanti, Lalita, others they knew.

Lalita was glad she hadn't broken any of Yale's rules and didn't need a family to help her, but she shivered thinking of how there was no room for her mistakes. How she could have been left homeless if she'd been the one to give in to her fears, cheat on an exam, and lose her place at Yale, her only safe place.

As the controversy about the rape wore on, Lalita was surprised by how much it hurt her personally. To be stared at, of course, by young women who called themselves "Sorority Girls for Wrongly Accused Americans"—to be called bad names on the street at Yale, which Lalita still called a "safe place," compared with her parents' house.

"Sand n-----."

"Fucking dink slut."

Lalita heard these slurs hurled at her while was waiting at Phelps' Gate for Tom to come pick her up after a few hours he'd insisted on having alone to go over the final draft of a paper he was submitting to a famous journal. She was smiling to herself with so much dreamy-eyed anticipation that she didn't notice the two basketball players standing in front of her until they had already come too close for comfort. They stood and stared at her—staring her down, she supposed, except she was already sitting on the stone ledge under the gate, and they loomed over her, as they must loom over most people just from their height, which laid end to end must have been as high as some of the houses she had seen and day-dreamed about buying one day with Tom. She met their gaze until one of them said, "Who are *you*?" with more contempt than she would have believed possible from someone she was not related to. They burst into laughter at her astonished look and walked away victorious.

The next day, she was walking across the New Haven Green with Noah, when one of his professors stopped them to say hello. He chatted pleasantly with them about the class—Advanced Composition, Noah had opted to major in music in the end—and how much he was enjoying the teaching so far. He thought Noah would assuredly get a wonderful job in the classical division of a record company after graduation.

"Try developing opera stars," the professor suggested to Noah, "since you're such a fan."

Then the professor—tall with thinning blond hair, attractive in that off-handed European way with tobacco-stained fingers, thin metal glasses and stubble on his face—turned to Lalita with a wink.

"Working on town gown relations?" he said to Noah. Both Noah and Lalita looked blank.

"What local school do you go to my dear?" he asked Lalita, putting a hand on her arm. For a second, she admired his long fingers rather than answering. It was Noah's professor, she didn't want him to walk away feeling as if his good intentions in bothering to talk to her in the first place, in taking the trouble to charm her, had been thrown back in his face. Did she?

"She goes right here," Noah said. "To that expensive school across the street. She's a philosophy major. The best student in the department."

"You go to Yale?" the professor asked with obvious surprise, but not the distaste Lalita had seen flittering over more than one face since the rape. "Well good for you." He smiled opaquely before continuing on. "Good for both of you," he stopped to add.

"He probably went to a community college himself," Noah remarked, putting an arm around Lalita's shoulders once they were clear. "Or like the equivalent in Denmark. He probably got hired here through connections."

Lalita laughed. Before the rape, she would have shrugged it off, joked about how open-minded Noah was for walking around in broad daylight with his townie girlfriend in plain view of his illustrious professors. But since the posters about Jayanti had gone up, Lalita felt that everyone she passed was watching her, questioning her presence at Yale. Even Lalita's aunt Shama, usually impervious, noticed a chill in the air when she went to Naples Pizza for a beer with Lalita. She had to wait nearly thirty minutes to get the bartender's attention.

"And you know it's not what I'm wearing," Shama joked, when she had finally come back to their table with the drinks.

Shama wore a long, belted leather jacket by Versace, over a red jersey dress also handmade in Italy, finishing with her favorite Jimmy Choo heels. Her make-up was immaculate, her hair falling in soft waves down to her shoulders exactly the same way it always had, the curve of her breast showing at the low neck of the dress as she sat down and opened her coat. But for once Shama's regal and sedate beauty appeased no one, provoked no smiles or offers of free drinks, only stares and curt replies to her questions. The men and women who worked in the small stores on York Street—not just the Co-op but the pizza place, the little store for used CDs, the flower shop, the grocery store—must have all looked at the posters about Jayanti on their way into work. They must have realized how much a boy like Dave Sheffield, the primary rapist—good looking, athletic, a regular at Naples' Thursday Nights—was one of them. He was that kid who left big tips and smiled at all the waitresses and clerks, at the cute girls with pierced noses and exposed belly-buttons who worked at the CD shop, at the middle aged woman who smoked and cursed as she sold flowers but wasn't too old or cynical to ask Dave "who was the lucky girl" each time he stopped by at her store.

It was a waste of time to dwell on it, Tom said, and Lalita agreed but couldn't stop herself from dwelling on the rape anyway.

Lalita bought a copy of the children's book Jayanti had illustrated, published in India, a book famous enough to be sold in a children's book and toyshop on Amazon. Lalita thought of the girl often though she had barely known her.

When Jayanti came back to Yale to finish up, after the hearing was over and all the rapists were suspended, then expelled, Lalita admired the way she held her head and walked as if she didn't care what people thought. Jayanti looked the same—a bit thinner, if anything, but still glamorously dressed and made up, still seductive. That was the most courageous thing about her, Lalita thought—that she'd been raped, had her beauty turned against her by someone abusive, and yet it didn't make her hesitate to showcase that very beauty, to put herself at the center of nearly any Indian party she went to. To even be a tease and flirt with all the uptight, Indian engineering types, letting them get their hopes up as she slid away at the end of the night, going back to the house where she lived now—the same safe house where Lalita had stayed when she first left her parents—alone.

Jayanti was so elusive, Lalita thought, admiring her independence while secretly grateful to be wrapped up in Tom's arms at night, not even minding it when he complained (as he had begun to in the month after the rape, when she clung to him even more than usual) that Lalita was getting in his way, that she needed to learn to take care of herself if he was ever going to get any work done and make it as an assistant professor. If they were ever going to make it through, long-term. If they were ever going to get married, he said, making her stop and look at him, wide-eyed. "That is where this is leading," he whispered. "It's what I hope."

When it turned out that Jayanti was in one of Lalita's classes, Lalita ended up inviting her to coffee. They sat at Atticus and she found herself against better judgment confiding in Jayanti how afraid she was of losing Tom. If Lalita had not been watching so closely, monitoring Jayanti's face for a sign, any sign, that she'd been traumatized, she would've missed the momentary, predatory gleam in the girl's eyes when Tom's name was mentioned.

"I think I've seen him around," Jayanti said, her eyes alert. Then all of a sudden, Jayanti was talking animatedly about Tom, Lalita's Tom.

"And of course, I noticed him when the two of you came to the Diwali dance. He's so good looking, maybe he's worth the trouble he's giving you."

Alrighty then, she's not crushed by the rape at all, Lalita thought, somewhat dispirited, then guilty for feeling so. But I shouldn't be the one to bring that up, she told herself. She changed the subject, asking about Jayanti's art, but the other girl was persistent.

"I mean, if you're not married, you can't expect Tom to give you such an exclusive commitment, to cater to your every need. Even if and when you do get married, you'll have to remain a separate person on your own. Maybe that's all that he's saying. Or maybe what the two of you need is to see other people for a while.

"Or come to big parties, so you won't become bored with each other. In fact, I'm having one in roughly one month's time. Do bring him. My gallery's showing."

So much for sisterhood, Lalita thought, hesitating before she gave Jayanti her phone number.

"Aren't you living with him now?" Jayanti said, writing the number down. "Because maybe then I should take his number too. I mean, if you're never at your place."

"No, I think you've got enough," Lalita said, a new steel in her voice, and Jayanti looked up, amused and taken aback. "I mean, that's really alright."

"I can always get the number from Tom himself later," she said playfully. "When he comes to my party, I mean."

"We'll probably be too busy that night to make it."

"Doing what?" The girl was unbelievable. Victim, my ass, Lalita thought.

"Fucking each other's brains out," Lalita replied.

Jayanti merely smiled.

"Oh, sorry, I didn't mean it like that." Lalita stood up to leave. "I really didn't mean to offend you."

"Not at all." Jayanti drew her *dupatta* (which in Lalita's opinion was too light a shawl for New Haven autumn weather) more tightly around her shoulders and shrugged.

"I'm just trying to make friends again since I had to go away. And your aunt Shama told me to look you up, so I was glad to see you in the class, I really was. I just wanted to be able to reach you."

Jayanti's arm and ugly bruises had healed, but she still looked translucent, vulnerable—in need of friends. It could have just been a talent she had, one of many, to look like that. But Lalita found herself giving her Tom's number, saying Jayanti should call them at his house when she knew the time of the party. She left, weakly hoping for the best, not hugging the other girl good-bye as she'd expected to. No one could blame her for being scared, even if the girl needed a friend, she thought, dialing Tom a few times on her cell phone before she realized he had turned his ringer off. He was working.

It was no surprise that Lalita ended up "forgetting" about Jayanti's party. It wasn't as if Tom noticed it; he worked through the entire weekend anyway, barely coming to the table when she made dinner and reaching for her in the dark half asleep, if at all. In her anxiety she really did forget to ask Tom if Jayanti had called. A few days before New Year's Eve, when they were walking past the Yale Art Museum they saw Jayanti coming down the steps. She stopped to say hello, prompting Lalita to watch Tom's face as they shook hands. Was there a gleam of anything? A fascination? So far as she could tell there was only politeness. But then, after they had started walking home again, he asked if that was the girl from the posters, the one Lalita had been distraught and jealous about. He teased her. "She seemed perfectly normal to me. A healthy red-blooded normal." Suddenly they were laughing and he was stroking her back, she had one leg between his and they were kissing like always.

"I love you," Lalita said, clinging to Tom.

"Me too, baby," he said, bringing her face close for a long kiss.

A few mornings later, Lalita found herself wishing Lucy good luck in Italy before hanging up the phone, glad for her friend who had decided to stay on in Italy, to study fashion and enjoy dating, now that Lucy wasn't engaged to Raymond anymore.

Raymond, while on his fellowship, had cheated on Lucy with an up and coming Black British academic in his cohort. The slightly sad but still somehow buoyant mood of their conversation made Lalita wonder if it was better to leave Tom of her own accord than wait for him to go. Or cheat on her.

Before his more and more frequent bouts of irritability turned into a permanent, level indifference that she wouldn't be able to charm him out of—"taking a break," people called it, although it felt like to Lalita that any kind of break would involve taking a jackhammer to solid wood under her feet, a plank of highest quality, that had thinned out and bent recently but was still strong enough to bear her weight and was still holding her on level ground.

Restlessly, Tom moved next to her in the warm winter bed, half in annoyance, half in lust, turning her so that Lalita faced away from him, her buttocks pressed against his front.

Lalita would be graduate from Yale in just five months. What then?

Eventually she and Tom woke up late, had breakfast together, like always. But this morning, unlike the other mornings of preceding weeks, Lalita was calmly observing, resolute (she told herself) in her decision to strike out on her own and stay that way. While he read the paper she reminded herself to save the housing section and start looking that afternoon for a place of her own. Shared apartments weren't too expensive in West Haven, for example, especially at the beginning of the year. She didn't have to stay here in New York with him. If she saved for a few years, till graduation, she might even have the money to put a down payment on a modest condominium—something her father had laughed at a few years ago when she brought it up, as a way to cut down her rental bills and invest for the future.

Surprisingly, the knowledge that these could be her last hours with Tom didn't prevent Lalita from enjoying a large bowl of milk and granola while he rubbed her thigh and read the newspaper.

Perhaps it was the fact that for once she didn't cling to him, or that her face looked less tense than usual when she was waiting for him to mention what time he would come home and if they would be able to have dinner together. He smiled at her, listening as she chattered on about a paper she was writing and collected the breakfast dishes. He put his own papers aside and took her waist between his hands, caressed her hips, then breasts. "Baby, tonight, let's go out," Tom said. "You're always the one left cleaning up, I'm so busy."

Lalita could no more explain the success of this morning than she could say why it was later that same day that she called a counselor with an office downtown whose name her aunty Shama had left with her a year ago. All she could say, when the counselor pressed her to give a reason, was that she'd had the feeling that morning of having averted some harm, having done something to protect herself from losing Tom. She didn't know what, but there it was—some internal shift, imperceptible to anyone else, but volcanic in its impact, forming plates and fissures between her old life and new one.

"Ah. Where to begin," the counselor said, smiling reassuringly. She was a white woman brown-haired, slender and stylish in a silk jacket over straight jeans, hazel-eyed. She was one of the most beautiful women Lalita had ever met and was also kind, without that hint of cool superiority that Lucy often projected. The woman (whose name was Marianne like the self-help guru, like Lalita's favorite poet) sat across from Lalita, her fingers templed. Her fingers were supple, Lalita noticed, the nails lacquered and shining. She was a psychiatrist who specialized in psychotherapy. She and Lalita's aunt Shama had gone to medical school and residency together.

Lalita wouldn't tell this unknown white woman anything. How could anyone like this understand what it was like to go to your mother's bed at night—not just to avoid another argument, but because it seemed like it was safe and warm, a refuge from all the rejections that her mother warned her about in great detail, as if they were inevitable blows that only her constant presence could shield Lalita from. Doing well in school meant having no friends—her mother had a story about how no one liked her because she always beat the curve on science tests, and not because she was never allowed to go to anyone's house at night or to the city with classmates after school. Not because her phone calls were monitored by her mother, by her father picking up the phone and listening in. Not because her mother never quite let go.

"But you think this kind of thinking even operates at *Yale?*" Lalita would ask, voice slightly muffled by her mother's fleshy upper arm as she lay in bed with her on another weekend night that her mother had insisted she spend at home. "Everyone there is used to doing well academically. A lot of them do serious sports, so they're good-looking too. Is it that big a deal, to master both?"

"Well, you're very beautiful too," her mother said, careful. "I'm saying they'll naturally be jealous of you for that. Many of those girls will be bright but not have your skin or your hair. It's too much for you to expect anyone to like you sincerely. The best you can hope for is that they don't actually *make problems* for you.

"That said, the problem of your looks," her mother would say with a harsh laugh, tracing the contour of Lalita's smooth cheek or playing with her silky hair, "fortunately or unfortunately, was not a problem I experienced. I can't give you any help with that. Except to keep away from boys, that much I know."

And her mother would pull Lalita close, pretending to sleep, her breathing growing heavier until Lalita, seduced into a feeling of safety, would ease out of her embrace, kissing her on the forehead, like a daughter, like normal.

No more and no less—a calm and collected Cordelia.

But then her mother would wake up suddenly, say in a wheedling voice, "Oh Lalie, could you massage my legs? With lotion? Use both your hands. That's my good girl. Go higher up," and contrive, one way or the other, to keep Lalita where she was, still in the bed with her mother, hands up to her thighs, ministering to her weary body and spirit for hours at a time as if there were nothing else a nineteen-year-old girl should be doing in life.

Waiting in her mother's bed for her father to come up the stairs, survey the two of them and shout, if he was tired by the effort of having to reclaim his own bed nearly every night, or laugh at them as he pulled out two pillows from under Lalita's head and surrendered his place. Home on a Saturday afternoon, evening. Home always the place where Lalita forgot herself, focusing her attention on what her parents did and said, threatened and hoped, their emotions like a Ouija board from which she, at her most fatalistic, would interpret her future.

"Still alone, after all these months of college," her mother would say suddenly, happening on Lalita in the kitchen, wearing shapeless, faded pajamas and reading an old paperback dispiritedly, crunching on a large, candied apple she had made as part of a batch, eating despite the uncomfortable awareness of her weight beginning to creep up again. "I told you it would be difficult for someone like you to make friends."

Now the therapist Marianne broke into Lalita's thoughts gently.

"I looked over the form you filled out. I noticed you left one question blank and I just have to ask you about this. I'm sorry if it's painful to contemplate, but I need to know: Have you ever thought about hurting yourself? Are you having any thoughts about hurting yourself now?"

Her gaze was intensely compassionate. She was a Buddhist, Shama Aunty had said. And yet, as intense as her gaze was, the lady still sat back in her chair, giving Lalita plenty of space, not coming too close as Lalita's mother inexorably would have.

Lalita felt tears come to her eyes. She shook her head no, about self-harm, and took a tissue from the box Marianne held out to her then.

There *was* one time Lalita had "tried to hurt herself"—though this phrase, Lalita thought now, made zero sense because if you were doing that kind of thing, you were already hurt badly. After the counselor had heard about it, and heard about the time just before then, when Lalita's father had come after her with a glass bottle that he said he was going to smash against her head, Marianne was quiet.

"Is this what they mean by the Freudian approach?" Lalita thought but didn't quite dare to say. "They just let you stew here in your own mess. You're just alone as usual. Goddamn," she almost said. Her anger and impatience must have shown, but Marianne looked unaffected, her surface still calm but careful. Physically she held back as well, not coming close.

Eventually the therapist said something Lalita wouldn't forget.

"In the work that we do here, these won't be the first or the only tears you'll shed.

"You'll cry, but each and every single one of your tears will be precious, because they'll heal you and make you free. And eventually, it will be as if you have a mirror in front of you, or a pane of glass, and everything your father says about you will reflect off that mirror, you'll be untouched and you will see that what he's saying is about him, is always about him. And what he tells you won't have the power to hurt you anymore, or ever make you want to hurt yourself again."

What Lalita remembered, many years later, was the image of the mirror, solid and cool like the mirror in her mother's room, where she had looked at herself before contemplating the end to her life. Where Lalita had spoken to herself without lies. In that mirror was hope, a self, some entity no one could touch or claim ownership to. Freedom like Marianne had said.

But what Lalita said in the session that day during her senior year of Yale, with the counselor—in a bitter tone that sounded like her mother's, she realized only afterward, when she was taking the bus back to the apartment with Tom and feeling angry and distressed about him too—was this:

"Oh great, a mirror made of tears. You mean I'll be reminded of them all the time, I'll have this barrier between me and everybody else, always making me different."

Marianne shook her head, then shrugged.

"We can talk more next time," the therapist said, "about what exactly the mirror image is about. And soon you'll be proposing your own images, your metaphors, finding your own way of out of this. But make no mistake about it—you will find your way. You will find recovery. The same impulse that led you to get on the train that day and leave your parents once and for all, to call your aunt, to call me—that's what's going to lead you home, to a real home where you can feel safe forever. Believe it."

That night in bed with Tom, a few hours removed from her first therapy session, Lalita was more quiet than usual. For once she didn't spill out everything that had happened in her day. For once she let him hold her without speaking, finding comfort in his touch and the awareness, never far from consciousness, of how different it was to be held by a lover than by her own mother—even though so many of the gestures were the same. Even the spooning, which her mother liked to do with Lalita when she turned sixteen, seventeen, twenty, her gnarled leg crossed over hers like a tree in an enchanted forest ensnaring the princess.

A mirror, Marianne said. In the early morning, Lalita woke up hours before Tom to do the meditation exercise Marianne had given her. Chanting in Pali the way she said, "Sarva buddho sangam." *Om nama shivaih*, she added. She kept her prayers secret from Tom, whose parents were Eastern Orthodox Christian and whose religious sentiment had given way to wry agnosticism by the time he reached puberty. In the morning light she looked in the mirror at her nude body, touched her breasts. *Lalita has a fat chest*, she heard her mother say. *Watch out for Lalita's boobsie-boobs!* But the day that she had tried to hurt herself was long past, too far away to picture in detail. Only Noah and Lucy knew about that—even her aunt Shama suspected but didn't have the details. She hadn't breathed a word of it to Tom, not yet. Her mother knew—she was the one who found her in the bathroom, reacted with surprising calm. But then, there hadn't been any blood or visible signs of injury.

"There's no need to go that far, Lalita," Lalita's mother said, taking the razor blade out of her hand and carefully wrapping it in one of her old saris, a rag. Her mother had thrown the razor away before Lalita had mustered up the courage to make even one cut. Her mother stood in the bathroom as she looked for a paper bag to throw the thing away, the evidence of Lalita's disloyal thoughts. While she searched for it Lalita sat silently—but her mother went on talking in her usual way—primly and cryptically. "No matter how bad things seem—and I know they must seem very bad to you—we don't commit that sin you almost did. We have to be strong no matter what your father says. We endure life."

And who was this "we"? Lalita's mother could have meant Hindus, Lalita thought, or Indians, perhaps, though her mother always said the women in their community had never befriended her because she was a professional woman, educated and not a stay-at-home. Her mother said they were all jealous of her, and rarely went to social gatherings.

But what her mother intimated, Lalita began to see, with therapy, was more the "we" of she and Lalita, impenetrable as long as Lalita herself stayed virginal, inviolate, distant from the rites of passage that marked her as separate from her mother, as a person. The "we" that held her father at bay. Held Lalita's own life permanently, at bay. Preventing her from ever feeling fully alive.

Another session with Marianne, this one a month after the very first session, after Lalita has had more than one fight with Tom, after he's said what she never imagined: "I can't do this anymore. It's just too hard. Maybe we should just end this now, stop dragging it out. I love you but I have to do my work. Nothing matters to you but your own feelings, you think the world revolves around your life."

At one time, it had seemed likely that she'd start the New Year without Tom in her life at all, and she clung to therapy. Still, sitting across from Marianne today, who looks lovelier than ever, Lalita tells herself there really isn't that much she needs to say.

Lalita faces the counselor, therapist, the woman she once sought so reluctantly, then eagerly, now as a matter of course. A duty, almost. Because she and Tom have made up by now, had a few weekends away where he just rested, celebrating the victory of a major academic publication that's given him more confidence about his career, and now they were talking about getting married once Lalita was done with college. Even talking about having children after that. And this duty Lalita has, what has made it bearable to sit in this room and expose, of her own accord, the vile disappointment of her own mother wanting to possess her—it's the duty of someone who wants to be a mother herself, who wants to make sure there is no way she'll love her own child in the wrong way.

She has begun to trust Marianne because of the way the sessions put her in a calmer mood for many days after each one—for how they seem to give her a moment's solitude even in the middle of an argument with Tom or her parents, where she perceives herself as free, where she remembers she has a choice. And so, Lalita complied when the therapist asks if there was anything else her mother or father did that Lalita had never told anyone.

Slowly scenes emerged in the word-paintings of therapy. Despite liking Marianne, Lalita resented being asked to recount them. They were like blunt hairs growing on her skin after she'd shaved and waxed her legs into a glossy perfection, those memories. They had an inevitability, almost an independent existence, unaffected by whatever heights she could manage to lift her life to. Her mother shouting at the sight of blood but standing passively behind Lalita's father, her mother looking on as he mocked her tears in an ugly voice and picked up a shoe to throw at her. The blood was from where her father had cut Lalita's palm open with a knife. The heavy glass bottle in his hand that one time, perhaps the worst—but before that, other weapons. A set of keys with a sharp appendage shaped like a corkscrew, zigzagging her arm when he hurls it, the wound light. Knives pointed to her cheek, "I'll scar you," he says in her memory. "I'll make you regret the very day you were born. I'll throw you down the stairs and break your neck." Once he'd hurled a rake from the garage at her when she'd knelt down and, in a moment of childish perversity (well she was only seven at the time) engraved her name in wet concrete using her finger and little stick. "Lali," it said. Her name in lights, she thought, whenever she had come back from college and was standing on the front steps, in view of the driveway where she'd once crouched down as a child, then as a young adult waited for her parents—since, out of the conviction that she'd lose it and some burglar would find it, they'd hesitated to ever give Lalita her own key to their house, unless they were leaving her at home for several days at a time and had no choice.

Lalita struggles to communicate with Marianne. More than scenes that she could describe was the feel of things—the sense of danger with which she awoke on most mornings, sheets soaked and Tom oblivious, until he joined her in the shower or breakfast, nuzzling her ear and whispering the half-playful question, "Who were you fighting with last night, sweetheart?" She laughed, asked him if she said anything in her sleep, hoping he won't have heard her, embarrassed when he does. "You said, she's coming and you're not going to let her. You said those people should watch out. Which people, baby? Who was hurting you?" He knows the answer but at the same time, by some miracle, does not. It has been his not knowing that makes her whole to him, a girl instead of a case, his flame instead of someone to feel sorry for. He knows that her parents are difficult, even that her mother in particular did something she's ashamed to talk about. He has guessed what, but didn't want to. His mind doesn't enter the same roads that hers does, doesn't make the journey with her, but it is his hand that she reaches for when she wakes up at night, his making love to her nearly every day that has taught her not to be ashamed of sex. She walks out of the shower naked sometimes, liking the way she looks, not startled anymore when he lunges forward with a sudden caress. She cannot seem to get enough of this physical affection, the first true affection that she's ever known where nothing is expected in return except her love, her loyalty, which must also somehow allow him his freedom. Even if she never learns the knack of it—the way to be close without clutching too tight, getting jealous of any female friend, or sobbing like the world will end when he slams the door after an argument or refuses to talk to her when he's working—she will always be grateful for this normalcy, an intimacy that doesn't leave a scar she has to tell a therapist about, that she has had to expose almost against her will, as a matter of conscience.

When Lalita got her mother's stiff letter in the mail, in her post office box at Yale Station, she panicked slightly at first, wondering if something bad had happened to one or both of them. From what they wrote in previous letters, their deaths were always imminent.

She scanned the pages quickly, then shoved it back in her pocket and forgot the letter was there until she was back in New York, making lemonade and cookies for Lucy, who had stopped by to visit, gossip and even tentatively start planning for Lalita and Tom's wedding that August, for after the end of senior year. Lalita pulled on her denim jacket again to walk Lucy to the train station and found the letter in her pocket.

"Don't read that now," Lucy said, recognizing the look on her face. "Just put it away."

"Look Lalita," Lucy added. "The hard things in life always find us. It's not like you have to *go* looking for them. It's the same thing about Jayanti's art show. Just put the invitation away and forget it.

"This is how life goes on, Lalita. Let whatever is too stressful just die quietly."

"That's just what my mother's afraid of. That she will die quietly, and I'll be nowhere in sight to hear her and feel bad about it."

"That seems unlikely. Even if you don't torture yourself over every single letter she writes, she'll find a way to make you hear her. She's just not the type to do things any other way. There are such good things happening for you now. Don't let your mother—don't let *anyone* make you lose hope."

Lalita waved to Lucy as she got on the train, then sat down on the bench on the platform of the West Fourth station and took her mother's letter out.

There were several pages with disembodied lists, just facts about how many boxes of Lalita's things were left, when she could come and retrieve them, mail from the government about her student loans her mother wanted to make sure she had received. *Important things*, her mother titled these pages.

Then another single page, small in the envelope, folded tightly as a winter bud. "The More Loving One," it read, in a script Lalita recognized as being photocopied from the collection of Auden's poetry she'd given her mother two years before, for Kamini's birthday.

But on earth indifference is the least
We have to dread from man or beast.

The rest of the poem was missing. Lalita thought that her mother had gulped down only the first lines of the poem in her usual ravenous state, had perhaps wanted to say, "I know that for all you care, I can go to hell"—to express love, bitterness, a feeling of maternal rightness and self-sacrifice in being "the more loving one."

Lalita was minoring in poetry and was not her mother's student, she remembered with relief. Now she felt certain that the rest of the poem belonged to her, not her mother, and that it described the intense discomfort she had felt in the heat of her mother's affections, the perpetual glare.

How should we like it were stars to burn
With a passion for us we could not return?

"If equal affection cannot be." Why couldn't it? Why couldn't Lalita be loved by anyone, with an intensity equal to what she felt for her lover? She crumpled the piece of paper into a ball that found its way back into her coat pocket rather than the open trash can near the subway turnstile. She felt certain of the way things were, at last. There was no opening anymore for her parents' distortions of reality, their accusations, their lies. This was her mother's problem, her sickness.

But the pain was shared between the both of them equally, wasn't it?

Lalita could never make it right, for her mother.

Lalita was sobbing when she got back to the apartment, grateful Tom wouldn't be home again for a few more hours. She sat on the couch in the twilight, not feeling hungry or energetic enough to make dinner. Her mood was broken only when one of the neighbor's children knocked on the door to tell her he was sorry for making so much noise with his soccer ball, which she hadn't even heard. His mother was probably standing in her kitchen across the hall, listening closely but not poking her head out because the boy was doing fine on his own. Lalita smiled at him and said not to worry, offered him a candy from the dish Tom liked to keep near the front door. When he had gone, Lalita was able to summon the presence of mind to retrieve her mother's letter from her coat and toss it into the garbage. She'd invite her to the wedding. That would be enough, she hoped.

She looked around the apartment, thinking of her books, her assignments, finishing her senior thesis on American poetry that her advisor said could even win a prize. Maybe applying to law school after that, or even a program her advisor told her about, for people brave enough to try writing poetry.

Here was the invitation for the art show Jayanti was putting up, and suddenly Lalita felt fearless, thought *Why not?*

It wouldn't be healthy trying to cling to him.

She and Tom would be going after all, that was that. It would be such an act of confidence for her to go with Tom, to walk over to where Jayanti would be standing, beautiful, invincible, and let her look up into his handsome face. She'd have to teach herself to be less afraid of losing him. She'd learn not to be bitter from the loss, if it came to that. Maybe even savor being free and alone. Maybe.

That night before Lalita went to sleep, with Tom's arms snugly around her, she thought of the remaining lines of the poem her mother had sent.

Were all stars to disappear or die,
I should learn to look at an empty sky
And feel its total dark sublime,
Though this might take me a little time.

How much was that? A little time. It had already been two years since she'd been in her parents' house, and had been their daughter. It had been nearly a year since she'd seen them in the restaurant in Morningside Heights, left the dinner early, without eating, because she'd been afraid of the looks on their faces, the blame, their certainty. Also afraid her parents would say something cruel, racist, even, to the Black proprietor, who ran after her that night with a small bag of sweets, patting her back as if he knew she needed this. Who was to say, how much time it would take, whether her mother would ever take a look at the distance between them—the gap between astronomer and star—and find it anything but frustrating? Nearly a year of her life had passed. Nothing had changed. Every single thing in Lalita's life had changed. But none of it was perfectly safe, not yet. How much time would it take, in the end? How much time before she could not be transformed back into the person she had been? Lying in the dark with Tom, her fiancé, she didn't know, and for the first time, didn't try to imagine.

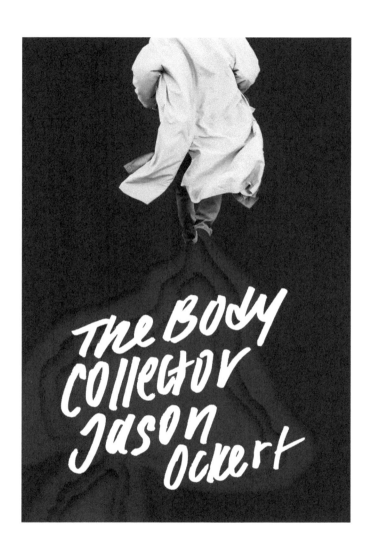

The Body Collector

JASON OCKERT

I.

The soft, wet, red lump sits on the paper-cutter board. The steel blade arm glistens in mid-December early light through the recently down-turned blinds. Donna notices rust-colored splotches—*maybe blood?*—on the mint-green carpet floor. Then she recalls that the office door was unlocked when she arrived this morning, which was peculiar, but then she forgot about it, and now, remembering, it's unsettling. Donna is always the first person to arrive at Strafe Brothers, which has earned her the privilege of carrying a key. Other than her two bosses and the security guard, nobody else has one. That she knows of. She is, perhaps, more bothered than most people by not knowing what transpires at the investment firm where she has worked for twelve years. At the moment, three unknowns loom in the small office supply room with her: *Why was the door unlocked? Where do those stains lead? What is that mass on the paper-cutter board?* A primitive part of Donna knows the answer to the last question—*it's a tongue*—but she is not ready to address that truth. Later, it'll make sense. For now, it's as if the Not Knowing Donna has looped a garrote around the Knowing Donna's windpipe and is preparing to tug. It becomes difficult to swallow.

The blood trail leads from the supply room, into the cubicle arena, past the receptionist's desk, and down the hall to the men's room. Donna takes a deep breath and cautiously opens the door.

Inside, it's dark until Donna takes two steps and triggers the lights that are on a motion detector. Fluorescent bulbs warm, buzz, and glow. As Donna says, "Hello," her vision adjusts and a person materializes. Draped across the sink is a slim man in a yellow jacket. He is doubled in the wall-mounted mirror and so is she. Donna sees her reflected self seeing what she sees, which causes her to blink rapidly. She's not sure where to put her eyes.

The man's head rests on the counter's edge. Blood has trickled from his gaping mouth onto the floor in a puddle. It doesn't look like he's still bleeding. Bags under his closed eyes are deep blue trenches. His face is so pale Donna is sure he's dead.

When she was younger, Donna wanted to be a veterinarian. People always said she was good with animals. She suspected people only said that because she wasn't very good with people and they wanted to be polite. Fifteen years ago, when she was working as a veterinarian's assistant at the local animal hospital, something happened which dashed her career ambitions. A rabbit named Hasselhoff died when she was helping the doctor in a neutering procedure. "Rabbit death commonly occurs," Dr. Bleyer had said even though Donna hadn't asked for an explanation. "Small animals don't fare well with anesthesia."

It wasn't Hasselhoff's death that rattled Donna, it was his resurrection. Shortly after Dr. Bleyer left her to clean up the mess, the hare's body rapidly twitched, it reared its tufted head, opened its pink mouth, and screamed. The impact of the sudden terrifying sound left a white streak in Donna's otherwise-auburn-colored hair. She's been dyeing it since. When Bleyer rushed in, wondering what was wrong, Donna explained, in a wavering voice, what happened. By that time Hasselhoff was dead again. And although the doctor said he believed Donna—it was a rabbit scream and not a Donna scream—his face couldn't conceal a shadow of doubt which has stained her confidence since.

Standing in the men's room with the blood-drained and ruined man and their reflections, Donna feels like screaming. Then she imagines what she would look like in the mirror if she did. Horrible. A scream amplifies wrinkles. She'd resemble a tired actor after fifty takes. To really let it out she'd have to stretch her mouth uncomfortably wide and expose a crooked incisor. And how might she sound? Like Hasselhoff? No, of course not. Bleyer must have been deaf to believe she was the animal. The rabbit scream held a shrill, taut, unwavering elegance. It contained a secret Donna still doesn't comprehend. By comparison, her scream would warble with insincerity. Anyway, thinking about screaming ruins the scream.

Swallowing her anxiety, Donna turns her attention to the maybe-dead man. She finds his jugular and waits ten seconds for a pulse. When there is none, she does her best performance of CPR.

The first time Duncan Weaver died was two and a half years ago. Back then he was thirty-three and weighed over 370 pounds. He worked from his apartment as a life insurance salesman. Every morning his supervisor emailed him a spreadsheet with names and phone numbers. His job was to work his way through the list and to fill out a digital form for every call. There were boxes to check and answers to provide. Did a person or a machine pick up? Did the phone keep ringing? If so, how long did you wait for an answer? Was the number still in service? When someone did pick up, Duncan followed the script provided in a color-coded instruction manual. If the prospect expressed even a hint of interest, Duncan read from the green section. If the potential client hesitated, Duncan first read from the yellow section and then, providing the caller didn't hang up, the green section. If the person said they weren't interested but didn't immediately terminate the call, Duncan quickly read from the red section, transitioned to the yellow section, and delivered the once-in-a-lifetime, hassle-free, bargain-basement deal found in the blue section. There was also a follow-up list. Duncan, his ears encased in a cushioned headset equipped with a microphone, dutifully scrolled down the infinite names for eight hours each day. Sometimes, he made many sales. Other days, he didn't.

When his workday ended Duncan's social life began. He made the phone calls in front of his laptop from the beige-colored couch next to the window overlooking the busy street in the living room of his second floor one-bedroom apartment. His wired, fast-as-blazes gaming computer was in the kitchen where he played *Blam!* with his internet friends. It was on one such occasion—when Duncan was obliterating online adversaries—that the game glitched and he lost an important battle. In response to this Duncan emitted four quick, loud, angry hoots and raised his arms to the ceiling. Then his heart seized and, tangled in cords, he toppled out of his video-gaming recliner. The impact from his big body crashing to the floor knocked a clock off the wall in his downstairs neighbor's apartment. When the neighbor stormed up the stairs to complain, he discovered Duncan and called 911.

At 10:32 p.m. on a breezy June 20th, in transport aboard an ambulance, a paramedic determined that Duncan had expired. Sometimes high-voltage defibrillator paddles can't coax a stubborn ticker into rhythm. The rig still sped with sirens and emergency lights to Chesterton General even though there was no real hurry.

While dead, Duncan missed out on the swirl of countless human interactions that unspooled in the city where he had lived his whole life. Amber Ludlow wrote a letter to her mother. Gabe Liston placed a forkful of birthday cake into his mouth. Bonnie Halber figured out how to whistle. Monte Jefferson crushed a cockroach with his wife's boot. Lenore Shringer observed the lights of an airplane blinking through Orion's Belt. Out of the corner of her eye, EMT Peggy Brantley witnessed Duncan Weaver twitch his finger.

The exact time Duncan returned to life was not recorded. Nobody knows the number of heartbeats he was gone. After he recovered, nobody—not even his parents—asked him what it was like to be temporarily deceased. Nobody—not doctors, nurses, his brother, the neighbor that discovered him—asked, "Where did you go when you were dead?" Duncan was not the kind of man who seemed capable of explaining life's greatest mystery—dying—to anyone. He was a mouth-breather who got easily winded and his voice was pitched an octave higher than pleasant. Not that asking, back then, would have made any difference; he wouldn't have known how to answer. In the hazy space of his awakening Duncan couldn't recollect any sensation or thought he'd had while dead. Nothing, really, and nothing was hard to explain.

Later, when the Body Collector returned to claim his debt, Duncan remembered. He couldn't comprehend, but he could explain. By then he was a completely new man, the antithesis of who he'd been. Anyone who knew the pre-death Duncan would not recognize the post-death one. The new Duncan had fashioned himself into a flâneur—a word and hobby that suited him well—always strolling through the busy streets without any hurry or direction. When he wanted, he could move with the crowd, through the crowd, or against the crowd. At all times the new Duncan blended. He was easily confused for an ordinary man in the process of going somewhere or else returning from somewhere. He'd quietly say, "Excuse me," if he and a stranger happened to bump into each other even if it was—as was almost always the case—the stranger's absentmindedness that caused the collision.

* * *

With the briny taste of blood still on her lips, Donna stands near the receptionist's desk surrounded by co-workers. When the chest presses didn't work, Donna performed mouth-to-mouth, and after several harrowing moments, the dead man coughed and opened his eyes. Donna was shocked to see how they looked just like hers—his eyes. They were round, focused, and knowing. She wondered what he was thinking about, just then—the millisecond before he was conscious. But there was no time to ask and even if she did, without a tongue, he had no way of answering. Instead, she called for help. Now, in the thrilling aftermath, she has become the office hero. Colleagues want details.

"Well, I came in early like I always do," Donna says, "and I started opening the blinds to let in the morning light. That's when I saw the object on the paper-cutter board."

"The tongue?" Sydney, the receptionist, interjects with her face pinched in disgust.

"I didn't know it was that at the time. I saw the stains on the carpet and I got a terrible feeling. I followed the trail into the men's room where I saw the man and, I don't know, adrenaline kicked in. Somehow, I remembered enough CPR to get him breathing."

"Did you perform mouth-to-mouth?" Sydney asks.

"Do you know him?" Heather adds.

"Yes," Donna replies, "and no."

"He's the light switcher-offer," Walter, in Accounts Payable, says. "The security guard knows him."

"The what?" Jeremiah, the Data Entry Clerk, asks.

"He comes into our building after hours and switches off all the lights people failed to turn off when they went home."

"That's a job?"

"Apparently. He's does the Mayberry, too."

"Why can't people do it themselves?"

"I know, right?"

"I do," Cathy, Office Manager, says, "but I don't think Amy does."

"How hard is to flip a switch before you walk out the door?"

"Why'd he chop his tongue off?" Yuri, in Public Relations, asks Donna. "And why here?"

"I don't know," Donna says.

"You're telling me that lump in the supply room is a tongue?" Cathy says. "Gross."

"Wait," Yuri says, "it's still there?"

All eyes turn to Donna, who is fiddling with her right earring. "I'll go look."

Sure enough, the fleshy lump is still there.

The others, who have followed Donna, hover at the door.

"The paramedics just left it here?"

"I mean, they were busy saving his life. Cut them some slack."

"Do you think they can stitch it back on?"

"Are you sure it's a tongue? It looks like a strawberry."

"Baby hamsters look that way."

"Sydney, you're going to need to order a new paper cutter. No way am I touching that."

Ignoring the others, Donna hurries into the break room, pulls a Pittsburgh Steelers coffee mug from the cabinet, scoops a handful of ice into it, and returns to the supply room where everyone is still chatting.

". . . didn't think the blade would be sharp enough," Walter says.

"What are you doing, Donna?"

"What does it look like she's doing?" Jeremiah says.

Using a yellow-colored legal pad Donna neatly slides the tongue into the cup.

"Hey," Yuri says, "that's my mug."

In the hospital room recovering after heart surgery, back in June and the first time Duncan died, a nurse visited. Foggy from the meds, Duncan didn't comprehend much of anything the young man—Nurse Brenner—said, which was: "There's good news and bad news. What do you want first?"

"The bood news," Duncan replied.

"The good news is you're still alive. The bad news is you're going to die—again—if you don't change your eating habits. Your heart can't support your body."

"My heart is too big?" Duncan asked.

"No. Body. Your body. You have to lose weight or you'll die. Again. It's simple, really: reduce your caloric intake and burn off the fat."

"Fatigue, fate, father . . ."

"You need to listen," Brenner said and glanced at his name on a nearby chart, "Mr. Weaver. You must change your current *death*style into a healthy *life*style."

"Deathstyle?"

"Your body only needs a fraction of the food you consume."

"Deathstyle?" Duncan repeated.

"Life. Think *life*. You weren't born with these excessive cravings. Once upon a time you ate in moderation. Once upon a time your body was a racecar. Do you remember when you were a racecar?"

"Deathstyle."

"*Life*style," Brenner stressed, his wide smile wilting. "I'll have a nutritionist contact you."

Deathstyle, Duncan thought, back in his apartment. He lugged the word to his beige-colored couch and put it on the plate with a half-eaten jelly sandwich he'd left before dying. Outside, the traffic complained. People passed on sidewalks. The sound of cars and voices became a single, flat, accusatory chant: *deathstyle, deathstyle, deathstyle*. The comment spun around and around in his head. It was a dark seed. In it he felt the hollow bloom of truth. A fissure opened in his recently repaired heart and a bilious vine wound up his chest, snaked through his esophagus, and penetrated his skull where it flowered in his brain and paralyzed him. There in mid-morning half-light he couldn't move. His breathing stuttered. Sounds muted. He wondered if he was dying again. His body was stricken by a dull pain and his head was encased in melancholy. A sharp burst of rain smeared the windowpane. An overhead light flickered and went out. A fly landed on the discarded sandwich and began to eat the word. *Deathstyle*, it said, *Deathstyle*.

"I don't want to die," he said to the insect, hating the meek sound of his squeaky voice. "But I don't know how to live."

Duncan was a decent son who remembered his parents' anniversary. When his detoxing brother needed him, Duncan was there. He was a faithful fiancé. Leslie was not. Though he played every week, he never won more than five dollars from the scratch-offs. He used to like music. Once, he pulled a woman out of the road who may have been crushed by a taxi. Because of his size, he always stood out in a crowd. Over the years, his skin became alligator-thick and he trained his mind to dampen the perpetual whispers from leering strangers with their weighted insults. When that poisoned word "fat" penetrated his eardrums Duncan morphed it into something else. The man in the herringbone blazer didn't say "fat," he said *fatigue*. It's just that Duncan couldn't hear the second syllable. It was a case of simple miscommunication. The girl in pigtails meant *fathom*. The bus driver said *fatal*, the waitress whispered *fatwa*. Over time, Duncan became impervious to the fatuous opinions of others.

He got through the day in this way, but there was no real pleasure in coping. Sitting prone in his silent apartment, having cheated death, Duncan had the wherewithal to admit food didn't please him. In fact, he couldn't recollect a time when he was really hungry—like, *starving*. Then there was *Blam!* Did his teammates—DuckyBoy, LOLita9, and Splatterz—notice his absence? Had he—Dr. DunDun—been replaced?

"Does it matter?" he said.

Deathstyle, the fly upon the sandwich buzzed. *Deathstyle*.

"I don't like that word." He couldn't think of any positive words that started with "death" to help shoo away the thought. Even the word "wish" couldn't brighten it. "Deathwish," he said.

Lifewish? asked the fly as it did the thing flies do with their legs.

"No. I haven't wished for life. Who does?" Duncan said, shifting into a more comfortable position on the cushions.

Duncan's life had been in decline for as long as he could remember. When, he wondered, did it peak? What was the tipping point? Life was nice when he was in love but it was impossible to conjure the good times with Leslie. The memory of discovering her having sex with the pizza delivery guy was seared deeply into his brain. That one moment erased so many wonderful times he'd had with her, which was a shame. Which he resented.

Had there been happiness in high school? No, no. Those were torturous years when he was unable to fit into the tiny seat-desk combos. And, PE.

"Middle school?" asked the fly. Hardly. He'd had a severe case of acne his mother insisted—in sixth grade, seventh grade, and eighth grade—would go away soon. Plus, there was Zach McLeider.

"Elementary school?" Back then his grandfather—who visited every other weekend—often whacked Duncan with a rusty spatula.

"Preschool?" Maybe. "Pre-preschool?" He'd had a handful of Matchbox cars and a train set. His stuffed koala bear was named Koala. Also, there was a playground a few blocks from home where his mother would take him. He'd had fun there, hadn't he? If memory serves, there was a slide which Duncan went down over and over again. From the top of that slide he saw into windows he couldn't see from the ground. That was a peak. There was happiness.

"Playground," he said to the fly, which had flown away. Duncan wiggled off the couch. Before leaving, he tossed the old sandwich into the trash.

In her coat and hat and with the tongue in the mug Donna takes the elevator down. She detests the cramped space and if it wasn't an emergency she'd use the stairs. She can't stand the way elevators amplify the radiating awkwardness pulsing off strangers, off her. With bodies so close to bodies people are compelled to say something inane or else blithely stare. The five occupants she's with now have small talk perched on their lips and bug eyes. Donna bites back a panic attack. To seem normal she raises the cup to her mouth and pretends to sip. The tongue has an earthy scent which reminds Donna of radishes.

By now she's licked away the blood. She faintly remembers the taste—like pickle juice—and wonders if, while she's at the hospital, she should get tested for AIDS. She knows absolutely nothing about the man she saved. He could be anyone. She hasn't had bloodwork done in many years and hasn't been sexually active for, *What? five years? Has it been five years?* Like most people she knows, Donna has been dutifully suffering through the malaise of heterosexuality with an anemic conviction someone special might manifest. Once upon a time, Donna had been in love. He turned out to be a whiff; a swing and a miss. How long has it been since she even had a kiss? Not since the sloppy make-out session with Greg Anderson at last year's Valentine's Day party. That's a memory she'd rather delete.

When the elevator doors part Donna exits in a foul mood. The tongue jostles against the ice and makes a hissing sound as she rushes past the security guard and outside. Her Camry is in the lot. She sets the mug in the cup holder and cranks the defroster. She doesn't bother waiting for the windshield to clear. The hospital is close. The glass is still semi-frozen by the time she arrives.

Inside, Donna approaches a small woman sitting behind a big desk. The receptionist says, "How may I assist you?"

"Here," Donna says, setting the mug on the desktop. She hopes the tongue will speak for itself.

"What is that?"

"It's a tongue. There's a man here missing it."

"Excuse me?" the woman says. "That's a tongue?"

"Yeah. I put it in ice to preserve it. Can it be replaced?"

"I'm going to have to look into this," she says, reaching for the phone. "Have a seat." Donna surveys the plastic, green-colored chairs in the lobby. She grabs the mug and finds a spot in the back row.

Walking was difficult when Duncan was big. After leaving his apartment and on his way to the park, Duncan counted each step in his head. It helped him focus on the task of moving and mute the word *deathstyle* which whispered in the swish of coats and pants of passing strangers.

Duncan's family no longer lived on Dell Street off Main. They moved to the suburbs in Lancaster after his little brother Brian finally admitted he needed help staying sober. Although it isn't anything he would admit, Duncan preferred Brian when he was an addict. He was less judgmental. Since finding sobriety (and Brian knows the exact number of days since he was last high) his brother feels entitled—*responsible* was the word he used—to offer an opinion about Duncan's weight. "Face it," he'd said on Thanksgiving, "you have a big problem. We inherited our addictive personalities from Grandpa Weaver. I learned from Dad that Gramps was a wicked gambler. Remember how we used to play Hearts at the kitchen table? He'd swat us with that spatula whenever we lowered our cards and he could see them. A fucking prick. Not that it was his fault. He lived and died with those demons. My point is, it's in us. Me and you. Food's your thing, bro. I can help you kick it. We'll start today. How about only eating one piece of pumpkin pie? Sans Whipped Cream?" Later, when his brother insisted that they break the wishbone—a tradition Duncan hated with unmitigated fury—and Brian got the bigger portion and won the wish, he just blurted it out. He'd said, "I wish that my big brother would take responsibility for his weight problem. I wish he could see how much he means to me. How much I love him and want him to get well." Technically, it was two wishes, but nobody objected. Instead, Mom and Dad nodded in agreement. They nodded and Brian nodded and Duncan snapped the short, brittle, turkey bone in half.

Duncan hasn't been home since. And he hadn't been to the playground in decades. Back then, when their mother took them, Brian was confined to a stroller.

That summer afternoon Duncan trundled past his childhood home and turned up Highfield. The park was right where it had always been. Although the fence around the playground was new, the equipment was the same. A seesaw leaned crookedly beside a mostly sand-less sandbox. The paint on the once-green merry-go-round had faded to a pea-soup color and the bars were flecked with rust. Only one of the half-dozen swings had a plastic seat and the chains on the others were looped over the metal set's top pole like jewelry on a lunatic. The numbers in the hopscotch pattern had worn away to nothing. The jungle gym was choked with weeds.

Near the bench, where Duncan situated himself and caught his breath, were two slides. One spiraled and one went straight down. As a kid, he'd play for what felt like eternity and yet he was never ready to leave. No matter where he started—the swings, the monkey bars, the merry-go-round—he'd always return to the straight-down slide. He'd climb up the metal rungs, rest for a moment at the top, and zoom down. Climb, rest, and zoom. Sometimes his body collected static electricity which he would try to hold until he could zap his baby brother.

If there ever was a place and time when he was happy, it was here and it was then. Sitting on the bench, having dodged death, Duncan felt the crush of sadness for the boy he once was who loved the slide so much. What part did he love best? Was it darting down the slick metal, the body in unabashed motion? Was it afterward in the anticipation of doing it again as he scampered up the rungs? Was it when he sat at the top and surveyed the city around him? From that vantage he could see the cars whizzing by and people moving with purpose. Back then he wondered where they were all headed and what they would do when they got there. When did he quit caring? When did he begin wishing all those people would disappear? When did he want himself to disappear?

Duncan didn't know the answers to these questions but it felt like the start of something to ask them.

Perhaps, he thought as he stood and began his slow walk home, the static-electric boy he'd been could reach across the years, place his small hands on his big, adult chest and jolt him out of his deathstyle.

Eventually, a man wearing blue scrubs approaches Donna, who is slumped in the unyielding plastic chair where she has been daydreaming. The ice in the mug has mostly melted. The tongue has darkened and it resembles a plum. She was just now thinking about the last time she was here—ten years ago—which reminded her of her grandmother which reminded her of love and how she lacks it. When her grandfather died from leukemia, Donna's grandmother swallowed a vial of sleeping pills. At the time, Donna felt embarrassed by the suicidal gesture. Now she cannot suppress a creeping envy rising in her chest. She wishes she had someone in her life she couldn't live without.

"It's about time," she says, standing. "This is going to need more ice."

The man is Nurse Brenner, who tended to Duncan during recovery the first time he died. He's helping again. Not that he remembers his patient. He doesn't recognize the tongueless Nearly Dead Duncan nor does he recollect the previous Nearly Dead Duncan and their deathstyle discussion. The hospital has been short staffed. Lots of people come and go. He plasters his face with a practiced toothless smile. "Ma'am," he says, "we're busy."

"I know, I'm sorry, it's just, I've been waiting . . . how is he?"

"And you are?"

"I'm Donna."

Brenner raises an eyebrow and exchanges a quick look with the receptionist who has been staring. A perk in her job is watching drama unfold in the waiting arena. Sick people and the loved ones of sick people can be fun to observe from a safe distance. "Donna," he says, "may I have the mug?"

"Of course. I only wanted to know if he's going to be okay."

"Unless you're family, I'm not at liberty to say." Brenner's plastic smile cracks.

"Really? You can't even tell me if he's going to be all right? He was dead, you know."

"Ma'am, the mug."

Donna suddenly contemplates running. She doesn't like this man, the hospital, the receptionist, the dim lighting, the antiseptic smell she's been marinating in for the past hour and a half. She's grown attached to the tongue and is not quite ready to part with it without learning something about the man it belongs to.

"What if I was his girlfriend? Could you tell me something then?"

"Are you?"

She could sprint across the frozen parking lot to her car, speed to her small apartment on Newbury, jam the severed muscle into the freezer, and keep it. Somewhat alarmed by this desire, Donna blushes.

"Do you even know his name?"

"I saved his life," Donna whispers.

"I'm sure you did," Brenner says as his smile returns. "Now hand over the tongue."

That June day two and a half years ago, when Duncan arrived at his apartment after visiting the playground, he found a medium-sized package outside his door. He carried it to the kitchen table. His name was written in cursive on a label without a return address. Inside was a cardboard box with the words Flavor Eraser printed on it. There was also an envelope which contained a newspaper clipping and a note. The newspaper was clipped from the Help Wanted section and the posting for a "Light Extinguisher" was circled in red ink. The brief, handwritten note read: *Mr. Weaver, Try this new patent-pending product. For best results, close your eyes and pinch your nose when you eat. It works! Also, apply for this job and tell Harvey I sent you. I'll check in sometime. Bood Luck!* It was signed, *The Nutritionist.*

At first, when he opened the box, Duncan thought it was a hoax. Inside were dozens of individually wrapped condoms. While he hadn't had the occasion to use one in several years, he still remembered what they looked like. Atop the pile was a small sheet of paper which explained what to do. According to the directions, you were supposed to put the condom—the Flavor Eraser—on your tongue before eating anything. Under *How It Works*, Duncan read the following brief explanation: *The thin rubber represses the microvilli—tiny, sensory hairs on your tongue's dorsum—and, as a result, your brain doesn't receive the dopamine splash you've become addicted to. Take away the pleasure and you can start thinking straight. You can concentrate on what's actually good for your body. If your head can't taste the difference between cake and broccoli, why not eat broccoli? If potato chips taste the same as apple chips, eat the apple. Flavor is the enemy of the heart. Take away your dependence on the pleasures of food and you will find happiness elsewhere.*

More was written, but Duncan quit reading. He was struck by the line, "Flavor is the enemy of the heart." It was a curious claim and made sense to him in a way he couldn't quite explain. So, he ordered an extra-large cheese pizza. After the delivery guy came and went, Duncan sat on his couch with a slice and a Flavor Eraser. He tore open the plastic wrapper and held the tongue condom to the light. The membrane-thin oval-shaped rubber had a pink hue. Placing it to his lips, he roughly jammed his tongue inside. The fit was snug with pressure at the stem. He ate the pizza. It tasted, he felt, a little bland, but not bad. Then he ate another slice. He closed his eyes and ate another. Still, the essence of pizza remained. As the Nutritionist suggested, he closed his eyes and pinched his nose and took a small bite. The flavor vanished.

Beneath the coffee table was a puzzle box with a picture of birch trees on the front. He and his fiancé used to put them together on lazy weekends. After removing a handful of pieces, Duncan ripped a slice of pizza into bite-sized chunks. He arranged both pizza and puzzle on his plate. Then, closing his eyes and pinching his nose, he ate everything and tasted nothing.

All night, Duncan tested the Flavor Eraser. He couldn't tell the difference between a Hershey's kiss and a clod of dirt from his potted fern. Cheesecake tasted like an old sponge, and vice versa. Marshmallows were Styrofoam. Pepsi the same as seltzer water. With his eyes closed, nose pinched, and wearing the tongue condom, everything was tasteless. Before easing himself to bed, he pried the Flavor Eraser from his tongue and pitched it into the garbage can. When he brushed his teeth he was startled by the minty flavor.

Before he died the first time, Duncan ate ceaselessly. With the Flavor Erasers, he began questioning his appetite. For the first week, out of habit, he ate like he always did. Even without flavor there was comfort in chewing. One day, as he mindlessly munched Cracker Jacks and watched a compilation video of professional *Blam!* players on his computer, he chomped something hard. When he spit the mouthful of chewed caramel-coated popcorn and peanuts into his cupped hands, he realized he'd bitten the plastic magnifying glass toy prize. Surely, if he swallowed it he would have choked and died. He switched to gum. One piece lasted several hours.

While the directions suggested the user only wear a Flavor Eraser before meals, Duncan kept one on all the time. It was more convenient.

Before he died, sometimes Duncan talked with his mouth full when he was on the phone with a potential client. Wearing the tongue condom caused Duncan to lisp slightly and he had to swallow frequently because of the extra saliva his mouth produced. Otherwise, he hardly noticed he was wearing it. Right away, inexplicably, he found his life insurance policy sales increased. He wasn't sure if his clients sympathized with his speech impediment and took pity on him or if, perhaps, there was a burgeoning confidence rising out of his body and spreading through the phone. Maybe, because he was taking life more seriously, they were taking death more seriously. At any rate, the boss was pleased.

Two weeks later, around noon, Duncan put on his best shirt and pants and walked the few blocks to the Easton building to inquire about the job in the paper which the nutritionist had left in the box. He was intrigued by the position—Light Extinguisher—and thought it might be nice to have a business card with that title upon it. By then, he'd already lost ten pounds and he noticed the difference acutely when he moved. He could almost swing his arms. Occasionally, he glimpsed the tips of his sneakers on the sidewalk as he strode ahead.

Although he didn't understand what a Light Extinguisher was supposed to do and he had no idea if the position was still available, Duncan followed the advice he'd received in the note. While he had no memory of meeting the Nutritionist, he had no reason to doubt him or her. To Duncan's surprise, when he told the doorman he was there to see someone named Harvey, Harvey—a middle-aged balding man with a quarter-sized coffee-stain birthmark on his chin—appeared. After a brief interview and a quick explanation of the duties (always lock up and return the master keys to the security guard), Duncan was hired.

The task of flipping a light switch off at the end of the day is too difficult for many people. Every night in Chesterton hundreds of lights are left on in empty offices. The electric bill for this simple oversight is substantial and it's the owners of the buildings that pick up the tab. Years ago, Gregory Easton—who had given up on politely reminding his tenants to shut the lights off when they left for home—decided to do it himself. He'd borrow the set of keys from the security guard around nine p.m. every night and make his way from floor to floor extinguishing lights. It brought him great pleasure to stand outside on the sidewalk around midnight and look up at his dark building. He could actually see the money he was saving. Jessica Mayberry, the owner of the adjacent building, noticed the darkness, too. Together, they created the Light Extinguisher position.

Monday through Friday, starting at eight p.m., Duncan walked to the Easton, grabbed the keys from the security guard, and rode the elevator to the top floor. He'd open doors, switch off lights, lock up, and move to the next office. All the hallways had cameras and from the desk in the lobby the security guard could watch him on a monitor if he or she wanted. When Duncan finished a floor, he'd take the elevator to the next floor, extinguish lights, and methodically make his way to the lobby. After the Easton, Duncan did the Mayberry. Six months later he was fit enough to forgo the elevator and instead climbed the stairs. Through the sweating and cursing, the turned ankles and blistered feet, the cramps and strained muscles, he persisted. He grew thin and swift.

Duncan found himself living a healthy lifestyle. He established a routine and rarely deviated from it. The first thing he did every morning was weigh himself on his sleek black scale which reminded him of a beetle's back. It pleased him to wake up weighing less than he did the day before. After showering and shaving, he'd savor brushing his teeth. Toothpaste was the only pleasure he allowed himself before jamming his tongue into a Flavor Eraser. Then he'd make his phone calls during the day and kill lights at night. Before bed, he'd remove the tongue condom and enjoy another good brushing. His teeth turned pearly white.

Duncan's diet changed dramatically. For breakfast, he ate granola because of the crunchy sensation. The sudden squish of a grape or pop of a cherry tomato in his mouth provided a pleasant jolt. While his tongue was rendered obsolete, the rest of his mouth could sense the cold of frozen bananas and the heat of a baked potato.

For lunch Duncan went to Bill's Cafeteria on Oak and Dovetail. Bill's had a soup special; after you bought ten bowls, the next bill was on Bill. Many people took advantage of this deal. Duncan would go there, sit in a corner with a cup of oatmeal and a mug of hot water with lemon, and spy on a parliament of old men who gathered together for lunch. The men—usually five or six of them—kept a strict routine. Each man unsteadily shuffled to their place with a bowl of soup, bag of oyster crackers, spoon, and glass of lemonade atop a sizeable hard-plastic tray. At their designated table—they always claimed a six-top near the bathrooms—they would carefully remove the items and place them upon the table. They piled the empty trays on the floor. These men did not always eat the same soup. A bald man with a beaked nose, Duncan noticed, might eat minestrone on Monday, tomato on Tuesday, cream of mushroom on Wednesday, and clam chowder on Thursday and Friday. Some men smashed their crackers in the bag before sprinkling them in the soup. One man wore a yellow-feathered fedora which he removed before eating. He set the hat on his lap and covered it with a paper napkin. A religious man always said a short prayer and a few men seemed to listen. Several men swallowed large, oval pills. A man with long white hair removed his dentures, wrapped them in a handkerchief, and set them by his elbow. They did not speak often and when they did Duncan was too far away to eavesdrop.

Duncan studied the way they ate. Hunched, with chins inches above the steam, the men dug in. Their shaky, age-spotted hands with stiff knuckles methodically dipped spoons from the soup into their mouths no matter if the soup spilled and the spoon was empty. They were pistons in some ancient machine that cranked away the lunch hour. Though he couldn't hear, Duncan imagined the wet sound of slurping. When the metal spoon collided against the teeth of the men who still had teeth, he felt a dull clink inside his own mouth. Their quick, old, speckled tongues worked the corners of their moist lips. When they were nearly done, the men who tucked napkins into their shirts lifted the bowl to their mouths, tilted their heads, and guzzled the dregs. A number of them dribbled soup on their shirt collar. When they were done, the feet of the chairs squealed as they pushed themselves from the table. Each man retrieved a tray, carried it to a conveyer belt and watched their dirty dishes disappear through a rectangular-shaped hole in the wall leading to the kitchen. Afterward, they lined up to use the bathroom, put on their coats, scarves, gloves and hats, and exited without goodbyes.

Duncan stared at the soup-eating men with such rapturous concentration it unsettled patrons who noticed. A woman with a turkey sandwich once tapped him on the shoulder and said, "Excuse me. Do you know them?" Duncan responded with a mutter and shooed the busybody away. "Don't you know it's rude to stare?"

Duncan was well aware of the placement of a stranger's eyes. *Rude* didn't begin to describe how it felt to be the object of someone's glare. The eyes aren't the problem. Duncan didn't bother to explain this to the woman. It was the judgment behind them that stung.

As far as he could tell, the men didn't know he was studying them. Their regimented procedure fascinated him. The intimacy of the consumption—raw lips, red mouths, pink tongues—repulsed him and yet he couldn't look away. A part of him enjoyed the queasy feeling their unabashed feeding produced. Their placid faces were devoid of pleasure. Duncan wondered if their taste buds had worn away. Maybe flavor was a distant memory for them. This thought provided comfort. He told himself he'd wander over to their table and ask them how the soup tasted, one of these days.

Donna knocks nervously on Duncan Weaver's apartment door and all of the things she planned to say evaporate. From the security guard she learned Duncan's name. His address was listed online.

Christmas has come and gone and now it is a new year. In the New Year Donna has decided to be a New Donna: more assertive, more brazen, more bold. She will behave like an executive, not an administrative specialist. She will be the veterinarian, not the veterinarian's assistant. She is a lifesaver, after all.

The Old Donna would have long ago buried her frequent thoughts of Duncan. She'd swallow him away with an extra sleeping pill while she tossed and turned at night. She would let the memory of the miraculous moment in the men's room when—after she'd pinched his nose and exhaled into his mouth—he coughed, took a ragged breath, and opened his eyes; she'd let that scene fade to black. She would repress her desire to ask him where he went when he was temporarily dead and what it was like. Were there lights? Pearly gates? Dearly departed? Beloved pets?

The Old Donna would deny she can still taste the tang of his blood. The New Donna emerged out of the bathroom mirror like a butterfly from a chrysalis and she has no intention of looking back in the hazy glass at who she'd been.

The hallway carpet has a maroon and gold crisscross diamond pattern with occasional threadbare white patches. Standing in her coat, hat in hand, she feels the oppressive heat from an overhead vent. The wide swirls of gray paint on the walls trigger a touch of vertigo. She should, she knows, eat something. It's noon now. Ordinarily, she returns to her apartment, walks Vincent, and consumes yogurt and a banana on her break.

She knocks again, this time loudly. After all the hours she has spent thinking about this moment she hasn't prepared herself for the disappointment of his absence nor is she ready to shuffle off in defeat. So she knocks again and again and again.

When the handle turns and the door opens Donna emits a quick yip and despite her desire to be a different person, as the man she remembers materializes in the doorway, Old Donna returns. She speaks in a rapid-fire burst: "Excuse me, I'm sorry to bother you, I didn't know if you were in there, I shouldn't have knocked so many times and I wouldn't if I knew you were inside but I wanted to introduce myself, well, we've already met but you can't remember me because you were dead, ha, well, you know, I mean I'm the one who found you and gave you CPR and retrieved your tongue and I hope I'm not intruding; were you taking a nap?"

With one hand on the doorframe, Duncan absorbs the barrage of words. Moments ago he was sprawled on the floor watching a galaxy of dust motes linger in a beam of blue sunlight and absent-mindedly waiting for the Body Collector. For a split second, he thought the pounding at the door might be him, but then he dismissed that idiotic notion; the Body Collector would never knock.

Duncan looks like a sleepy version of the man Donna remembers. His hair is frazzled. There's more color in his thinly beard-stubbled face and fewer bags tugging at his cheekbones. Her attention is drawn to his green-blue tinted eyes that are exactly like she recalls; precisely like hers. She wonders if the hue of his irises takes on different shades—more blue or more green—when he wears different-colored clothing. Before her thoughts can scatter, she takes a deep breath. Then says, "I hope I haven't disturbed you. I can come back at a more convenient time. We have the same eye color!"

For a while, Duncan doesn't move. He stands rigid and tense like a condemned pirate on the edge of a plank in a troubled sea. Donna fiddles with the earring on her right ear. She's wearing sterling silver seagulls with wings extended. Slowly, Duncan lifts his clenched fist to his face as if he is going to throw a punch. He extends his pointer finger toward his mouth. For a moment, Donna wonders if he is going to open his lips and if he does she is excited about the possibility of what she might see. Will the tongue she carried be there or will there be a nub of angry red flesh? To her disappointment, Duncan's expression doesn't change and his lips remain zipped. He's pointing at his mouth to tell her he cannot speak.

"Oh. That makes sense. It must be hard. I hadn't thought of that. Well, it crossed my mind but then skedaddled. That happens. Anyway, it's no big deal. An easy fix. You'll see. I'll swing by tomorrow." Spinning on her heels, Donna marches to the end of the hall, enters the stairwell, and behind an avalanche of nervous energy, she bounds down the stairs.

The next day she only has to knock twice before Duncan appears. She notices he has combed his short, brown hair and is wearing a shirt with buttons. Though he hasn't shaved, it's hard to say if he's attempting to grow a beard. She is wearing a black pea coat, a green, recently laundered blouse, and the lightest spritz of rose-scented perfume. "I brought this," she says triumphantly. In her hands she's got a whiteboard and a package of markers. "Maybe we can communicate?"

Inside, the apartment is sparse and immaculate. Donna takes it all in; there's an unfinished puzzle of a snowy pastoral landscape on a kitchen table, a bonsai tree on a planter beside a window, a walnut-colored coffee table, a navy-blue couch which looks as if nobody has sat upon it, a bookshelf containing many hardbacks, and an off-white rug with a zigzag pattern. She's not sure if she should take off her coat. On a rack beside the front door is his familiar yellow jacket. She can see bloodstains on the collar.

"May I sit?" Donna asks.

Duncan sweeps his hand toward the couch. He pulls a chair from the kitchen and situates himself in front of her, the coffee table between them.

"It is kind of you to let me in. I certainly don't want to be a bother. It's just, ever since that day, I've been thinking about you a lot. I was hoping you were getting better. My colleagues wondered why you did what you did where you did it and though I'm curious, too, I realize it's none of my business. Oh, and Yuri wanted to know if he would ever see his Steelers mug again. But he's a huge jerk."

Duncan runs a hand through his hair. He beckons for the whiteboard and a marker. In clear, even cursive he writes, *Are you the Nutritionist?* and puts the board on the table where she can read it.

"Ha! Well, no. I should introduce myself. I'm Donna. Donna Langford. I work at Strafe Brothers. I found you in the men's room. I know I wasn't supposed to be in there, but I couldn't help myself. When something unusual happens at work, I'm the kind of person who needs to figure out *why* it happened. I read a lot of mysteries but my real life is super boring."

Duncan nods, then stands and walks into the kitchen. He opens a drawer and returns to his seat with a brown dishtowel which he uses to erase his question. He writes, *I don't have the mug.*

"Oh, that's okay. It's not important. To be honest, Yuri doesn't even know I'm here." Donna sits with her back straight on the couch. She crosses her legs at the knees and fidgets.

Duncan picks up the marker, erases what he'd written, and writes on the whiteboard. *Are you friends with Harvey?*

"I don't know anyone named Harvey. I got your name from Melanie at the front desk and your address from the internet. I'm not stalking you or anything. I just . . . I'm glad you're better. I didn't know what happened to your tongue."

It's back, Duncan writes. *Regrettably.*

Although Donna is dying to pursue the conversation further, she doesn't want to push. She's been called pushy. *Nosy*, even. Her grandmother told her to shut up when she visited her in the hospital, after the old woman's failed suicide attempt. Donna was talking incessantly about whatever, filling empty space with sound. She can't help it. Silences are dangerous. When someone is quiet they're normally thinking. Those thoughts, she has learned from experience, wander into criticism about some facet of her—what she's wearing, how she's standing, if she's smiling when she should be frowning or frowning when she should be smiling. A person's judgmental opinion is always betrayed in the eyes.

But blathering and worrying about what a person is thinking about her are characteristics of the Old Donna. The broken man she saw in the bathroom still looks shattered. Just because he's alive doesn't mean he wants to live. He might try to harm himself again, and Donna does not want that. She read somewhere that there is an art to getting a person to open up. One way is to be aloof instead of eager. To play hard-to-get.

"Well," she says, standing, "I'd love to chat further but I've got to grab lunch before my break ends. I'm glad that you're on the mend." She scoots by him to the front door. Then, without thinking about it, she lifts his jacket off the coat rack and hides it behind her back. Before leaving, she asks, "Do you mind if I come by tomorrow?"

Duncan hasn't moved from his spot in the chair. His gaze is on the window. When she poses the question, his head jerks down ever so slightly, which Donna takes as an affirmation.

The next day, to her surprise, Duncan has made her lunch: a ham and cheese sandwich with lettuce and tomato. There are two dill pickles on the plate next to a nest of potato chips.

"You shouldn't have," Donna says when she's sitting at the kitchen table. The puzzle has been put away. "This is kind of you."

Duncan shrugs and sits across from her. He keeps the whiteboard between them.

"Aren't you going to eat anything?" Donna asks as she nibbles on a piece of lettuce.

Duncan shakes his head.

"You're not hungry?"

On the whiteboard, Duncan writes, *Tell me about you.*

Between bites, Donna talks. Duncan learns she is a vegetarian, she enjoys musicals, she has an opinion about waves, her dog is a five-year-old half-shepherd, half-retriever, she buys Amish soap, and she hiccups in tight, clipped, thrilling undulations. Her lunch hour vanishes. "Vincent will have to hold it today," she says. On her plate she leaves the ham in a tidy pile.

"Tomorrow," she says, sliding on her coat, "will you tell me about you?"

Duncan mouths the word, *Yes*.

The next day, a Friday, Donna walks Vincent before visiting Duncan. There's a bowl of potato soup waiting for her at the table. After hanging up her coat she finds her seat and thanks Duncan profusely. In one hand she picks up her spoon, in the other she lifts a marker. "I'll eat, you write," she says.

Taking the marker, Duncan writes on the whiteboard. Then he holds it in his lap so she can read it. He has written, *What do you want to know?*

"I want to understand why you did what you did, I guess, but I don't want to be a nag about it. Back when I was a teenager, I was the best secret keeper in my friend group. These days, I don't have many friends and the ones I have don't share interesting secrets. I don't know why it matters so much, but I want you to trust me."

Duncan stands, retrieves the dish towel from the kitchen, erases the board and then writes, *I'm not sure I can trust you when I don't trust myself.*

"Try me."

With his left hand, Duncan uses the cloth to erase and with his right hand he writes. Then he reveals the words to her. *I don't have much time left.*

"Why not? Are you expecting company?"

Duncan sighs heavy. He stands and adjusts his chair so that he is sitting beside Donna. This way, she can read what he has written as he's writing. *A couple of years ago I had a heart attack and died.*

"Oh, no. I'm sorry."

Duncan erases and then quickly writes, *I didn't stay that way. When I was dead I made a deal.*

Donna blows lightly on her soup. She tries to make eye contact, but he's focused on the whiteboard. "With the Devil?"

With the Body Collector.

"Ah," Donna says. "Care to explain?"

Raising his head, Duncan meets Donna's gaze. He finds a mixture of care and concern in her face. It's the same look he remembers seeing when he returned to life in the men's room. Turning back to the board he writes, *You won't believe me.*

"Fine," Donna sets the spoon beside the bowl and rests her hands in her lap. She straightens her spine and waits for Duncan to give her his attention. "How about you and I make a deal? You write whatever you want. I won't judge and I won't interrupt. I know a thing or two about believing in things that other people don't believe. Someday, I'll tell you about Hasselhoff. Deal?"

And you'll finish your lunch?

"Yes." Donna smiles and extends her hand for him to shake.

Duncan is ready to tell the truth. He was thinking about this moment, back in his bed tossing and turning, all last night. Although, with her help, he cheated death again, now that his tongue has been stitched into his mouth, he is back to his doomed weight. There is no hope, but there is also nothing to lose. If he puts his story into her head, a part of him might carry on. At least until she forgets. By then, he'll be long gone and nothing will really matter.

Two days before Christmas, after undergoing a thorough psychological examination, Duncan was discharged from the hospital. Doctors had to weigh the option of sending him home with Prozac or Vicodin. In the end, they chose the pain meds and insisted he check in soon.

Home in his apartment, the first thing Duncan did was step on his well-worn scale. Shaking with anticipation, he covered his face with his hands and hesitantly peeked through fingers at the result. Sure enough, he still weighed 186.2 pounds. Nothing had changed. The cursed number remained. In his mouth, a brick of pain pulsed in erratic intervals. Ignoring the medication, he positioned himself spread-eagle on the kitchen floor. With his arms and legs wide he resembled a kid in a patch of snow about to make a snow angel. Christmas came and went. The Ball dropped. The phone rang, his neighbors shuffled above and below, snow fell quietly, sparks of laughter caught in the hallway. He didn't eat and couldn't sleep; he wasn't hungry or tired. On occasion, he'd drink from the faucet. The pain lessened. A fly buzzed above and landed on the ceiling which seemed odd to Duncan; he'd never seen one in winter.

During the hours and days of psychological evaluation Duncan never mentioned his deal with the Body Collector. Although doctors didn't believe him, he insisted the tongue evisceration was an accident. He claimed he was dehydrated and, as a result, he fainted, banged his head on the edge of the table, and unwittingly pulled the handle down. Psychiatrists were dubious but couldn't prove what he said *didn't* happen. He was reluctantly released into the wild.

Weak and alone, Duncan listlessly waited for the Body Collector to arrive and fetch his tongue. Then he heard the knock on the door, struggled to his feet, and saw Donna—a woman he couldn't place at the time but remembered last night—through the peephole.

And now she's here and he's here and the events are ready to be shared. Written then erased. Believed or not believed. Remembered forever or forgotten immediately. Retold or never repeated. Who knows. What matters is the purge. The unburdening. Getting it out. The weight of the story throbbing in his skull is a million times heavier than his body has ever been.

Taking her proffered hand, which is cool and dry, he shakes it and seals their deal.

II.

We're all born into a body. It's a gift. What we make of it is, for the most part, our choice. When we die, our flesh becomes ash or dust. Does our non-corporeal self receive the reward of eternal life? I can't say for certain. I wasn't dead long enough to find out. Instead, I returned. I re-entered my old body. But my body no longer belonged to me alone. I'd promised it to the Body Collector.

At night, on my way to work I pass the "that'a way guy" on the corner of Charles and Bloom. He sets himself up on the sidewalk in front of the Easton. Although it's not his name, I call him Charlie B. He's a busker with a stunning voice and a peculiar sense of rhythm. He plays notes on his guitar that somehow exist between beats. When you think you've got the pattern in your head, Charlie B. bends the tune slightly enough to make you listen harder. He's really good and I always put a dollar in the yellow pail. He is someone I never would have met if I hadn't died, and I am thankful that I knew him. Whenever you give Charlie B. money, he'll stop, look you in the eye, and exclaim, "He went that a'way!" Then he'll point ahead of you or behind you, to the left or right, before diving right back into his song. People get a kick out of it. I've watched them smile and shake their heads. Nobody knows who Charlie B. means. *He* is who, exactly? Someone you were pursuing? Someone pursuing you? God? In early December, I found out.

I used to be big. Too big for my heart. When I died two and a half years ago I weighed 372.4 pounds exactly. They weighed me at the hospital and wrote it on the chart. Before the paramedics brought me back to life I existed somewhere else. I can't say where I was because there isn't language for it. I couldn't see, but I wasn't blind. I felt entombed, but not constricted. I may have been in a pod or I may have been in a womb. If you can imagine the afterlife as a mansion, with space and dimension, I was in the foyer. And if I had to describe the wisp of dark energy that wavered in front of me as an entity, I'd describe it as a spine of smoke. If I were to say this creature and I spoke, I would be wrong. There was no mouth. There was no space to carry sound. There were no words. And yet, we communed.

The thing offered me a choice: I could resume living or resume dying. As far as I know, I was never given a glimpse of what the next stage of my post-life would be like, if there was one. I decided to return, obviously, and when I did my memory was wiped clean. Suddenly, I was back in the ambulance. I remember the perplexed face of an EMT. Her eyes widened and she said, "Holy shit, he's alive!"

Everybody dies and nobody has proof about what happens when we do. Even people like me who have peeked behind the curtain can't offer anything concrete about passing. One moment I was playing *Blam!*, then nothing, then the ambulance. No lights. No tunnel. No kaleidoscope of memories. If anyone asked, I would have said waking out of death was precisely like waking up from a dreamless dream. What do you say when someone asks what you dreamed when you didn't? Dreamlessness, some say, isn't possible. "You dreamed," a psychoanalyst might say, "you just don't remember it." The same can be said about death. Believers say nothingness is impossible. "There was something, you just don't remember it." Maybe that's true. Maybe memory is all that matters.

Losing weight isn't easy even when faced with the certainty that your heart will surrender if you don't. Addiction can't be cured with the snap of a finger or the wave of a wand. My craving for food and *Blam!* consumed me. Years ago the joy in eating and playing was gone, but I had no desire to do anything else. Call it lethargy, or gluttony, or lack of ambition. The nurse who visited me in post-op after my heart attack said I had to change my deathstyle to a lifestyle. Easier said than done. Little did I know, I had a business partner with a vested interest in my weight loss.

Upon returning to my apartment one afternoon, I discovered a box. Inside were Flavor Erasers and a job advertisement. Presumably, these items were sent by a nutritionist. When I tried to track this person down, I got nowhere. Doctors, nurses, the receptionist, none of them could give me a name. When I went to ask Harvey, he was gone, too. Retired to Bermuda. Supposedly. I have my doubts if he was real, either.

My best guess is that the Nutritionist—and maybe Harvey—were henchmen for the Body Collector. Because there *were* Flavor Erasers. They don't exist now—I've scoured the internet and can't find them anywhere—but they did then. My slimming is proof. You know how they fatten a cow before they slaughter it? It's like that, only the inverse. I needed to shed pounds, and the tongue condoms combined with the Light Extinguisher gig, they sculpted me into what I weigh now.

Hindsight. I like that word. It's unusual when you read it. "Hind" isn't something we use on its own. You can add "be" and create "behind." Essentially, it means *back*. To clearly see what has already transpired is dangerous. The "seeing" must happen "now" and we do it not to benefit the person we were but to benefit the person we might become. Fool me once, shame on you. Fool me twice, shame on me. I am both You and Me and always the fool.

I had a premonition on Valentine's Day when I was in ninth grade, a glimpse of my impending death. That morning I woke up, dressed, and got ready for school. As I was brushing my teeth I looked at myself in the mirror and instead of seeing my face I saw my skull. All the flesh and muscle had been stripped away. The rest of my body was normal. When I put my hands to my head, I felt my ears and my nose, but I couldn't see those features. I thought there must be something wrong with my eyes, but when I left my bathroom and saw my little brother at the breakfast table, I couldn't see his face, either. When his jaw chewed cereal I saw it turn to mush between his teeth.

I made my way through the day desperately trying to repress my disquieting anxiety. Everywhere I turned I saw ordinary bodies carrying fleshless heads. At lunch, I kept my eyes on my shoes to avoid observing all the skulls eating sandwiches and chips. Without skin to hide how we chew, masticated food is repulsive. Everything becomes an off-white-colored glob—like a dollop of bird shit—before being swallowed. I didn't eat anything all day.

I've always been irked by the way hearts are depicted. The shape on playing cards, chocolate candy, and emojis bear no resemblance to an actual heart. The human heart resembles a clenched fist coated in sticky blood. Take a teenager who has been in a brawl with twenty bullies and consider his fist as he stands exhausted and triumphant over a heap of beaten bodies. That's what a human heart resembles.

Skulls, though; they look like skulls. Although it was disturbing not being able to make out facial features, that night in my bedroom, alone, and away from mirrors, my appetite returned. I devoured an entire bag of Hershey's kisses and a tin of Valentine's Day sugar cookies. The next morning, to my great relief, everything returned to normal. People had faces again. I had no way of explaining what happened and I forgot all about it.

With hindsight, I know the truth.

I have a love/hate relationship with words. They are little mysteries with histories that get trapped in my brain. I never bothered to weigh myself before I tried to lose weight. What's the point? The numbers only went one way—up, up, up. Besides, I didn't need a scale to tell me I was heavy. My whole life, people incessantly reminded me. As a baby, I was pleasantly plump. As a kid, I was big-boned with a hearty appetite. I grew from plus-sized to obese. Then I became morbidly obese. That word—*morbid*—stuck in my head for a long time. It's a sick thing to call someone with a weight problem. It makes you feel like a monster. Like people want you to die or else disappear. And those were the "acceptable" labels that fed my feast of shame. The unacceptable insults—the ones whispered in the school hall—included Tubby, Lard-ass, Blimpie, Butterball, Roly-Poly, Porker, and my favorite, Duncan-Da-Donut. Such silly-sounding chastisements rolled right off my back. But when a word is chiseled with hate and hurled by boys with hard, cruel eyes—I'm thinking of Lester and Jake from high school—it can leave a scar. For four years those kids made bullying me their life's goal. It was like a part-time job. The names they called me—and I won't repeat them—were more like bullets and knives than sticks and stones. They turned my self-worth into Swiss cheese. In response, did I become a gym rat, sculpt my body into one sleek rope of muscle and beat the crap out of those clowns? No. I didn't. I hid in my room with a bag of Whatever and played video games. A habit that eventually killed me.

While I didn't step on a scale that Valentine's Day when I saw skulls, I'm certain I weighed 186.2 pounds. That's the doomed number I weigh now. It's also the amount of flesh I promised the Body Collector.

There was a caveat to my resurrection. You see, the wisp that greeted me when I was dead was me. Not me as I'd always known myself; more like a post-me pulse of displaced energy. *That* me—the Body Collector—would become the me I discarded. Every pound I lost seeped into that nether world and coalesced around the spine of smoke. My flesh provided it with muscle, sinew, and bone. The body I shed became its body and when we both weighed exactly the same—186.2 pounds—the deal was complete. The front door would crack open and he'd charge through. My death weight was his birth weight. He'd take over my life and I would resume dying.

I knew all this I just didn't remember. The Body Collector enshrouded my thoughts and made me forget until it was too late. He manipulated me all along. He made me believe in myself. He tricked me into thinking *I* had the discipline and courage to lose half of my weight. He lured me away from my deathstyle and convinced me there would be happiness in a new frame. He duped me into having hope and convinced me that pleasure wasn't elusive. That joy exists in striding through the street amongst strangers. When the body and the mind wander, there's serenity. For a while I had faith bliss exists in the meditative distancing of the self from the self.

At first, after two weeks without seeing any fluctuation in my weight, I thought there was something wrong with my scale. It wouldn't budge from that cursed number. Unlike the old me, the new me was cognizant of every calorie I consumed and every calorie I burned. I weighed myself religiously each morning and became giddy as the pounds sloughed off. After I'd lost 150 pounds and excess skin hung from me like I was half-melted, I underwent abdominoplastic surgery to have it removed. The loose dermis they shaved off weighed over nine pounds. I bought a new wardrobe and felt better than I ever thought it was possible to feel. No more backaches. No more acid reflux. No more worries heartburn was a heart attack or a twitch in my cheek meant I was having a stroke. And, best of all, no more trailing whispers from strangers when I passed them on the sidewalk. I was perfectly capable of blending. For the first time in my life I wasn't the object of a stranger's gaze. I became the watcher, not the watched.

As I walked, I took note of the city I've lived in my entire life. Suddenly Chesterton seemed foreign. My eyes swiveled with a reckless abandon without the fear of scornful, judgmental glares. Most people I saw looked genuinely happy. This came as a shock. I figured they were at least a little like me—discontent with the shape and sway of the world. I learned, for the most part, my fellow citizens were blissfully unaware of where they were going and what they were doing so long as they were in the company of people who looked like them. For most of my life, until I'd lost half my weight, I stood out. I was a hippo on the sidewalk. Of course I avoided eye contact with strangers, but I could still feel their stares and scowls. My big body offended them. I put others in a bad mood. For them, I only existed so that they could situate themselves in relation to me. I was a warning of who they might become if they quit dieting and exercising. My existence forced them to evaluate what they had for lunch and what they were planning on having for dinner. Above my head flashed a sign which read: "Eat more vegetables or else you'll be like me." And they hated me for the reminder.

The new me meant nothing. Let me tell you, it's so much better to be ignored than judged. For a while, I was fascinated by my well-earned invisibility and closely watched people glide by me as I glided by. Over time, the surprise of their indifference to me wore off. I became like them when they became nothing to me, too.

Then I reached my destined weight. I woke up on the Monday after Thanksgiving feeling anxious. It was as if someone had confined me in an emotional straitjacket. Other than not being able to taste—which, after spending so much time wearing Flavor Erasers, I considered a blessing—there was nothing wrong with me. I was, in fact, in the best shape of my life. My head felt as clear as it had in years. I'd even exchanged a few pleasant emails with my ex-fiancé. I was genuinely happy for her happiness—she and her husband were expecting their first child—which, in my mind, proved I'd moved on from her.

I tried to ignore the paralyzing belief something awful was impending. I expected the phone to ring with news my father or mother had died or my brother relapsed. On my walk, I kept looking over my shoulder, certain I would be mugged. Cars passed closer than usual. At Bill's I ate a big, tasteless plate of turkey with gravy, mashed potatoes, stuffing, and pumpkin pie and I wondered if each bite might be my last. Finally, I made it through the day and cautiously anticipated the night.

I love—well, loved; I've been let go—my job as Light Extinguisher. At night, the buildings are so quiet. Except for the low hum of electricity the only sound I ever heard was of my own making. There was the jangle of the keys in my pocket and the echo of my footsteps in the hollow of the stairwell. Every night I'd sign a form indicating I was in possession of the keys which the security guard handed me. I'd climb the 252 stairs to the top floor of the Easton and make my way up and down the hall. Whenever I spotted light spilling out from under a door I'd unlock it and enter.

At first glance, all corporate working spaces look the same. Propped in a dusty frame on every brown desk is a photograph of a kid, a spouse, a dog, or a sunrise. Paper is strewn on the desktop or else arranged in a neat pile. Computer monitors angle toward swivel chairs the backs of which are often worn by sweaters or jackets. There are many knickknacks. Potted plants try to survive without the sun. For the most part, my eyes pass right over everything before I turn off the light.

It's always the same people who fail to switch off their lights. We are our habits. But we're not the same. For example, there's a man named Frank Davis who works at Darlingco. It's easy to learn names from paperwork. Frank never turns off his desktop banker's lamp. From the family photo, I'd say he and his wife were in their mid-fifties and his boys were teenagers. Frank keeps a bowl of candy on his desk for co-workers to enjoy. When he fills it with mini-chocolate bars it's empty in a week. When he puts butterscotch hard candies in the bowl it takes about a month to be eaten. At first glance this triviality meant nothing to me. But then I noticed a pattern. When there was chocolate, Frank's desk was more organized than when it was filled with butterscotch candies. His mouse was centered on the mouse pad, his keyboard dusted, and his stapler sat straight next to a neatly arranged cup of pens. The only thing out of place was the family photograph. One Monday night, as I reached across the desk to yank the chain on the banker's lamp, I discovered the picture was face down. I wondered if this was an accident. The next night, though, it was still overturned. That Friday night there was only one candy bar left and the picture was still toppled. The following Monday, when the hard candies returned to the bowl, the family photo was righted. His desk quickly slipped into disarray. This pattern continued for about a year until, one night in February, I noticed the candy bowl was gone. Also, the family photo on his desk was replaced with a picture of Frank shirtless on the beach with a dark-haired woman whom I recognized from a photograph on a desk in an adjacent office. Her name, I discovered when I double-checked, is Violet Hopewell. She is in her mid-thirties, has a cat named JoJo, and enjoys sky-diving.

The candy in that bowl told a story Frank didn't realize he was telling. Violet liked chocolate. When she'd visit his office for an afternoon piece he made sure his desk was tidy and his family absent. After their weekend dalliance, he'd feel temporarily guilty. The butterscotch acted as a barrier. He probably told himself he'd break things off and that he still loved his wife. His willpower dwindled with the hard candy. How eager he must have been to replace the chocolate. The affair teetered and tottered until Frank's wife demanded a divorce.

None of that was any of my business. Frank doesn't know I exist. He's merely a fool who fails to turn off his light. I never swiped a single piece of his candy. He isn't part of my story, but telling you makes it temporarily real. And that does matter.

When I made my way to the ground floor, I'd sign out and return the keys to the security guard. Then I'd walk next door to the Mayberry which has 336 stairs from bottom to top. Afterward, I'd return to my apartment and slip into a deep sleep.

To my surprise, when I weighed myself Tuesday morning, shortly after Thanksgiving, I still weighed 186.2 pounds. This was unusual considering the feast I'd eaten the day before. By my calculation, I should have weighed at least 186.6 pounds. All day, I went about my business, distracted. I didn't make a single sale. For lunch I choked down three burritos and a bag of Doritos. I did not enjoy a single bite. Then I weighed myself. I was still 186.2 pounds. I ate a dozen jelly-filled doughnuts. I consumed a bucket of chicken and three hamburgers. I climbed on the scale. 186.2 pounds. Desperate for a change, I fasted. For five days I subsisted on nothing but water and bananas. I should have lost five pounds. Since I no longer had faith in my scale I went to Beyond Baths and weighed myself on ten of theirs. On every one, I was 186.2 pounds.

It's hard for me to remember a time when mass didn't matter. The only way you lose as much weight as I have is by setting goals and sticking to them. When I committed myself to a healthy lifestyle, my first challenge was to get under 300 pounds. After reaching that important milestone, I celebrated by going to the movie theater—something I hadn't done in two decades. I dropped under 250, 200, and 190. How far did I want to go? My destination was 174 pounds. The last time I saw my little brother—over three years ago—he bragged about weighing 175 pounds. My plan was to surprise them all on Easter in my new racecar body. I know now that will never happen.

On December 3, around nine, I made my way to the Easton. Like always, I passed Charlie B. He was playing something slow, as I recall. Something full of sorrow. I put a dollar into his bucket and continued. After a few paces, I realized something was off. Charlie had stopped playing, but he didn't exclaim, "He went that'a way!" Curious, I turned to see what was wrong.

Charlie's eyes were wide and his face stricken. He had a shaky finger placed over his pressed lips instructing me to be quiet.

"What is it?" I said. "Which way did he go?"

Charlie shook his head while his eyes stayed locked on mine. Then, very slowly, he lifted his hand past his nose, beyond his head, until his arm was outstretched and he was pointing at the sky.

When I looked up I saw snow drifting through the light from illuminated offices. It was, to my knowledge, the first snow of the year. It melted the moment it touched the ground.

"He's that'a way," Charlie whispered, "and he's waiting for you." There was conviction and worry in his voice and my instinct was to assure him he was mistaken. As my eyes scanned the staggered rectangles of light dotting the building, I noticed something peculiar. In one bright window, on the seventh or eighth floor, there was a human-shaped silhouette. It looked, from where I stood, like the person had their hands pressed to the glass as if they were trying to push out into the frigid night. When I extinguished the lights it was extremely rare for me to encounter anyone other than a janitor. No janitor I knew would ever make a handprint on glass. Although the person was too difficult to see clearly, I had the distinct feeling he or she was staring down at me.

Then I was startled by the sound of Charlie playing his guitar again. I averted my eyes to him and when I squinted back up at the building, the figure was gone.

Unsettled, I did my job cautiously. I was already flustered by my inability to free myself from the shackles of my weight. Now my mind was occupied by a stranger lurking somewhere inside. On every floor and behind every door I expected the person to materialize. And then he did.

I was on the sixth floor and had entered the law offices of Crenshaw and Milligan when I saw him. He was standing in a tunnel of light at the end of a hallway. I couldn't see his face clearly; it was cast in shadows. He didn't move or speak but he gave off a familiar and menacing aura. I knew—felt it in my blood—I was in danger. So I fled. I scampered out of the office, down the stairs, and to the security guard. That night Melanie was working. You know her. She is a no-nonsense retired police officer who, like me, abhorred chit-chat. I explained there was an intruder. Perhaps, if I hadn't earned her trust over the course of the years, she might not have believed me. But, after asking me a few questions, we rode the elevator to the sixth floor. The figure was not in the hallway. Melanie searched every office and found nobody. To be on the safe side, she reviewed the security footage. The only person on the recording was me.

 I did what anyone else would do in my shoes: rationalize. "It must have been a trick in the light. It was a hat rack. It was my reflection bouncing off a smooth surface. It was all in my head." I attempted to comfort myself with the familiar platitudes meant to explain away the unexplainable and I continued to do my job.

 Then I saw him standing behind a desk in the overhead light of an accounting office on the twelfth floor of the Mayberry. Which was impossible. The door was locked and there was no way he could have slipped past the security guard and gotten there so fast. This time, though, I could see him clearly and what I discovered is he was me. The arms dangling to his side were my arms in my shirt and jacket. His shoulders sloped like mine. The cleft in his chin indented my chin. His eyes were my eyes. The scar on his forehead was the same size and shape as the one I received when my gaming computer chair toppled over on my face after I'd suffered a heart attack, collapsed, went into cardiac arrest, and died.

 I tried to blink my double away. I attempted to shake him out of my head. It was no use. Finally, I said, "You're not real," and switched off the light. To my delight, when the room went dark he disappeared. A great wave of relief washed over me. He was, I thought, a figment of my imagination, after all.

 A few floors down I found him again. This time he was in a supply closet. Like before, when I flipped the switch, he vanished. This pattern continued all the way down the building: the doppelganger appeared in a patch of light, I'd make it dark; he'd go away and reappear in a different space. Before handing the keys to Wayne, I feebly asked him if he'd seen anyone in the building. He hadn't, of course. Just me.

 As far as I know, while there's addiction in my blood, there is no history of mental illness in my family. I explained this to a therapist who offered free first-time consultations. He had a number of theories for my supposed inability to gain or lose weight and my visions. He suspected I was experiencing symptoms of multiple personality disorder I'd been suppressing, perhaps, all my life. He wondered what might have triggered these episodes. I didn't know. He said it was important to figure out and he strongly encouraged me to make an appointment for next week. My time had expired. I never saw him again.

The following night I decided to confront my double. I found him beside a photocopier in the Hudson office. When I asked him what he wanted, he simply stood there staring. After a long while he lifted his clenched fist and slowly raised it to his face. Then he pointed to his mouth. I leaned forward in anticipation. I was certain he was going to explain himself. I would finally learn why he was tormenting me and, maybe, I could give him want he wanted and be rid of him. When he opened his mouth, he didn't utter a word. I peered into the emptiness inside before snapping off the light.

I spent the next day pacing my apartment trying to come up with a plan. Up to that point I had been playing by his rules. He's the one who decided when and where to appear, not me. Although I'm the one who switched off the light, he had the power to randomly reappear. I wondered if there was a way I could trap him and force a standoff. By then, I was so tired of being chased. It's no way to live. That was the point, of course. I was supposed to die.

I made my rounds like always and when I sporadically encountered him I quickly snuffed him out. I turned off every light except for one. That way I knew where he'd be. I'd force him to me.

We know now the light I left on was the one in the office supply room at Strafe Brothers. I chose it at random. You can tell your co-workers I didn't have any ulterior motives. It wasn't anything they did or didn't do. And while I say that my choice was random, I wonder if that's really true. If I didn't confront the Body Collector there, you wouldn't have discovered me in the bathroom. If that were the case, I wouldn't be here now. Were you part of some kind of divine intervention? Or were you simply in the right/wrong place at the right/wrong time?

When I left Strafe Brothers, I didn't lock the office door. In the stairwell on the ground floor, I propped open an emergency exit. Then I returned the keys to Melanie and circled around the building to the ajar door. I climbed back to the eighth floor, moved through the hallway between the gaps in the video cameras—I knew them well—and returned to the office. In the supply room, I sat with my back to a stack of boxed paper and waited. I had to fight every instinct to turn off the light.

    I don't know how much time passed before I drifted off and I can't say for sure why I awoke. Maybe he nudged me. When I opened my eyes sunlight was pushing through the edges of the blinds. Sitting beside me was him. We were so near our shoulders touched. Up close, there was no mistaking his likeness to me. We weren't similar, we were exactly the same. When I blinked, he blinked. When I raised my right arm, so did he. I stood, he stood in unison. For the briefest of moments I felt a sense of agency. He mimicked me which meant *I* was in control. Such foolish wishful thinking! I prepared to explain what I believed to be true: he had been defeated. I outlasted him by refusing to extinguish the light. This time, when he disappeared in the daylight, it would be permanent. But when I began to triumphantly speak, he did not. He opened his mouth and kept opening it. It stretched wider and wider. I clenched my jaw, willing him to do the same. Instead, the gaping hole encircled with teeth grew larger. His mouth began to swallow his features. First went his nose and chin, then his eyes and eyebrows. I stared, horrified, expecting to hear an explosion of cracking bones. When it became too much, I tried to look away. Though I fought to turn my head, I could not. He wouldn't let me. He made me face him. To look—really look. To see what was absent. To acknowledge what he was missing. To accept that there was still something left for me to give.

    That's when I remembered our deal. I understood, as I've already explained. It was as if a blanket had been removed from my brain and the memory came back. The Body Collector clicked on a light bulb in my skull and it scorched me.

    The average tongue weighs about two and a half pounds. The Body Collector didn't need the whole thing, but what he wanted was more than I wanted to lose. That was to be my last payment. Our bargain was to be fulfilled. He'd kept good on his promise—after all, I was still alive. But my borrowed days were over and it was his turn to occupy my body.

    I wonder if it was me or the Body Collector who slowly lowered our head to the table beside the paper cutter. Which of us stuck our tongue out and said, "Ahh"? Did I fumble for the handle and yank the blade down or was it him? Was I the prisoner or executioner?

    I can tell you, the pain was unlike anything I've ever felt. Since it was supposed to be the last thing I ever experienced, what did it matter? Suffering is only suffering after it's over and you have survived. When you have time to think about it as you recover. Which was never meant to happen.

From there, in the supply room, things are murky. I don't remember staggering down the hall. I don't know how I got into the bathroom. I don't know what time it was when I died. There's one thing I do know: I promised not to make any more deals for my life.

But I'm alive. So I might have, right?

The funny thing is, when I unpeeled my eyes and saw you, for a split second I thought I was in Heaven or else some nice post-death place. You have that kind of face. Then again, it could have been the overhead light above that made you glow a little.

Tranquility didn't last long. I was whisked to the hospital, a familiar purgatory, and reality set in. I'd dodged death again. I didn't know how, exactly. Had I lost my will and made another pact? Or, maybe there was some kind of trial in that dark mansion and I successfully pleaded my case with Death. I mean, what more could I have done? I gave my doppelganger what he demanded. It wasn't my fault that I returned instead of him. I'd won, I reasoned, fair and square.

Then the nurse showed up with my tongue. I wordlessly begged them not to stitch it back on and make me whole. If they did, I'd return to my doomed weight which meant the Body Collector still had a claim. It meant I'd died for nothing. A cruel joke. Death was a cat playing with me, the mouse, before ripping me to shreds. How I tried to get the doctors to understand. They had to be blind not to see terror in my eyes. It was no use. I thrashed my head until they sedated me.

Before being discharged, doctors told me that when the swelling goes down, I'll talk again. They said, someday soon, I could return to my old life. Which old life did they mean? It's only a matter of time until the Body Collector returns. All those days recovering in the hospital I stayed on my back with a liquid diet. Any ordinary person would have lost at least five pounds. The first thing I did when I returned here is climb on my scale. You may wonder if I felt frightened when I saw I still weighed 186.2 pounds and nothing had changed. I didn't; I don't. Don't get me wrong—I don't want to die, permanently. But I'm unwilling to live in a world in which I'm always the quarry. I don't want to be haunted and I don't want to be a ghost. When the Body Collector decides to visit, I'll pluck out my tongue and willingly fork it over. I'm done, I'm done, I'm done.

Where will I go the next time? My last time? After the deal is finally complete and he is me? I can't say with certainty. Will I become someone else's spine of smoke? Will I offer a big, desperate man a shady deal? If every day we're one step closer to death, perhaps every day we're dead we're one step closer to tricking ourselves alive again.

III.

Duncan clicks the cap on the marker and sets it aside. He leaves the last line on the whiteboard.

Donna, who had been leaning forward, leans back. She does not know how much time has passed. Certainly, her lunch break has expired.

Only fragments of Duncan's story came through. He moved frantically without much pause. With his right hand he scribbled, and with his left hand he wiped away—write/erase, write/erase, write/erase—like windshield wipers hitched to the highest setting. Donna figured out early on that it was more important for him to jot his thoughts down than it was for her to read them. The basic gist came through: he was a lonely, unsettled man who had undergone major psychological trauma when he had a heart attack two and a half years ago. Since then, he'd been doing his best to live well. Which is hard to do when you're all alone. Clearly, he hasn't been able to shake away the creeping sensation that nothing he does will ever be enough. All that seems pretty normal, to Donna. She doesn't mind emotionally complicated men. They can be exciting. Her ex was one. With him she made the mistake of smothering his issues with unfounded optimism and encouragement. What he needed was time, a gentle hand, and a good listener who said the right thing at the right time. The old her was not prepared.

Mostly, while Duncan wrote, she stared at him and daydreamed. When she rescued him he was clean-cut and diminutive, a little like a vampire. He was, after all, nearly a corpse. Now, though, in the early stages of a beard and with such a voracious intention to put words down, he feels bigger. Fuller, somehow. He parted his mouth every time he erased the board. When he did, the slightest tip of his tongue protruded. This habit turned a crank in Donna's head around and around. In a box on a table in her brain resided a forbidden thought. She knew what was inside the box since she was the one who put it there. It was not a question of whether or not she would engage the idea—she would—it was a question of how much she would obsess over it. When the Jack in the box popped out and teetered maddeningly on the table in the chamber of her mind, Donna did not try hard to cram it back, return it to the million other passing fancies that trigger and fade in a given hour. Instead, she fed it. By the time he had finished writing and capped his marker, her desire to touch her tongue with his was a plump, naughty, mischievous hobgoblin. She knew with absolute certainty she would kiss him.

"You sure have a lot going on up there," Donna says, pointing toward Duncan's head. Cold potato soup remains in the bowl. "Have you thought of growing a beard? If it's bushy enough—like Amish men wear—it might give you an extra ounce or two and you could break the spell."

To the surprise of them both, Duncan laughs. It's a messy, sputtering, staccato burst: ha-ha; ha-ha-ha; ha-ha. Donna puts her hand to her mouth and titters behind it. After regaining his composure, Duncan erases the whiteboard and writes: *I never thought of that. Maybe I'll try.*

The next day, a Saturday, Duncan takes the stairs to the street where he is meeting Donna and Vincent. Yesterday afternoon, before leaving, she told him that she had a surprise. He finds her standing on the busy sidewalk with her leashed dog and his yellow jacket.

"I had it dry-cleaned," Donna says when he's near. "Good as new."

Taking the jacket from her, Duncan slides into it. It's an unexpectedly warm afternoon and people are walking around in bright spirits. In the sky are more birds than clouds. The dirty chunks of gutter ice have melted. When Duncan says, "Thank you," it sounds like, "Kunh Ku."

"You're welcome. Here," she says, straightening the collar. "Much better. And this is Vincent. He's my best friend and the reason I get up in the morning."

The mutt wags his tail when Duncan scratches behind the ears. Vincent grins the way that canines seem to do when they're happy.

"Let's walk," Donna says. She's wearing a bright red scarf. "You lead."

Keeping his hands in his pockets, Duncan cuts up Livermore. The weekend traffic is moderate. The entire town of Chesterton seems to be in a pleasant mood. Drivers aren't honking their car horns. Most pedestrians have their heads raised and not bent to their cell phones. Someone is grilling burgers nearby. Duncan is a fast walker and he discovers that Donna is, too. The dog trots casually. There's slack in his leash.

They cross Meadows, wind down Main, and find Dell. Duncan leads them up Highfield to the old playground. When they arrive Donna lets Vincent off his leash. "He'll be fine," she says, and arranges herself on the old bench. "What a wonderful day."

"Eh-kiz," Duncan says. There's a puddle beneath half of the bench which forces him to sit close to her on the dry side so his shoes won't get wet. From his jeans pocket he removes a small notepad and pencil and writes; *I used to come here when I was a boy.* In order for Donna to read this, she has to lean into his shoulder. She detects the faintest hint of cologne. "It's nice."

Vincent dances between drips from a row of melting icicles on the swing-set frame. A squirrel chits in the branches of a sugar maple. Someone has graffitied the word *Pleasureboat* in orange bubble letters on the backside of the Playground Rules sign. Duncan's childhood self is perched atop the slide watching and waiting to swoop down.

From her purse, Donna removes two candy canes. "These are left over from Christmas," she says, handing one to Duncan. "You need to help me finish them. I can't stand being reminded of the holiday when we're so far away from it. My parents used to leave the lights up until Groundhog Day and it drove me nuts."

Duncan uses his fingernails to open the wrapper. He slides the stick end between his lips. Donna does the same.

There are a lot of things Donna would like to say. Like how the light turns Vincent's fur orange. And how she used to want to be a veterinarian until the incident with Hasselhoff. How, like the rabbit, Duncan wasn't really dead, either. Not that it's the same thing—it's not, obviously—but she was there to bear witness both times and that was something, wasn't it? And yesterday, when he mentioned how, after he regained consciousness and saw her face, plain old Donna, he thought she was an angel! Well, he didn't use the word *angel*, but it's what he meant. Nobody in this whole wide world has ever said anything so sweet. Hearing it made her body grow warm all over.

She wants to say more. Much more. Like, she's certain she was meant to find him. And how vulnerable he looked in the men's room. She wanted to scream but found courage to fight for his life by seeing her mirrored reflection. Like him, she was given a choice: run away or else act fast. She seized the opportunity and she's still seizing it. She wants so badly to seize him but if he doesn't want to seize her or doesn't want to be seized by her, than premature seizing might screw things up.

As Donna is thinking about all this, she feels a fluttering in her side and, before she even realizes she's doing it, she places her hand on his hand and leaves it there. She slowly counts to ten believing if he doesn't move it after that amount of time it means they're holding hands. After thirty-five seconds Donna musters the courage to turn her face toward him. There, she finds his eyes are stretched wide in horror. The candy cane hangs loosely from his mouth.

"What's the matter?" she says, pulling away. She's about to offer an apology when he fumbles in his lap for the notepad and pencil. In his familiar looping cursive Duncan writes: *I can taste this!*

That night, alone in his apartment, Duncan feasts on mint chip ice cream and thin mint cookies. The flavor is wild in his mouth. He falls asleep beneath a blanket of crumbs. Awakening Sunday morning, Duncan represses a pinch of optimism as he enters the bathroom and stands upon his sleek scale. He hasn't allowed hope into his life for as far back as he can remember.

When he sees what he weighs—187.6 pounds—he lets out a quick yelp. "I cam beave hit," he says. "I," he repeats because it sounds like it should. "I. I. I." He kicks the scale and it slides beneath the sink. "I'm free."

Standing before the mirror, Duncan celebrates by brushing. His toothbrush circles his teeth a hundred and fifty times and he vigorously scrapes the morning film from his semi-operational tongue. He wonders what other flavors he can taste and suddenly feels ravenous. He'll visit Bill's Cafeteria and sample every soup. He'll sit where he can't see the platoon of soup-slurping men—forget about those old geezers. Then, later, he and Donna have plans to go to a movie. He'll order the biggest bucket of popcorn and squirt a pound of butter over it. If things go well—and why not keep on hoping now that he is free?—the night might end with him tasting her lips. How long has it been since he kissed someone? Too long to worry over.

After he's rinsed, Duncan contemplates shaving. The man in the glass with the unfinished beard appears either dirty or dangerous and he isn't sure if Donna prefers his face this way or smooth. He took her joking comment about growing a heavy beard half-seriously. His straight razor is in a drawer. As he's rooting around, without announcement, his trachea is gripped with a tourniquet of dread. It becomes difficult to swallow. Every positive thought evaporates. His heartrate skyrockets. He's certain that if he makes any sudden moves he'll careen into cardiac arrest.

Before Duncan raises his head to greet his reflection, he knows exactly who he's going to find. There, staring back, is his 372.4 pound self. Plump, crimson cheeks gobble up his nose and the semi-beard looks like the prickly jowls of a wild boar. A staircase of chins tumble down his face in a meaty bib over his neck. Duncan in the mirror opens his sneering, chubby lips and says in a clear, falsetto voice: "You're gaining weight."

Everything returns. Duncan remembers exactly what it was like to be big. He remembers the pull of gravity on his knees; the impossibility of standing for long. He remembers the sound of his labored breathing punctuated by a spontaneous wheeze; remembers shortness of breath. He remembers *morbidly obese*, Zach McLeider, and *deathstyle*. He remembers strangers—remembers family—and the way people positioned themselves in orbit around his body. He feels the angry red rash in the folds of his belly. Remembers assessing how much weight a chair could hold before cautiously sitting. Swollen ankles. Stretched veins. Barely earning enough money to pay for food and rent.

In a flash, Duncan imagines every moment since he died, in reverse. He's sucked backward out of the men's bathroom at Strafe Brothers, away from the paper-cutting board, down the stairs, past Charlie B., and into his apartment. He undoes every step, turns on every light, re-packages every Flavor Eraser. From the morning he died on December 4th all the way back—897 days—to the night of June 20th when *Blam!* glitched and his heart quit; it all rewinds. Every ounce of who he'd been coalesces into the familiar stranger.

Duncan lifts his huge arm and guides the razor to his mouth. All he needs to do is say, "Ahh," stick out his tongue, sever the sutures, undo the work of doctors, hand over what he owes, and, uninterrupted, bleed out on the dirty linoleum bathroom floor. He'd told himself he wouldn't resist when the Body Collector returned.

Duncan pinches his eyes closed. He sticks his battered tongue out between his teeth. He touches the blade to the delicate muscle. But then, he pauses. He hesitates. Something feels off. The Body Collector was him, halved, not who he'd been whole. The man he'd been before dying the first time hadn't committed to selling his flesh. The monster in the mirror is no monster at all, it's a memory.

Duncan puts his tongue where it belongs. He lowers the razor. He opens his eyes, meets them reflected in the mirror, and instead of seeing Old Duncan he pictures Donna. Like she noted, their irises have a similar hue. While that's true, they don't perceive things the same way. He tries to imagine what it was like when she found him in the bathroom and what he might have done if the roles were reversed. If he spotted her in the women's room. He would have done what most people would do: call for help. By the time the paramedics arrived, she'd be dead. Dead-dead and cold with no hope of coming back. Then she wouldn't have had a chance to meet him. And vice versa.

Duncan knows better than to ask Donna why she saved him. If he did, she'd say, "Because you needed help," or, "I couldn't stand there and do nothing." There's a word for this. A label for her—*Good Samaritan*. That's what she is. A very good one. She would have aided anyone in need. "Even you," Duncan says to the melting man in the glass.

Donna's kindheartedness explains why she gave him CPR, but it doesn't elucidate what she saw in him that was worth saving. What she still sees. Maybe, in time, someday he'll see someone in the mirror he can live with.

Duncan returns the razor to the drawer. He'll give a beard a try. As he turns away, he thinks, *Samaritan*. It's a promising word. He can't come up with a single instance when it's used with *Bad*. Sure, there are bad humans, but he has never heard them referred to as *Bad Samaritans*. Probably, they're out there. If he spots one, he'll walk on by. Or, when he's able to speak, he could try talking to them. He misses discussions. Misses chatting with real people in real life, not spamming potential customers on the phone. It might be nice to rediscover his voice. He can't recollect saying a single meaningful thing in years. If he can manage to make it through the day and then survive tomorrow, he promises to approach a stranger on the sidewalk and strike up a conversation, whether they're good or bad. It's possible that he'll discover that most people are ordinary Samaritans, like him.

Before leaving the bathroom—the word and its possibilities expanding in his skull—Duncan snaps the light off.

ABOUT THE AUTHORS

Mauricio Montiel Figueiras is a writer of prose fiction and essays as well as a poet, translator, editor, and film and literary critic. He is the author of fifteen books in different genres. His work has been published in magazines and newspapers in Argentina, Brazil, Canada, Chile, Colombia, Italy, Peru, Spain, the United Kingdom, and the United States. He has been Resident Writer for the Cheltenham Festival of Literature in England (2003) and the Bellagio Study and Conference Center in Italy (2008). In 2012 he was appointed Resident Writer for the prestigious Hawthornden Retreat for Writers in Scotland. In 2020 he was selected artist in residence for the Saari Residence in Finland. Since 1995 he lives and works in Mexico City.

Jeff Parker is the author of several books including *Where Bears Roam the Streets: A Russian Journal*, the novel *Ovenman*, and the short story collection *The Taste of Penny*. He teaches prose in the MFA Program at the University of Massachusetts Amherst, and he is the Co-Founder and Director of the DISQUIET International Literary Program in Lisbon, Portugal.

Chaya Bhuvaneswar is a practicing physician, writer, and PEN/American Robert W. Bingham Debut Fiction award finalist for her story collection *WHITE DANCING ELEPHANTS: STORIES*, which was also selected as a Kirkus Reviews Best Debut Fiction and Best Short Story Collection and appeared on "best of" lists for *Harper's Bazaar*, *Elle*, *Vogue India*, and *Entertainment Weekly*. Her work has appeared in *The New York Times*, *Salon*, *The Sun*, *Narrative Magazine*, *Tin House*, *Electric Literature*, *Kenyon Review*, *Masters Review*, *The Millions*, *Joyland*, *Michigan Quarterly Review*, *The Awl*, and elsewhere. She has received fellowships from MacDowell, Community of Writers and Sewanee Writers Workshop.

Jason Ockert is the author of the novel *Wasp Box* and three collections of short stories: *Shadowselves*, *Neighbors of Nothing*, and *Rabbit Punches*. Winner of the Dzanc Short Story Collection Contest, the *Atlantic Monthly* Fiction Contest, and the Mary Roberts Rinehart Award, he was also a finalist for the Shirley Jackson Award and the Million Writers Award. His work has appeared in journals and anthologies including *Best American Mystery Stories*, *Granta*, *The Cincinnati Review*, *Oxford American*, *One Story*, and *McSweeney's*. He teaches at Coastal Carolina University.